Save the
Last Dance

NEW YORK TIMES BESTSELLING AUTHOR

SHELLEY SHEPARD GRAY

Save the Last Dance

BLACK STONE
PUBLISHING

Copyright © 2020 by Shelley Shepard Gray
Published in 2020 by Blackstone Publishing
Cover and book design by Alenka Vdovič Linaschke

Printed in the United States of America

First edition: 2020
ISBN Fiction / Romance / General
978-1-982658-58-8

1 3 5 7 9 10 8 6 4 2

CIP data for this book is available
from the Library of Congress

Blackstone Publishing
31 Mistletoe Rd.
Ashland, OR 97520

www.BlackstonePublishing.com

To Connie Lynch—a tireless supporter of writers and readers, and one of the kindest women I've ever had the pleasure to meet. Connie, I hope this book makes you smile.

Letter to Readers

On Thursday, December 13, 2018, Nicole Resciniti, my longtime agent, called with the incredible news that the team at Blackstone Publishing had just offered a contract for my Dance with Me series. I know this date because we had just started our drive from Cincinnati to Colorado Springs. We'd moved out of our house the night before, signed the papers for the new owners that morning, then started driving. And in the middle of that first morning—somewhere in the middle of Indiana—I received the call!

I've often thought about how timely that call was. Like the women in the Dance with Me trilogy, I was about to start over in a new town. I was also excited about the prospect and sad to be leaving everything familiar. Since the day of that phone call, Tom and I moved to Colorado. We also remodeled most of a house, made new friends, found a new church, went through a lengthy shoulder surgery, and shoveled a whole lot of snow. In the midst of all of that, I wrote *Shall We Dance?*, *Take the Lead,* and *Save the Last Dance*.

Now, like Shannon, Traci, and Kimber, I've at last settled into a new home and will be forever grateful for the opportunity I was given to start over.

I'm honestly a little sad to say goodbye to all the characters and places I made up in the fictional town of Bridgeport. I loved writing all six books set here, both the Dance with Me trilogy and the original Bridgeport Social Club books.

I'm so pleased to share that I've recently been given another contract from Blackstone. These books will be more romantic suspense in nature and take place in Ross County, Ohio. They feature English characters but many Amish secondary characters—which of course, are close to my heart. I hope you enjoy *Edgewater Road*, the first book in the series, which will be published in 2021. The first chapter is in the back of this book!

I always say I write books not just for myself but for my readers. So, dear reader, thank you for traveling to Bridgeport with me, and I'll look forward to greeting you in Ross County very soon!

With my blessings and my thanks,

Shelley Shepard Gray

CHAPTER 1

December 1

She couldn't get off the phone fast enough. Pacing the length of her small bedroom, Kimber Klein fiddled with her earpiece and tried to come up with a legitimate reason to end the call. Esme wasn't making it easy, though. Her girlfriend approached most conversations in the same way she directed her modeling career—with grit and determination.

"Kimber, you never answered my question. Is that guy still stalking you?"

That guy was Peter Mohler. Peter, who had worked on one of her photo shoots a year ago, had been trying to get closer ever since. Peter, who'd sent her flowers, cards, and creepy lingerie. Peter, who her agent Brett seemed to think she was making too big a deal about.

She didn't feel the same way. Even thinking about Peter Mohler made her feel sick. "I don't think so." She really hoped not.

"You mean he finally stopped sending you those creepy notes?"

"It looks like it. I haven't gotten anything from him in weeks." Of course, she'd also moved from New York City to small-town Ohio . . . and essentially stopped modeling.

"You aren't sure?" Esme sounded confused.

Kimber couldn't really blame her. She was confused by her behavior as well. She'd always been assertive and direct— sometimes to a fault. When she was a teenager, she'd been proud of herself, feeling like a "real" New Yorker.

Over the last year, she'd changed a bit, though. She was more patient, more subdued. Hesitant.

Peter's constant notes and gifts had made her uncomfortable. His sudden appearance at one of her modeling shoots had freaked her out. About to call the police, she'd touched base with Brett. He'd been upset on her behalf and told her to relax because he was going to take care of Peter.

But then she'd discovered that he'd never done a thing.

"I don't really think about Peter anymore," she lied, focusing back on their conversation. "He's in my past."

"Oh. Well, that's good," Esme said. "It's probably healthier, huh?"

"It is. I feel better. I mean, all of me feels healthier now."

"I still don't understand how you were able to walk away from your whole life, Kimber," Esme said with a new spike of incredulousness in her voice. "Grand Cayman was gorgeous and the designer gave us all samples. I got the most divine silk chiffon gown in spearmint. You would have loved it."

Kimber barely refrained from rolling her eyes. That was how she used to talk too. She used to be amazing at describing items of clothing in a way no one who didn't work in the fashion business would even think about. "I bet."

Esme paused, obviously waiting for some more envy-laced comments or another couple of questions. When Kimber remained silent, she added, "You would have had a ball."

"It does sound like a good time," she murmured, because modeling bathing suits on a beautiful tropical island had once been her dream job. She'd loved the beach and the downtime and the gorgeous clothes and samples that she'd been given. "I would have loved those days on the beach . . . if I wasn't retired."

Esme cleared her throat. "You didn't have to be, Kim. We were all talking about you. John Creek swore that you could have gone another five years."

John Creek was one of the top photographers in the business. For him to say such a thing was a compliment—and very generous.

Kimber guessed it was maybe too generous. She might have had three more years modeling, and that would have been stretching it.

She could have gone for a while longer . . . if she'd been willing to continue the same grueling pace.

That was, she would have had a ball modeling bathing suits and ball gowns for high-end fashion magazines while getting paid an obscene amount of money to pose on the beach on a Caribbean island.

All she would've had to do was stay hungry, swallow her pride, and pretend that nothing else mattered to her except being photogenic and having a hefty savings account.

But that was the thing—for the last year, none of that really seemed to matter anymore.

Or maybe it never had.

Feeling drained, Kimber said, "Esme, it's been nice talking to you, but I've got to go."

"How come? What are you doing these days?"

She was currently doing a lot of nothing . . . except for her new volunteer gig at the elementary school library. "I'm still getting my bearings, though I have been volunteering lately."

"That's it?"

"Hey, don't knock it. Doing nothing feels pretty good." Before Esme could reflect on that, Kimber softened her voice. "I am real glad you called, Ezzie. You didn't have to think of me. I appreciate it."

"We're friends, right?"

She felt terrible. "Right. We are friends. I'll call you next time."

"I hope you will. Oh! Door's ringing. I've gotta go. Bye."

"Bye," Kimber replied, though the line was already dead.

After swiping the screen a couple of times to check that she didn't have any messages or emails, Kimber set the phone down. If the last phone call hadn't done it, the lack of anything would have cemented the state of her life. She was currently doing next to nothing with her life.

She'd thought it would feel a lot better than it did.

* * *

"Everyone, let's say a big Coyote hello to Miss Klein and tell her thank you for being our reading volunteer today!"

Kimber smiled then tried not to step backward as the group of nine-year-olds howled at her. Someone needed to tell them to tone it down a notch.

When the librarian looked her way expectantly, Kimber said, "I don't have to howl back, do I?"

"Absolutely not, dear."

"Whew. I was a little worried there."

She'd been serious, but everyone in the room chuckled—the kids, the librarian and her aide, and even the kids' classroom teacher.

Actually, everyone seemed pretty amused by her except for

Jeremy, who was standing in the back of the room with his hands stuffed in the pockets of his worn jeans. She'd learned during her first visit that the dark-haired fifteen-year-old was earning some volunteer credits this semester. He came to the elementary school a few times a month and helped various teachers for an hour or two. Mrs. Lentz, the librarian, loved having him shelve books.

Kimber figured she normally wouldn't have given the teen a second thought, but there was something about him that called to her. Maybe it was because he looked just as uncomfortable in his skin as she felt. There he was, wearing faded jeans, tennis shoes, and a pullover and looking pretty much like every other fifteen-year-old boy in the area. But there was something in his blue eyes that seemed far older than his years.

Not for the first time, she wondered what his story was.

"Miss Klein, would you like to begin now?"

"Oh. Yes. Of course, Mrs. Lentz." Holding the picture book up, Kimber said, "This is one of my favorite holiday stories, *The Christmas Mouse.*"

As she began reading through the well-loved story, everything that had been bothering her began to fade away—the doubts, the boredom, Peter Mohler and his creepy fixation with her.

One by one, the kids stopped fidgeting and got caught up in the story. Little by little, they began to smile about the little Christmas mouse's adventures.

All except for Jeremy. He kept shelving books but stopped frequently to listen. She loved that. However, every time their eyes caught, he looked away, like he was embarrassed.

When Christmas Day came and the little mouse had a cozy home all his own, Kimber closed the book with a satisfied sigh.

"So what did all of you think?"

Hands shot in the air. Laughing, she called on the little girl with the red pigtails in the front row.

"I want a Christmas mouse."

"I do too. Does anyone have a favorite part?" She called on a boy in the back corner.

"When he was almost caught in the trap. That was scary."

Kimber nodded. "I thought so too."

Mrs. Lentz joined them. "Everyone, it's time to line up. The bell's going to ring soon and we need to get you back to class."

Immediately, all twenty-four of them jumped to their feet and hurried into line. They'd already completely forgotten about her and were excited to move onto the next part of the day.

After the kids left, she glanced at Jeremy. He had picked up the book and was examining the cover.

She walked to his side. "It's a cute story, huh?"

"Yeah."

"I'm a fan of picture books. I'm always in awe of the illustrations. Do you like them?"

"They're all right, I guess. I . . . I'd just heard this one before."

"Did your mom read it to you when you were little or something?"

He paled. "I've gotta go." Looking like he couldn't get out of the room fast enough, he spoke a few words to Mrs. Lentz, held out a card for her to sign, then grabbed his coat and strode out the door.

Unable to help herself, Kimber watched him until he was out of sight.

"He got to you, didn't he?" Jeanie Lentz said.

"I guess he did, but I'm afraid I just scared him off. I don't know what I did, though. Sorry about that."

"Don't worry about it. Jeremy is a good kid, but he's a little aloof."

"I know you can't share too much, but is he okay?"

"I think so." She paused, then said, "He's in foster care, with a single dad."

"He's a foster kid? Poor guy."

"People say he's been through a lot." Jeanie smiled softly. "I heard his parents died in a car accident or something a couple of years ago, and he's been in a couple of homes since then."

Now she felt terrible. "No wonder he took off so fast. I asked him if his mom used to read *The Christmas Mouse* to him."

Jeanie shrugged. "No reason to feel bad, dear. You couldn't have known about his parents. As a matter of fact, I wouldn't have been too surprised if he had told you all about his mom. He might have enjoyed sharing that memory with someone."

"Maybe." Thinking about her own mom—who had adopted her when she was just a baby—Kimber nodded. "Well, I guess it's time for me to get out of here as well. Thanks for letting me come back."

"It's my pleasure. You have a great rapport with the kids, and it's obvious that you love the books too. I'm delighted that you're volunteering."

"Thanks."

"Actually, no pressure, but if you'd like to do more around here, I'd love it."

"You mean read to more classes?"

"Yes. And help check books in and out. Maybe do a little bit of tutoring."

"Wow. Let me think about it."

"Sure. Like I said, it's all unpaid, so just do what you want."

"I'll let you know next week."

"Perfect. Now, you better get on your way. The final bell's about to ring. If you're not careful, you won't be able to get out of the parking lot for another twenty minutes."

Kimber grabbed her purse and coat. "See you soon," she said before rushing down the hallway. After making a quick stop at the volunteer desk, she trotted out to the parking lot.

Her pace slowed as she realized it was too late—she was going to be there for quite a while. There was already a long line of parents waiting to pick up kids.

Then she stopped at her brand-new, gleaming-white, all-wheel-drive Mercedes. Two of the tires were flat.

Flat like she wasn't going to be *anywhere* anytime soon. Flat like they'd been slashed on purpose.

And then she spied a familiar-looking note with the familiar-looking handwriting tucked under one of the windshield wipers.

Peter Mohler had found her again.

Standing there in the middle of the Bridgeport Elementary parking lot, Kimber tried her hardest not to burst into tears.

CHAPTER 2

"*Amazing grace! How sweet the sound*
That saved a wretch like me.
I once was lost but now am found,
Was blind but now I see."
—JOHN NEWTON

Never in his life had Gunnar Law seen such a pretty woman have such a royal hissy fit in a school parking lot. He'd been sitting in the parent pick up line, flipping through the radio stations, trying to find one that wasn't already playing Christmas music— honestly doing nothing but biding his time until he could pick up Jeremy and get home.

He'd been bored, a little stressed, thinking about the car he could have been working on at the shop . . . when, there she was. A tall woman, at least five foot nine, slim, with gorgeous hair that hung in rich, dark waves to her shoulder blades. She had on dark jeans, black boots, an ivory sweater, and a form-fitting light-blue parka.

She was stunning, there was no other word for it. Heck, he hadn't even known that word was in his vocabulary until it popped into his head.

Sitting behind the tinted windows of his Chevy truck, he watched every step she took. Then, in spite of the distance, he found himself worrying about her when she drew to an abrupt halt in front of a gleaming-white Mercedes sedan, dropped open her mouth and froze.

For a split second there, he'd been sure she was petrified.

She inhaled deeply, preparing to let out a full-on scream, but then she seemed to catch herself at the very last minute. To his surprise, she covered her mouth with one gloved hand and stomped her feet. It was kind of cute.

It was also kind of odd.

He didn't know a lot of beautiful Mercedes-driving women— okay, he didn't know *any* beyond the ones who owned the cars he worked on—but that didn't mean he couldn't tell when something was wrong. He finally looked down where she was staring.

Two flat tires.

And he knew right away that he wasn't looking at two tires that had come into contact with a couple of stray nails on the road. No, someone had done some real damage to her car.

BEEP.

He jumped, then realized he was holding up the car line. He moved forward, catching sight of Jeremy standing off to the side. The boy looked calm and a little removed from his surroundings.

This wasn't new.

As far as Gunnar could tell, the kid wasn't ever bothered in the slightest to be the only high schooler in the vicinity. This time, he was also staring in the same direction as the small group of elementary age kids. He, along with at least half of the young kids, was watching the riled-up woman.

Rolling down his window, he called out to him. "Jeremy?"

The boy immediately stepped forward and climbed inside the truck.

"Hey," Gunnar said. "You good?" he asked as the boy tossed his backpack in the back of the cab and buckled up.

"Yeah." He paused, then blurted, "I was just watching Miss Klein. Gunnar, I think something's wrong with her car. She looks real upset."

"Are you talking about that woman who's standing next to the white Mercedes?"

"Yeah."

"I noticed her too." He pulled over to the side so the cars behind him could leave. "Now, who is she? I don't remember you mentioning her before."

"Miss Klein is a volunteer in the library. She reads stories to the kids while I shelve books. She's nice." Still watching her, he added, "She's usually kind of quiet too. I've never seen her so mad."

Noticing that she was currently staring at her cell phone but not doing much else, Gunnar said, "I was thinking maybe we should see if she needs help. What do you think?"

"I think we'd better do something. She looks pretty confused, Gunnar."

"All right, then." He drove back into the parking lot, parked in the first empty spot that his truck would fit into, then looked at Jeremy. "Ready?"

Jeremy didn't say a word. Just hopped out.

When they got to Miss Klein's side, she was on the phone but didn't look any happier. She frowned when they approached, but then smiled at Jeremy. "Hold on a sec, please," she said to whoever was on the phone. "Hi, Jeremy, right?"

Jeremy nodded. "Yep. We saw your car."

"I'm on the phone with a car place now." Sounding aggravated, she added, "I couldn't believe it, but the dealership said my flat tires weren't their problem." As if suddenly remembering that she had put the place on hold, she said, "Oh, shoot. Hold on!"

Gunnar exchanged a glance with Jeremy as they listened to her try to convince whoever was on the line to take care of her problem immediately. She sounded both naive and bossy—the woman pretty clearly had no idea about cars, mechanics, or flat tires. She needed a hand.

Luckily, he was in a position to help. "Excuse me. Ah, Miss Klein?"

She pressed her hand against the face of the phone again. "I'm sorry, yes?"

"I can help you out. Go ahead and tell whoever you're talking to that you've got it handled."

"But I don't—"

"It's okay," Jeremy blurted. "Gunnar knows how to take care of things."

Miss Klein stared at him a moment before speaking into the phone again. "Thanks, but I've found someone else," she said as she disconnected.

He couldn't help but grin. "Wow. That was abrupt."

"Ugh. I guess I was." Seeming to shake it off, she shrugged. "I grew up in the city. Old habits die hard, I guess."

"What's the city?" Jeremy asked. "Are you from down in Cincinnati?" Bridgeport was one of Cincinnati's northernmost suburbs.

"Not that one. I'm referring to New York City."

"Wow," said Jeremy.

Turning to Gunnar, she held out a gloved hand. "Since you're saving me and everything, I should probably get to know you. My name's Kimber."

"You're name is Kimber Klein." He couldn't help but smile at that.

12

Looking mildly sheepish, she nodded. "Yes. And before you ask, I also know that my full name has a cute little ring to it."

He shook her hand. "I'm Gunnar Law. And it looks like you and Jeremy have already met."

Smiling at the boy, she stuffed her hands in her coat pockets. "We sure have. We met at the library."

"So you're the librarian?" He would have read a whole lot more when he was in school if the librarian had looked like her.

She laughed. "Not at all. I'm just a volunteer."

"That's nice that you take the time to do that." He paused, hoping that she might give him more information, but she didn't.

When he realized Jeremy was trying not to smirk at his attempt to chat in the cold parking lot, Gunnar got down to business. "Look, this is your lucky day. I work at a mechanic shop, and I just happen to be buddies with the owner. His name's Ace."

"Ace?"

"I promise, he's a good guy. I grew up with him. Let me give him a call and get you some help."

"You sure that won't be any trouble?"

"It's a phone call. No big deal."

She seemed to need a minute to think. After glancing at Jeremy again, she nodded. "Thank you. I really appreciate it. Honestly, I didn't know what I was going to do."

Gunnar felt like he'd just passed some kind of test, and he was pleased about it—which was pretty odd, considering that he was trying to do the woman a favor, not date her. When he noticed her shoving her hands in her pockets again, he said quietly, "It's cold, Kimber. Do you want to sit in the truck with us while we wait? We could turn the heat on."

"Oh, that's okay. I can sit in my car."

"All right, but it might be a few. Might as well sit with us, yeah?"

Glancing at Jeremy again, she said, "Are you okay with that?"

"Yeah," Jeremy said.

"Maybe try for a *yes, ma'am*?" Gunnar murmured.

"Ma'am."

For some reason, the kid's reluctant effort to adopt Gunnar's old-school manners melted some of her veneer. She grinned at Jeremy. "Let's go get warm then. It's freezing out here."

Gunnar walked to the passenger side door and opened it for her. She got in. Jeremy hopped in the back cab. Already calling Ace, Gunnar walked to his side.

"Law, what's up?"

"I'm calling in a favor. I'm at the elementary and there's a lady here who's got two sliced tires. She's gonna need a tow."

"Can't you just put on a spare?"

"It's a Mercedes, and no. Both of the tires are flat as pancakes. Honestly, I'd feel better if you helped me take care of it."

"I can't go, but I can send someone out."

"Perfect. Thanks. You won't miss us. I've got my green truck and it's parked next to a flashy white Merc."

"I'll tell Carter."

"I owe you."

"Nah, the lady will owe me. They're her tires, right?"

"Yep," he replied, though for some reason he was feeling a little protective of her. "I'll pass on the word."

Ace chuckled before disconnecting.

Gunnar shook his head as he got into his vehicle. Immediately, he caught the scent of her perfume. It wasn't sweet and cloying, or even flowery. He wasn't good at descriptions—he could only categorize it as *expensive*.

Why he was even analyzing her scent was a mystery.

Hoping to cover up his awkwardness, he said, "Ace can't come, but a guy who does a lot of work for him can. The guy is probably already on his way."

"This is really nice of you both. I bet I'm putting you out."

"You're not. We weren't going to do much tonight, except maybe go hunt down a Christmas tree."

The woman looked over at Jeremy. "Oh no! I'm sorry. I'm spoiling your evening."

Jeremy grinned. "I didn't even know we were gonna do that. It's fine."

"We don't have our tree up yet."

"Do you and your husband get a real one or an artificial?"

"I'm not married. I live with some girlfriends." Looking puzzled, she said, "To be honest, I hadn't even thought about Christmas decorations yet. I guess I should."

"Probably. It's coming up."

Kimber grunted. "I heard that. Hey, Jeremy, is he always so literal?"

Jeremy grinned. "If you mean, does he always tell the truth, then yep."

"That's a good quality," Gunnar said.

"It is if the person you're talking to wants to hear it," Jeremy joked.

"You got me there, boy." He was about to add more when he noticed that Jeremy was grinning widely. Like was exceptionally pleased. Gunnar was floored. Jeremy hadn't looked this relaxed or happy the entire time he'd been living with him.

Looking at him, Kimber said, "Where did you learn that? From your mom?"

"From both of my parents, I guess. Neither are much for liars."

She smiled back at the boy. "I guess this means he's raising you right. You're a lucky young man."

"Oh, Gunnar isn't my real dad. I'm just his foster kid."

And *that* . . . turned the atmosphere in the truck about twenty degrees cooler.

"Ah. So how's it going? So far, so good?"

Gunnar bristled. What was that supposed to mean? They were strangers, so why did she think that *any* of what they were doing was her business? Feeling protective, Gunnar said, "Excuse me, but why are you asking him that? I'm his guardian."

She cut him off. "I'm not talking to you, Mr. Law. I asked Jeremy." Her voice gentled. "So?"

The boy rolled his shoulders. "I guess it's going all right." His eyes narrowed. "Why? What do you know about foster care, anyway?"

"My sister was raised in foster care and then in a group home. She told me that it wasn't easy."

While Gunnar sat there and processed that, Jeremy seemed to wake up. His focused sharpened, and he seemed to push aside some of his natural reticence.

"Your sister was in foster care but not you?" he asked.

Looking pained, she nodded. "It's a long story, but I'm one of three sisters. We were split up when we were hardly more than babies. I was adopted, and so was Shannon. Our middle sister wasn't."

"That's tough," Gunnar murmured.

She turned to him. "I'll be honest. I never knew I had sisters until recently. But when I realized that Traci's life was so different from mine? Well, it was hard to come to terms with." She lifted her shoulder. "But everyone goes their way in life, I guess. Even folks who grew up with their real parents don't always have it easy."

"Maybe you're right," Gunnar said.

"I know she is," Jeremy corrected.

While Gunnar gaped at the boy, Kimber laughed, and the sound was low and husky while feminine enough to make every one of his nerve endings take notice.

She winked at the boy before turning back to him. "If you

aren't certain about that yet, you just might be the best thing that has happened to Jeremy here."

This was really the oddest conversation he'd ever had. Who talked about such things so boldly?

Luckily, Carter and the tow truck appeared. "Looks like we're going to get you on your way real soon."

She smiled up at him. "You didn't lie, did you? I don't know what to say except for thanks so much."

"It was no problem." He kept his words short and sweet, but the inside of him was already wondering about that comment. Who had been lying to her so much that she expected it from the get-go? And why the heck did that bother him so much, anyway?

CHAPTER 3

*"O, Christmas tree, O, Christmas tree, how
faithful are thy branches?"*
—"O CHRISTMAS TREE"

Watching his foster dad was pretty entertaining. Though Gunnar was acting all cool and collected, Jeremy thought it was pretty obvious the guy only wanted to keep staring at Kimber Klein.

Jeremy thought it was funny. During the five months that he'd lived with Gunnar Law, the guy had never acted like he'd even noticed there were women in the world. The man was stable, methodical, and completely focused on three things: his work, his friends from West Virginia . . . and Jeremy.

Actually, he'd been *really* focused on Jeremy, which had been sort of nice but also a little overwhelming. He might've had a rough go of it, but he wasn't a kid. He didn't need Gunnar to worry about the little things like if he had eaten his breakfast or done his homework.

Unfortunately, no matter how many times Jeremy had told him that, Gunnar still made him bacon and eggs every morning—and sipped coffee while Jeremy ate.

But now? Well, now, the guy was acting like Miss Klein was all that. Jeremy didn't really blame him—Miss Klein *was* really pretty. But he'd seen a lot of pretty women in Bridgeport. He wondered what Gunnar saw in her that was so special.

After the tow truck disappeared and Gunnar was still frozen in place, Jeremy said, "Are you okay?"

"Hmm? Oh, shoot." Gunnar shook his head like he was trying to clear it. "Sorry about all that. Probably the last thing you wanted to do today was help some lady with her vehicle."

"I didn't mind. She really needed some help. I'm glad you knew who to call." He grinned. "She looked pretty clueless, standing there by her car and staring at her phone."

"I thought the same thing." Still not putting the truck into gear, Gunnar said, "Hey, I never asked. Do you know her well?"

Jeremy tried hard not to smile that Gunnar was fishing for information from a teenager. Starting to feel kind of sorry for the guy's instant crush, he said, "I don't know her at all. She helps out in the library when I'm working in there, but it's not like we talk or anything. I've only spoken to her a couple of times."

"Oh."

"She seems nice, though," he added, because they still weren't going anywhere.

"She does. She's got a heck of an accent, doesn't she?"

Jeremy privately thought Gunnar was the one who had a heck of the accent. But he knew better than to say that. "I should've asked her if everyone from the city sounds like that."

"It's good you didn't. That would be pretty rude."

"Yeah, maybe you're right." After a couple of seconds of silence, Jeremy cleared his throat and looked pointedly down the street. He was long past ready to go home. He had a ton of homework and was starving.

Finally taking the hint, Gunnar put the truck into gear and started for home.

Glad that they were finally moving, Jeremy leaned back in his seat, wondering what Miss Klein's real story was. All he could think about was her comment about how she'd been adopted but her sister hadn't. That didn't seem right.

Though he usually would have kept his question to himself, his question bubbled out: "How do you think that works, with her being adopted and her sister going into a group home? What do you think happened?"

Gunnar glanced his way when he came to a stop sign. "I wondered the same thing. I don't know. To be honest, I don't know much about how the whole system works except for how things went with you. You probably know more than I do."

He'd told Jeremy several times that after considering fostering for a good year, he called his social worker, who he'd known through church, and asked her questions. It turned out Melanie had been anxious to put Jeremy someplace better and had expedited the paperwork and house calls. Just six weeks after Gunnar's initial call, Jeremy had been moving into his house.

"I thought I knew some stuff, but I didn't think child services did things like that."

"Did what, exactly?"

"You know, I didn't think the social workers and courts split up siblings."

"I don't think they do anymore. That would make a hard situation even harder, I reckon."

"Yeah." Jeremy had always wished he'd had a sibling, but after hearing about Miss Klein's situation, he was kind of glad he didn't.

What would he do if they were separated? "Do you think she was telling the truth?"

"I do." He rubbed a hand over his face and seemed to contemplate that. When he looked at Jeremy again, his hazel eyes looked puzzled. "I mean, why would someone make that up?"

That made sense.

As Gunnar pulled into the driveway, he said, "Jeremy, since we're being real honest and all, I have to tell ya that you caught me off guard when you pointed out that you were *just* my foster kid."

"How come? It's the truth, right?" What he didn't want to say was that he was too afraid to call Gunnar his real dad. What if Gunnar changed his mind?

"You're right. But we've been together for a while now. Five months." He unbuckled but didn't move. "Listen, when we talked about going through with the adoption, I thought you were on board with wanting to make things permanent too. But, if you think it's too soon, or you're not sure . . . you just have to tell me. There's two of us, you know."

Even thinking about leaving Gunnar's house and getting stuck in some stranger's house made him panic. "Are you saying you changed your mind?"

Gunnar shook his head. "No. No, not at all."

"But—"

"Jeremy, bud . . . this is all hard enough without you putting words I wasn't even thinking into my mouth. That's not what I said at all. You know I want you with me, but you're fifteen, not five months. You have a say in your own future," he added gruffly. "I want you to feel good. Not just settle, you know?"

Jeremy knew what he should say. He knew he should say that he hadn't changed his mind, that he liked Gunnar. That he wasn't settling. But it was like all the words in his head got sideways before making their way out of his mouth.

21

So instead he just nodded. He felt like crap keeping silent, but he didn't know if he had it in him to give Gunnar anything more. "Okay. Glad we talked. Let's go on in. It's freezing."

Jeremy climbed out, grabbed his backpack, and walked to the front door of Gunnar's house. As he'd done every time since he'd first seen the place, he reflected on how crazy it was that he lived there.

Gunnar Law not only worked as an auto mechanic for Ace, he did carpentry work on the side. He'd built his house over two years, and it was cool. Like, amazingly cool.

For one, it was way bigger than it looked from the front. It was a sprawling walkout ranch-style house with four bedrooms, a media room, five bathrooms, and a kitchen–dining room combo that practically ran the length of the house. Crazier still, before Jeremy moved in, Gunnar had lived there all by himself.

He'd later learned that Gunnar had built it for a woman he'd been dating, but they'd broken up while he was building it. He'd finished it out with the intention of putting it on the market, but the real estate market was in a slump and no one was looking. Sometime after that he'd decided to just stay.

And now Jeremy had a huge room right next to the kitchen. Crazy.

After unlocking the door, Gunnar motioned for Jeremy to go in while he punched a series of numbers on the keypad.

"I was thinking chili tonight. You okay with that?"

"Yep."

"Do you have homework?"

"Yep. A ton."

Gunnar raised his eyebrows. "You always say you have a ton."

"That's because I always do."

"Do you need some help?"

"No."

"Are you sure?" Looking uncomfortable, Gunnar folded his arms over his chest. "I'm not too good at math, but I can help you study history or something. I wasn't great in school, but I didn't flunk out or anything. I also know a couple of people who could tutor you, so don't be shy."

"Thanks, but I'm good. I'm gonna head to my room now."

"All right. I'll call you when supper's ready."

Walking the short distance down the hall to his room, Jeremy walked inside and closed the door. And, at last, he felt himself relax.

The truth was, he wasn't all that good at school. He wasn't failing out, but he mostly got Bs and Cs. He'd always been okay with that, since he'd been basically just trying to get by. But now that it looked like staying with Gunnar could actually happen, he started thinking about other stuff. Like a future. He was a junior, halfway through the year even. If all went well, he could be graduating high school in a year and a half. Melanie, his social worker, had told him he should even start thinking about college or trade school.

Jeremy hadn't ever believed he'd have the money for either, but now he was starting to think that she hadn't been just giving him a pep talk. Maybe he *was* going to have a future after all.

His phone buzzed, pulling him away from his worries. Looking at the screen, he saw it was from Phillip. Phil was his best friend at Bridgeport High. They'd met in biology. Their teacher had made them partners when the class was dissecting a frog. Both of them had been trying hard not to gag but had somehow gotten the best grade on the test, which inspired them to work together again.

Which kind of turned them into friends. Now Jeremy ate lunch with the guy and his whole crew.

And that was really amazing, given that Phillip was friends with just about everybody.

> Hey. Have you asked anyone to the
> Christmas dance yet?

Jeremy rolled his eyes. Bridgeport High held a fancy Christmas dance every year, a couple of days before Christmas. He thought that was a weird time to have a school dance, but everyone said it was tradition and that they'd been holding the dance in the school gym right before Christmas for decades. Some people even planned their vacations around it.

He hadn't thought much about the dance for a number of reasons. But, he guessed if he was a guy like Phillip DiCenzo, he would be. Every girl in the school probably was waiting on him to ask her out.

> No. Have you?

> I'm taking Carson.

Should've known. Phillip and Carson weren't official yet, but everyone knew that they liked each other. Phillip walked her to class every day after lunch.

> Carson said that Bethany Seevers
> likes you. What do you think?

> About Bethany? IDK

> She's hot.

Yeah. But I don't really know her.

Get to know her so we can go together.

Whatever.

I'm serious.

Fine. I'll think about.

Good.

Jeremy watched the screen for a minute more, but true to form, Phillip had signed off and was focused on the next thing.

Sitting down on the big La-Z-Boy that was in the corner of his room, Jeremy thought about Bethany. She was in their science lab too. She *was* hot. She had really long hair, and he'd always thought she was one of the prettiest girls in school. She didn't have lots of curves like Phillip's Carson. Instead, she looked kind of willowy.

But as he thought about Bethany, he realized he didn't think about her looks all that much. Instead, he liked how she was so nice. A lot of people their age were only nice to their friends. Not Bethany, though. She seemed to go out of her way to talk to everyone.

Yep, she was really sweet. And that sweetness—combined with her light brown hair and green eyes—well, he couldn't think of a better girl in the junior class.

But he didn't know if he even wanted to go to a dance.

Girls, in his experience, liked to talk. She might want to know about him.

Then he'd have to tell her his whole story. About how Gunnar Law wasn't really his dad and this cool house wasn't actually *his* house.

And if she still asked him questions, he'd have to share that he'd been in four other foster houses and that he'd never had a dad. And that his mom had been real sweet until she'd gotten shot at an ATM.

He could just imagine how cool Bethany would think he was then. Obviously, not very.

Which meant before long, Bethany wouldn't like him anymore—and worse, she would probably tell everyone about his parents and how he used to live. And then everyone would know how different he was.

That was something he wasn't ready to deal with just yet. Shoot, he didn't know if he would ever be able to deal with that.

CHAPTER 4

CLARA: *A young girl who receives a Nutcracker doll for Christmas and dreams that he comes to life.*

December 5

Kimber had started helping her sister Shannon clean up her dance studio on the bottom floor of their building once a week. It was a good way to spend time with her sister, since Shannon was married and wasn't around that much at night anymore.

Kimber also had a natural affinity for organizing and cleaning. She didn't mind doing either and loved seeing a room with everything neatly in its place.

Shannon, on the other hand, did not.

Their third sister, Traci, sometimes offered to help, but more often than not she took a pass. Kimber didn't fault her for that, however. Traci was a cop for the city of Bridgeport. She not only had a demanding job, but she was also a new mom. Several months ago, Traci had met a pregnant teenager named Gwen and took her under her wing. A lot had happened, but in the end, Gwen became Traci's unofficial little sister, and Traci became the adopted mother to Gwen's baby boy, Bridge. So Gwen had a lot on her plate . . . and a doctor fiancé to boot.

Since Kimber was taking a break from modeling and wasn't sure what to do next, she'd been trying to help Shannon out in the dance studio. Shannon had been appreciative of everything, which was very like her sister.

But, what Kimber hadn't seen coming was Shannon's need to try to teach her to tap dance. No matter how many times Kimber had protested that she really, really didn't want to learn how to do a time step, Shannon tried to convince her to "just give it a try."

Like she was currently doing.

Grimacing at both the ugly tap shoes on her feet and the fact that she couldn't make a single clean *tap* like Shannon did, Kimber was already counting the minutes until the impromptu lesson was over.

Shannon, however, seemed to think of Kimber's talentless toes as a wonderful challenge.

"Come on, Kimber," she coaxed, standing by her sister's side. "This will be fun."

"It won't." It had never been fun.

"I promise, you'll get the hang of it. Soon, you'll be tapping up a storm."

She was so far from tapping up anything. Annoyed, and barely keeping her thoughts to herself, Kimber eyed their reflections in the mirror. Here she was—feeling a little frumpy in faded jeans, an old sweatshirt, heavy socks, and fake-leather flats with taps attached to the soles. Next to her was little petite Shannon looking perfect in form fitting black pants, a violet tank top, some kind of cute knit-wrap thingy, and legitimate, two-inch-heel tap shoes that were actually very pretty.

Added to the disparity was the fact that Kimber was a good ten inches taller than Shannon. Kimber always felt like a giant next to her. Now, she not only felt huge, she felt like a clumsy oaf too.

"Shannon, it's real sweet of you to get me tap shoes, but I'd really rather clean."

As she should have expected, Shannon looked really confused. "Don't say that. No one would rather clean than dance."

Oh, yes they would! Choosing her words carefully, Kimber added, "To be honest, I'm not enjoying this all that much." Like, at all.

"That's because you're rushing, Kimber. Now, let's just take each step slow. Before you know it, you'll be agreeing with me that tap dancing isn't so hard."

"It's always going to be difficult because I have no sense of rhythm." She also had no interest in learning how to time step. As in *none*.

Shannon did some kind of fancy footwork to illustrate her point. "You'll get the hang of it soon. You just need some muscle memory. That's where good old-fashioned practice comes in."

"But—"

"Come now. Don't give up," she pressed in her sweet southern drawl.

Kimber was getting tired of being ignored. "Shannon, one last time, I came here to clean, not dance." She also had come in to talk. She really wanted to talk to Shannon.

Looking deflated, Shannon stared at Kimber in the mirror. "You're serious."

"I promise, I'm so serious." *Please*, she silently added. *Don't make me pull a New York attitude.* It was on the way though, because her patience had left a good five minutes ago.

"Fine." Pointing to the three closets on the back wall. "How would you feel about helping me organize the costumes for our

Christmas ballet? You know, all my students will be performing different dances from *The Nutcracker*."

Kimber did know. She was excited to help Shannon and to see it too. What she *didn't* want to do was dance. "I'd love to help you—as long as you don't start trying to make me tap dance anymore. My feet already hurt."

She chuckled as she sat down on a bench and carefully removed her tap shoes and slipped on some black leather flats. "I'm sorry. I just have a feeling that you're going to be a really great tap dancer. But I don't mean to continually put you on the spot."

"Thank you for that." After taking off the ugly tap shoes, Kimber put back on her favorite running shoes.

"Oh brother. Well, let's get started." Moving over to the closet, Shannon started pulling out boxes and plastic tubs. "So how are things going? And, before I forget to ask, where's your fancy new car? I didn't see it parked on the street when I got here this morning."

"My car's in the shop because someone slashed two of my tires while I was helping out in the library at the elementary school."

Shannon's face went slack. "What? When?"

"Yesterday."

"I can hardly believe it. Bridgeport is such a safe place. Who do you think could have done it? Do you think it was a kid?"

"I don't know what to think. If it was a kid, it feels kind of random. I mean they're just little kids at that elementary school."

"You're right. Maybe someone was trying to rob you or something?"

"I don't think so, but who knows?" Because it hurt too much to think about Peter Mohler being so close, Kimber knelt down on one knee and pulled another large plastic tub out of the closet. On its heels slid out two shopping bags stuffed to the gills with fabric.

Looking at the hodgepodge of costumes, plastic tubs, holiday decorations, and what looked like old and discarded socks, she wrinkled her nose. "Shannon, this closet is a clown car."

Her sister frowned. "I know. It's a real mess. I don't know how it got so bad."

"Me neither. We've barely been here a year."

"Obviously, I need to give it more attention—it's always last on my list, though. I'd much rather teach or dance."

"I know." It was really cute the way Shannon loved to dance so much.

"Thanks for helping me."

"I'm happy to help, but this closet needs more than a little TLC." Shannon was going to need a better organizational system, because this really wasn't working. "I think we need to find a system for you. Hmm. Do you want me to start a list on the computer? We could catalogue it . . ."

"No, I want to get back to your tires getting slashed. Did you call the police?"

"No."

"Why not?"

"I don't think it's a police matter." The truth was that she hadn't wanted to go down that road again. No one in New York had cared about her stalker, since he hadn't actually ever hurt her or her property. Plus, their sister, Traci, and Shannon's husband, Dylan, were cops. She wasn't ready for her sisters to become involved either.

"Really?"

No, not really. "I was thinking maybe I drove through a construction site or something."

"I've never heard of two tires getting slashed from stray nails on the road."

Kimber hadn't heard of that either. Plus, the guys at Ace's

shop said the damage had probably been made with a knife or a box cutter. "Don't worry about it. The important thing is that my car will be as good as new by this afternoon."

But Shannon didn't seem to want to let it go. "If it wasn't a teen, who could it have been?"

Maybe her stalker? "I'm not sure."

"Hey. You look worried. Are you scared? Do you want me to call Dylan?" Sounding more positive, she added, "I know he'd be happy to help. I bet he can come right over and take a statement."

Her offer was pure Shannon. She was so eager to assist, so determined to help someone in need, and she was willing to do whatever it took to make that happen—even volunteer her busy, newlywed cop husband.

Though, Kimber figured Shannon volunteering Dylan wasn't much of a stretch. He would probably be as willing as Shannon to help her out. She just wasn't sure he could do anything.

Shannon's desire to help everyone and get Dylan involved was cute, and it made Kimber happy that Shannon had that support system. But it wasn't how she handled things. Kimber handled them on her own. "I didn't tell you so you could fix me."

"I wasn't trying to do that."

She heard the hurt in Shannon's voice. "I'm not trying to be mean, I'm just saying I've got it handled." She attempted to chuckle. "I mean, I only told you because you asked where my car was."

"So if I hadn't asked, you would have kept your car troubles to yourself?"

"It's not that I don't trust you, it's just that it's my problem and not yours."

Shannon looked even more hurt. "Okay," she said. Then she turned back to the closet and pulled out another plastic tub.

"Look, I'm sorry . . ." Kimber's voice drifted off. Because really, what was she going to say, anyway? That she was being secretive because she'd been burned by revealing too much to the wrong people? That she was hesitant to talk about anything because she'd been followed around by a creepy stalker guy for the last year and never said anything?

It was time to change the subject. "In other news, I met a great guy in the parking lot while I was waiting."

"What?"

"The man was the guardian of the high school helper in the library. When they saw me freaking out in the parking lot, they came over to help."

"He was a guardian?"

"Yep." Pulling out a couple costumes, she started organizing them in piles. "The boy is a foster kid. And the guardian is practically a walking advertisement for gorgeous men who are competent."

"So he's a hunk with a good heart. Those are my favorite types of guys."

Kimber wasn't usually so dreamy, but she couldn't deny that Shannon had a good point. "I think they're mine too."

"Is he married?"

"I don't know."

"You didn't check? Was he wearing a ring on his hand?"

"No. But that doesn't mean anything. I'm sure that even back in West Virginia, there were plenty of married men who didn't wear a ring." She'd sure encountered lots of married men who didn't believe in rings when she'd been modeling.

"Oh, come on. I'm small town, but not that small. Did you get a married vibe from him?"

"Shannon, you are a piece of work. No one has a married vibe."

"Some people do. I do."

Even though both Shannon and her husband wore rings, they

did have an "I'm married don't mess with me" vibe. Some people *did* have that kind of way about them. "Fine. If I had to guess, I'd say he was single."

"Then he would be perfect." Opening another tub, Shannon smiled. "Ah, here we go. These are going to be sublime for my little snowflakes. Help me count, would you?"

Kimber pulled one of the costumes up. The white leotards were embellished with silver sequins and rhinestones through the midsection. Wide silver and white ribbons were attached to the side seams, then trailed down for a good eight inches. No doubt the ribbons would flutter in the air every time a dancer moved. "These are really pretty."

"Thanks. My mother made them. She's the best." Shannon carefully shook each one and laid it neatly on the floor around her. "We'll have to put Traci on it. She can look him up."

"Wait . . . Why not Dylan?"

"He's not the type of guy to get into that. He'd say I was meddling and wouldn't listen when I tried to tell him that I was only looking out for you." She rested on her knees. "Did you count twenty?"

"Only seventeen."

"That's what I was afraid of. I'm going to have to order more—my mom's on a river cruise in Europe."

Shannon looked so put out by that, Kimber chuckled. "Do you even know where to order dance costumes from?"

"Of course. Dancer's Warehouse." She pursed her lips. "I mean, I'm pretty sure they have costumes for little girls. If not I'm going to have to do more hunting tonight."

Comments like that were why Kimber felt like she needed to help Shannon out as much as possible. "Girl, you need help."

"I know. I love to dance and I love to teach dancing. But all this other stuff? It's overwhelming as all get out." She shrugged. "But what can I do? I've got a building to pay off."

"You can ask your sister to help you with the payments. And for the record, I'm talking about me, not Traci."

Shannon's eyes got big. "I can't ask that of you. You're busy."

"I'm not that busy. Plus, you know I can pay for things."

"No way. I don't want your money."

"I have money to spare. And . . . I could also be your assistant."

"You don't have that kind of time."

"I do, and you know I do."

Looking around at the pink fluff surrounding them, Shannon blew out a burst of air. "Then I accept. But be warned. Being in my studio means you're going to be surrounded by teenage girls and ballroom dancers."

"I promise. I've already figured that one out. As long as you don't make me start tap dancing, it's all good."

CHAPTER 5

THE NUTCRACKER: *Clara's new toy that comes to life. He is magically transformed into a handsome prince and accompanies Clara on her adventure.*

Gunnar couldn't look away as the contractor at the front of the long line he was in pulled an attitude with Suzanne, the clerk who was in charge of approving building permits. No matter what she said, the contractor argued with her. They were loud too. Loud enough to be clearly heard over the canned Christmas music playing throughout the building.

Usually that kind of thing pissed him off. He didn't like to waste time and he really didn't like to watch idiots self-implode.

But it was bitter cold outside and spitting snow. At least here inside the county office it was warm, and there was a good sandwich shop next door. As soon as he got his paperwork finished he was going to grab a cup of soup and a roast beef sandwich.

Plus, he wasn't the only person in the room watching the interaction with interest. The other eight or so men and women were focused on the argument as well. Who could blame any of them? Suzanne was as grizzled as any of them and didn't put up with much. Besides, the contractor was a real bonehead.

"My money's on the clerk," Hodges said behind him.

Gunnar grinned. "Well, yeah. Of course Suzanne is going to win—she doesn't put up with much. No, I'm thinking the bet needs to be on *when* she's going to win, not *if*."

"I say less than four minutes," the woman in front of Gunnar said. "Suzanne is beginning show signs of irritation. She's repositioned her glasses twice now."

"I'm going with eight minutes," Gunnar said. "Suzanne looks like she's playing with him the way a cat tortures a mouse." Lowering his voice, he added, "I think this is her fun."

Hodges and his partner jumped in. Each made a bets, one declaring that Suzanne was about to call for security within two minutes, the other saying that he didn't think the clerk took anything personally and she was just slow.

As the clock ticked, they all watched intently—even the old guy at the end of the line who seemed like he didn't hold with the way they were joking around.

And then . . . six minutes later, Suzanne pointed to the door and the arguing dude slumped out, looking equal parts ticked off and dejected.

Hodges and his partner had just whistled low when Suzanne focused on the lot of them and glared.

That shut all of them down immediately. Everyone knew better than to piss off Suzanne. As she'd just illustrated, she could make a person's life quite difficult—bring an entire construction project to screeching to an abrupt halt.

"Next!" Suzanne called out.

The woman in front of Gunnar stepped right up and presented her file. Two minutes later, Gunnar did the same.

Suzanne, all hard lines and silver hair, held out a hand. "Sounded to me like you were having yourself a good old time in line, Mr. Law."

"I didn't mean anything. No disrespect intended, ma'am."

"Uh-huh."

Gunnar decided to keep his mouth shut then, only speaking when she asked him questions.

Finally, with a long-suffering sigh, Suzanne stamped his paperwork and handed it back to him. "You have a good day now."

"You too, ma'am. I sure appreciate your help."

She half rolled her eyes at his good boy act. "Next!"

Grinning to himself, he neatly folded the permit in his wallet and waited in the line at the sandwich shop. Luckily, it moved much faster, and in less than ten minutes, he was sipping hot potato-cheddar soup and biting into a thick roast beef sandwich.

He was almost done when Ace called. "Hey, Gunnar."

"What's up?" He wasn't scheduled to work for another two days. "Do you need me?"

"Nah, nothing like that. I was just wondering if you've seen that Mercedes gal again."

"Why?"

"Have you?" Ace pressed.

"I haven't. Why?" he asked again. Ace wasn't the type to call him with random questions like this.

"Oh, no reason. No reason, other than it looked like there was something between you two."

Oh, for Pete's sake. Was his buddy seriously trying to play matchmaker? Weighing his words carefully, he said, "I don't know if there was something between us or not. It's doubtful that I'll ever see Kimber again."

"Oh, yeah. That was her name, wasn't it? Kimber."

Shoot. He'd said too much. "Any reason you're pushing this?"

"No reason. Not other than this Kimber seemed real sweet." He lowered his voice. "She also asked about you when she picked up her car. She seemed disappointed that you'd already left for the day, Gunnar."

Even though a part of him was pleased about that, Gunnar did his best to play it cool. "I don't know why Kimber would be disappointed or not. I mean, all I was doing was helping her out."

"She's real pretty and she seemed sweet too. Not every woman is like that, you know."

Gunnar knew. Avery, his ex-girlfriend, had seemed sweet—until she'd opened up and turned into a demanding, conniving shrew.

"You got lucky with your wife, Ace." His wife, Meredith, was one of the sweetest ladies Gunnar had ever met.

Ace's voice brightened. "True that. Now, I know I'm sounding all in your business, but you've been alone for a while now. You might want to think about giving Kimber a call. She seems like a woman who would be worth your time."

She'd been a mystery, that's what she'd been. Beautiful, direct, and confusing. And, most likely far too *city* for a hick from small-town West Virginia like him. "I've got enough going on with Jeremy, Ace." Moreover, he didn't necessarily want anyone digging into his personal life.

"Fine. I hear you."

"Appreciate that."

"You're off the schedule until Monday. But will I see you Friday night?"

"I'll be there." Ace's son Finn had just signed with a college to play ball next fall. Ace was beyond proud and was hosting a big spaghetti dinner in his honor.

39

Just as he got up to toss his trash, his phone buzzed, signally an incoming text.

Looking at the screen, he sat back down again.

Speak of the devil, it was Miss Kimber Klein.

> Hey. Just wanted to thank you for your help the other day. I've got four working tires again. Everyone at your shop was great.

As he read her text a second time, he felt a quick little burst of adrenaline when he thought about texting her back.

Lord, he was so out of practice dating. Finally, deciding that it would be rude to not text back, his thumb hovered over the screen before finally replying.

> No problem.

One minute later, she wrote back again.

> Hope you don't mind that I got your number from Jeremy. I promise I won't start texting you all the time.

To his surprise, he realized that he wouldn't mind if she did. But then what would they do? He didn't date . . . Did he?

He decided to keep it simple.

> Glad you're all good again.

He pressed Send before he did anything stupid and asked her out.

He stared at his screen, saw those telltale dots that meant she was forming a reply . . . Then they disappeared.

She was going to write him back but then changed her mind. He felt a burst of disappointment before reminding himself that he didn't have the time or the inclination to date again.

But as he walked to his truck, he knew he was lying to himself. After the Avery debacle, when he'd literally discovered her with another mechanic at his shop, he'd been afraid to put himself out there. He'd been burned, it had hurt, and he wasn't in any hurry to get burned again.

He was gun-shy. That's what he was.

As he contemplated that bit of truth, Gunnar realized that he was a lot of things, but he'd never been a man who was afraid of things. Not to move to Ohio from West Virginia. Not to start contracting in addition to his auto mechanic job. Not to finish building his dream house, even when his girlfriend exited his life.

Not even to decide to foster a teenager, even though he had next-to-no experience parenting.

So to be afraid of starting a new relationship didn't sit well with him. It didn't set well with him at all.

He just wasn't sure about what to do next.

CHAPTER 6

"Just as I am—though toss'd about
With many a conflict, many a doubt,
Fightings and fears within, without,
O Lamb of God, I come!"
—CHARLOTTE ELLIOTT

So her whole texting thing with Gunnar Law had been a mistake. Every time she reviewed their messages over the last week, Kimber blushed like a schoolgirl, and she was pretty sure that she'd stopped blushing a long time ago. Until now.

When she'd first seen Jeremy at the library, she'd kept everything easy and cordial with him. At first, she wasn't going to mention Gunnar but then later decided that it would be rude not to fill the boy in about what happened.

Her chance came soon after the last bell of the day rang. "I think your foster dad is a hard nut to crack," Kimber told Jeremy when she ran into him in the elementary school parking lot.

For a second, it looked like the boy wasn't sure whether to act like he knew her or not . . . but then her words registered. "Huh?"

"After I got his number from you, I texted him in between classes. I told him thanks for helping me out the other day, but he didn't write much back."

A reluctant smile appeared. "Gunnar isn't real good on the phone. He hates texting too."

"I got that impression." Kimber smiled back. "Thanks for passing on his number, though. It was real nice of you to do."

Though he looked pleased, he shrugged off her words. "It wasn't any big deal."

She figured Jeremy didn't realize it, but Gunnar had almost said the same exact words to her last week. Hiding a smile, she added, "I hope he didn't get mad at you for passing it on or anything."

"He didn't get mad. Gunnar doesn't get mad about things like that."

"No? Well, that's good." Gunnar Law didn't seem like the kind of man to get riled up about much. Probably wouldn't break a sweat about anything that he didn't care about too deeply. She wondered what he *did* care about. Was it just Jeremy? Or was he already seeing someone and she was making a fool of herself? "Hey, Jeremy, sorry if this is too personal, but is Gunnar seeing anyone right now?"

He raised his eyebrows. "Seeing, like does he have a girl-friend?" His voice had risen an octave.

"Yes. Like that." Or, like, a wife.

"No, he doesn't." The boy almost smiled again, but something just beyond her seemed to have caught his attention.

"Oh. Well, um, thanks."

"No problem." He stuffed his hands in his pockets then glanced across the parking lot. Kimber followed his gaze and saw he was looking at a group of cute girls standing together. No, it was obvious he was gazing at one of them in particular.

Kimber had noticed the girl right away. She was a pretty thing with truly gorgeous long, light-brown hair. She'd also been casting covert glances at Jeremy whenever he looked the other way.

Deciding to do Jeremy a favor, since he'd helped her out, she said, "This isn't my business, but it's been my experience that if a guy doesn't make the first move, a girl assumes that he doesn't like her."

Jeremy's head whipped around to stare at her. "Really?"

"Honest. Girls might be all 'this is 2020,' but some things don't change. They don't want to make the first move." She grinned. "I don't lie about relationships."

When Jeremy looked longingly over at the girl again, Kimber decided to give him some space. "Well, I'm outta here," she said. "Have a good evening."

He shoved his hands in his pockets. "'Kay. You too."

After inspecting her tires and releasing a sigh of relief that nothing was damaged today, she got in her car and left the school grounds—pleased to notice that Jeremy and the girl were now chatting up a storm. Well, maybe things were going better over there.

Kind of like her day had gone better than the other days she'd volunteered. The kids weren't looking at her strangely as much and Mrs. Lentz was giving her more to do. So those things were a plus.

Though she loved books and she liked reading to kids, she now knew that working in a library wasn't going to satisfy her, career-wise.

She just wasn't sure what her dream job actually *was*.

That was frustrating, because she seemed to be harboring a sense of confusion about *who* she was too. She'd always been kind of reluctant to model. She'd liked it, but she'd never gone out of her way to talk about her modeling life to anyone. It hadn't been because she'd been shy about the traveling, long days, or the success she'd achieved.

Actually, she'd felt the opposite—she just hadn't cared that much about it.

Traci had once accused her of being modest, but that hadn't been it either. Oh, she'd been pleased with her success and the way everyone in the business had seemed to like how she looked. She liked doing things well, so she'd worked hard to garner a good reputation. She'd arrived on time for shoots, been easy to work with, and been diligent about maintaining her measurements. Designers hated it when models' weights fluctuated and they had to make emergency alterations.

But although she'd done a good job, she'd felt nothing but relief when she'd finally made the decision to quit.

But now? Now she realized that she'd looked at her profession as who she was.

So if she wasn't Kimber Klein, the successful model . . . she didn't know who she was.

As if her mother was reading her mind, her cell phone rang. Glad that everything was all connected via blue tooth in her fancy car, she clicked on the icon on her steering wheel. "Hi, Mom."

"Kimber, I'm so glad I caught you."

Her mom sounded a little breathless. Worried now, she said, "Why? What's up?"

"It might be nothing, but we got the strangest call on the house phone last night. I was going to call you right away, but your dad told me to let you sleep."

"Let me sleep? How late was that call?"

"After ten."

She wouldn't have been asleep, and she doubted her parents had been asleep either. But it still seemed late.

Her parents refused to get rid of their landline, which meant they got a good handful of phone calls from telemarketers every day. "Mama, I've told you, those telemarketers are trouble."

"It wasn't one of them, honey. It was from Brett."

"You mean Brett, my agent?" What in the heck was he doing,

calling her parents? Was he hounding them about something? If so, she was going to kill him.

Her mother's usually bright voice turned more tentative. "Yes, I mean, I believe so. I don't know any other agents, do you?"

"No."

"Well, then . . ."

Her mother was a chipper sort of person. She was also a successful financial advisor, opinionated, and into everyone's business. Her mother was not tentative. Ever. So hearing that unfamiliar note in her mom's voice was not a good thing. She was going to give Brett Day a piece of her mind if he upset her mother.

Feeling protective, she pulled into the parking lot of a church and got ready to listen. "Mama, what did my agent have to say?"

"Well, dear, that's what I wanted to talk to you about. It was all very strange."

"What was?"

"He . . ." She paused. "See, Brett told me that he's been having trouble getting ahold of you and he was getting worried."

"He said that?"

"Almost word for word. Kimmy honey, I tell you what, I didn't know what to think or what to say. I mean, I knew you hadn't changed your phone number."

"No, I have not." Oh, she was peeved.

"I think you have the same email too. I mean, I'm not one to send you emails, but I think it's the same. Right?"

"I do."

"So why would he lie about all that?"

"I couldn't begin to guess." But it couldn't be good. After all, Brett absolutely knew her phone number by heart. She was also 100 percent sure that he knew she hadn't changed it.

In addition, she also knew that he hadn't tried to contact her in weeks. "Is that all he said, Mom?"

"Pretty much." She paused. "Except, now I don't want to talk bad about him, but Brett sounded off, actually. Almost like his voice was slurred."

"Slurred?"

"Yes. I thought it was so strange, I signaled for your father to pick up the extension and listen in too."

Just like they were on a cop show or something. "What did Daddy think?"

"Your father thinks the same thing that I did. We think that maybe he was drunk and forgot your number." She took a breath. "I'm not saying that would be right, but I guess it's possible, even on a Wednesday night."

That was her mother. In her mom's world, no one imbibed on a school night. "Hmm."

"What do you think, dear? Could that be it?"

"I couldn't begin to guess. But don't worry about it, okay?" she murmured. "I'll call him and figure out what he wants."

"Oh. Okay," her mom said, already sounding relieved. "I hope nothing is wrong. I mean, you said you quit modeling."

"I did." Thinking quickly, she said, "Maybe he got a payment for one of the shows I did last month and he's trying to forward it to the right address."

"Oh." Her voice brightened. "Well, now, that would make sense."

"Yes. Again, please don't worry, Mama. I bet he was just confused. No big deal." Realizing what she'd just said, she shook her head. Now she was sounding like Gunnar and she didn't even know him.

"All right then. So . . . how are things with you?"

"So far, so good."

"Are you missing modeling?"

She allowed herself to think about it for a moment. "No, not really. I mean, I do miss parts of it, but I was ready for a change."

"I, for one, am glad that you're going to put your mind to use now. God gave you a good one, you know."

"I know." She'd also heard that same reminder from the time she started school.

"Any chance you want to move back to New York soon?" Her mother's voice held a note of hope in it. "Daddy and I sure miss you. I can't believe we won't be seeing you until after Christmas."

She missed them too. She hadn't seen her parents all the time when she was in New York, but it had been nice to be able to hop on the subway and see them in their brownstone in Brooklyn. "I'm going to hate not seeing you too, Mom, but January will be better. We can have a nice visit then. It won't be rushed."

"Have you found a permanent place to live yet?"

"Not yet. I'm still enjoying living with all the girls and getting to know Traci and Shannon."

"All right. I understand."

She still sounded sad, though. "Mom, if you want, you and Dad are welcome to come out at Christmas. It's going to be hectic, but if you want to be in the midst of the chaos, you're welcome to be here. You could meet Shannon and Traci when you're here too."

"I'll talk to your dad. I do feel bad that we haven't met your sisters, and a little bit of chaos might do us some good."

"Then book a ticket or drive on down."

"You know what? Maybe we will. I want to get to know those girls." Her mother's voice sounded a little wistful.

"Hey, Mama?"

"Hmm?"

"Did you only want to adopt one girl?"

"Kimber? What are you talking about?"

"Did you know that I was one of three siblings?"

There was a pause. "No, dear. All we'd done was fill out the paperwork and said we were hoping for a baby."

"Would you have taken all of us?"

"I . . . well, I think so." Her mother sounded stressed. "Kimber, dear, of course I'm sorry about what happened with Traci and Shannon and that the three of you were separated. No one ever told us you had older sisters needing homes too."

"I know."

"Is there a reason you're asking me about this now? It was all a really long time ago."

"You know how I told you that Traci was in foster care and never adopted."

"Yes?" Her voice was strained.

"Well, Shannon's mom said that she never knew there were three of us. I just wondered if the adoption agency told you the same thing."

"We'd wanted a baby. We'd been on a waiting list for years. Hearing about you was the best news ever."

Kimber noticed that she didn't exactly answer the question. But suddenly, she wasn't sure if she really wanted to know. It wasn't like the past could be changed anyway.

Kimber pulled back out onto the road and when she hung up after a few more minutes of conversation, she was pulling up to her building. The Christmas lights that they'd hung together in the small front yard and around the door were twinkling merrily. It had been a small miracle that they'd done such a good job. It had turned out that each of them—Jennifer and Gwen included—had had strong opinions about how to decorate a house for Christmas. Boy, they'd laughed and argued . . . and then gotten mugs of hot chocolate and stood together in the front yard to admire their hard work.

Kimber had loved every second of it.

Now, looking up at the house, she realized that she might not be exactly sure who she *was*, but she did know one thing for certain.

At last, she was home.

CHAPTER 7

THE MOUSE KING: *He's the mischievous king of the magical soldier mice. The Mouse King declares war on the Nutcracker and his tin soldiers and a battle ensues.*

Bridgeport High was pretty big. Each day, there were at least four hundred students in the building. That meant that there was always someone walking in the halls. There were always a lot of people. That was fine, but it made it kind of hard to have a private conversation with anyone.

Jeremy had been pulled out to speak to Melanie in the office. They were supposed to talk twice a month and every once in a while she liked to meet with him at school instead of at Gunnar's house. They had talked—and really, there hadn't been too much to say; everything was good with his foster dad—and now he was walking back to class.

And then there, coming toward him, was Bethany. He couldn't believe it, but they were the only two people in the whole hallway—they were essentially by themselves.

It felt like fate. Every other time he'd seen her, they'd both been surrounded by a ton of people. Well, mainly she was. Bethany had been in Bridgeport since kindergarten and seemed to know everyone at the school.

When she saw him, her steps slowed. She lifted a hand and brushed a chunk of hair behind her ear. "Hi, Jeremy."

"Hey, Bethany." He stopped right in front of her. Knew he needed to say something smart sounding—or at least something that made sense—but all he seemed to be able to do was stare at her.

As the seconds passed, she looked up at him expectantly, obviously waiting for him to say something. A line of worry formed on her brow when he didn't say another word. "Um. Well, I'll see ya."

Telling himself to *Get. A. Grip.* He called out, "Hey, wait."

She turned back to him. "Yes?"

"Listen, sorry." He paused, then realized that he had nothing to lose by telling her the truth. "The truth is that I just came from seeing my social worker and I didn't know how to tell you that. I was embarrassed." And that was the truth. He was embarrassed that his life was so different than hers. But, what could he do? He hadn't asked for this messed up life but it was his.

"How come you have a social worker?" Her eyes widened right before she slapped a hand over her mouth. "Oh my gosh, forget I asked you that. Sorry."

"No, I don't mind if you ask. I mean, it's not a secret." He took a breath and decided that he didn't mind telling her the truth, but he sure didn't want to tell her all his ugly during their first real conversation.

He shrugged. "I don't have any parents." He briefly considered making things sound better than they were, but decided it would all come back to haunt him if he did. "I never knew my dad and my mother was shot a couple years ago."

Her green eyes widened. "Oh my gosh!"

"Anyway, um, after my mom, uh, died, I was put into foster care. Gunnar, the guy I live with? Well, he's my foster dad."

"Oh. I didn't know about that. Does anyone know?"

"Not really. I don't like to talk about it much. But, um, it's not a secret or anything. I don't mind talking about it—though we don't have to." When she kept staring, he felt like slapping himself. Why had he gone and shared so much anyway? "Sorry I brought it up. I just wanted to tell you the truth. That's all."

She stared at him for a few seconds, obviously processing what he said. "What does that mean? Are you going to have to move away?"

"No. At least, I don't think so anymore. Gunnar wants to adopt me." *Jeez.* How did he go from not wanting to tell her anything to word vomit?

"That's great. I mean, I think it is?"

"It is. He's a good guy." He really needed to stop. Like, right away. "What are you doing out in the hall?"

"Me. Oh." She grinned. "Nothing that exciting. I had to go to the bathroom."

Awkward. "Sorry." Boy, he knew he was blushing. "I'll see you." But just as he was about to turn away, Bethany called out to him again.

"Hey, Jeremy?"

"Yeah?"

"I'm glad you told me about your meeting."

She was? Thinking that there could only be one reason why, he murmured, "I guess you think something's wrong with me, huh?" Even though he knew he sounded like a loser, Jeremy figured he might as well just put it out there. After all, if she did think he was pathetic or something, he wouldn't be surprised. Half the time he thought something was wrong with him too.

But instead of nodding her head, she said, "No, I think you're really strong."

"Strong?"

"Yeah. I mean, a lot of people go through bad stuff but they wear it on their heart." Those green eyes he kept thinking about clouded. "It's always the first thing they tell you. But not you." She smiled at him before turning away and rushing down the hall.

He couldn't believe it. He'd shared the worst thing about himself, and she hadn't made fun of him or acted weird.

Actually, Bethany acted as if his past was something to be proud of. He almost started smiling too as he entered his world history class.

"You're late, Jeremy," Mrs. Cook announced from the front of the room.

He handed her the pass. "Sorry. I had a meeting in the office."

After scanning the note, she nodded. "Get the notes from someone."

"Yes, ma'am."

Though a couple of the kids snickered, Mrs. Cook looked a little happier with him.

Right now, he didn't care about either his teacher's approval or the fact that most kids in Bridgeport hadn't been raised to stick *ma'am* on the end on practically every sentence.

Bethany had made him feel like he wasn't as weird as he constantly felt. That was huge.

CHAPTER 8

"And she brought forth her firstborn son,
and wrapped him in swaddling clothes, and
laid him in a manger, because there was no room
for them in the inn."
—LUKE 2:7

"What took you so long?" Karyn asked when Bethany slid into her seat.

"What do you mean?"

Karyn tossed back a chunk of her dark auburn hair. "Ha, ha. Don't look so innocent. You were gone for a *while*. You also might as well tell me why you look so pleased with yourself."

"Stop. I look normal."

"Ah, no. You look like you're sunbathing at the pool instead of sitting in the middle of Spanish in December."

Bethany would usually tell her best friend to shut up, but she knew Karyn was telling the truth. After double-checking that Mr. Hernandez was still talking with two kids at his desk, Bethany moved an inch closer. "As a matter of fact, something did happen." She was so pleased, she couldn't help but sound as smug as she felt. "I finally talked to him."

"To who?"

Two girls in the row in front of them turned around and giggled.

Bethany gave them a pointed look until they turned back around. "Keep your voice down," she hissed. "And you know who I'm talking about. Jeremy Widmer."

As usual, Karyn's sharp mind started firing off questions. "The new kid with the dreamy blue eyes? Everyone's been trying to flirt with him, but he always acts like they don't exist."

"He's not stuck up. He's shy. But anyway, the two of us were alone in the hall and talked for at least five minutes."

"No way."

"Way." And, for the record, Jeremy absolutely *did* have dreamy blue eyes. Not that she'd ever admit it to him.

"Well, tell me everything. Who spoke first? What did he say? What did you say back? How was talking to him? Was it awkward? Easy?"

She glanced at Mr. Hernandez again. He was still talking to the same students. As the clock ticked away, everyone else started talking quietly too. Satisfied that nobody was eavesdropping, Bethany continued. "Jeremy was walking out of the office and I was walking toward the bathroom. We met in the hall . . ."

"Well . . . what happened?"

"He said *hey* and I said *hi* and then we just kind of stood there for a minute. And then, at last, we started talking."

"About what?" Karyn's voice was impatient and it had risen a tiny bit.

Bethany knew right then and there that she wasn't going to reveal Jeremy's secret. She didn't think it was bad to be a foster kid, but she realized that he kind of did. She didn't want him to think she was gossiping about him either. "Nothing special," she said at last. "We just kind of started talking about stuff."

Karyn looked unimpressed. "Did he ask for your number?"

"No."

"So even though you got to talk to him, it wasn't about anything special."

No, she kind of thought it was. Still determined not to actually come out and share Jeremy's secret, Bethany lifted her chin. "What did you expect? We hardly know each other."

"I guess that's true. Too bad he didn't want your number though."

Bethany was kind of starting to think that too. But pushing that disappointment to one side, she added, "I promise, it was a good conversation. Really good. I understand him a little better now. I actually think he's kind of shy."

Karyn still looked unimpressed. "He better ask you to the Christmas dance soon or someone else is going to."

"I don't know about that." It wasn't like she was the most popular girl around or anything.

"Bethany, give yourself some credit. You're going to get asked by someone in our group."

Put that way, Karyn was probably right. They were part of a pretty big group of friends. Though some of the guys and girls were paired off, most of them weren't. That meant that even though she wasn't tight with any particular guy, there was a good chance one of them would ask her to the dance. In fact, she'd overheard some of the guys talking about that during their lunch the other day. One of them had pretty much said that he'd rather take a girl in their group to the Christmas dance than someone out of it.

Until she'd met Jeremy, she'd thought the same thing.

"The dance isn't until right before Christmas. Jeremy has time to ask me." That is if he wanted to ask her.

"Not that much time."

Karyn had a point. Pretty soon, all the guys were going to start choosing their dates. And once that began, the girls would start freaking out if they hadn't been asked.

Things would get weird as gossip and rumors went crazy.

Eventually, even the more reluctant boys would start asking someone so they wouldn't have to deal with the pressure anymore.

Days later, the rest of the popular, more vocal girls would get snapped up, and girls like her would be left to either go with friends or stay home and pretend they were glad they weren't spending hundreds of dollars on a dress, shoes, and a mani-pedi.

None of that had started yet, but that didn't mean she had much to entice Jeremy to ask her. "He might have someone else in mind. Or, he might not even want to go."

"Of course he will." Looking alarmed, Karyn leaned closer. "Hey, you kind of look like you're gonna cry if he doesn't ask you. He will. And, like I said, *someone* is going to."

When she noticed that the girls in front of them were looking at her again, Bethany shrugged. "It doesn't matter. Let's just drop it, okay?"

Karyn raised her eyebrows. "Okay, if that's what you want."

"It is." After opening up her textbook, she leaned back in her chair. When Mr. Hernandez started talking, she even tried to care about what he was teaching.

But as the minutes passed, she knew conjugating verbs in Spanish was a lost cause. Her mind drifted back to Jeremy's secret.

Bethany made a mental note to try to figure out what it meant if someone was a foster kid. Did they even get to stay in the same house for very long?

Or did they even get to do things like date and go to dances? She might be preparing for disappointment no matter what.

She was still thinking about him when she got out of class

and headed to her locker. And after lunch, when she was walking toward choir, there he was. Jeremy was standing with about five other people near the front door.

Even though she knew it was stupid, she was pretty sure her heart started to race.

When he saw her, he smiled.

Pulling herself together, she strode forward. "Hi, Jeremy. What are you doing?"

"Waiting for Mr. Glover. He drives us to the elementary school today. I help out in their library a couple of times a month."

"I almost signed up to do that. Do you like it?"

"Yeah. It's easy. All the librarian usually makes me do is shelve books. Plus, the kids are kind of cute."

"I bet they are."

Adjusting his backpack on his shoulders, he spoke again. "It's too bad you didn't end up doing your hours there. We could have gone together."

"I wish." When his eyebrows rose, she hastened to explain. "I mean that would have been fun, but I didn't have room in my schedule this semester. I'm on my way to choir now."

He grimaced. "I'd rather shelve books than do that. I can't sing a note."

"I can sing, but my voice isn't anything special. I'd rather dance."

"Dance?"

"Yeah. I've been taking ballet forever."

"That's cool. Can you get on your toes and everything?"

She giggled. "You mean *en pointe*? Yes."

"I heard that's hard. You must be really good."

"I'm okay." Though it was rude to brag, Bethany knew she was actually a pretty good ballerina. Not fantastic, but better than a lot of other girls in the class. "I'm in a dance company. We're performing *The Nutcracker* for Christmas."

"That's cool." He looked impressed, which made her feel kind of good.

"Jeremy, now!" Mr. Glover called out.

"Sorry, Mr. Glover!" He turned back to her. "Hey, I've got to go."

She giggled again. "I know. I do too." But still, she didn't move. And neither did he.

He smiled at her. "So, well . . . uh, have fun. I'll call . . . Shoot, I never got your number. What is it?"

He was asking for her number!

"Jeremy!"

"One sec!" Turning back to her, he winked. "So . . . can I have your number?"

He was a good three feet away now. No way was she going to call it out to him like that. "Maybe I'll give it to you tomorrow."

He grinned at her before running to catch the car.

She smiled all the way to choir. There was something good happening between the two of them, she was sure of it. There was something so good that she didn't even care that he was new to the school and not a part of her group of friends. Or that he was a little shy and kind of awkward.

Not even that he was a foster kid and had a social worker. No, all she really cared about was that he seemed to feel the same way about her that she felt about him.

CHAPTER 9

THE LAND OF SNOW: *Where the Nutcracker takes Clara after defeating the Mouse King in battle. There, they dance among a flurry of snowflakes.*

Gunnar was close to losing his mind right there in the middle of his living room. After taking a deep fortifying breath, he said, "Mama, what did you just say you were fixing to do?"

"I said that I'm going on a swing cruise right after Christmas."

Hearing that a second time over the phone line didn't make the statement easier to handle. Had the moment he'd been dreading just arrived? Was he going to have to start parenting his parent? Keeping his voice firm, he said, "I don't think you should do that."

"I don't know why not. Everyone says it's a lot of fun."

He was now beet red. "Have you told anyone else about this?" Thinking of his eldest brother, he added, "Have you told Martin?" Because Martin was going to have a fit.

"No, dear. You're the first."

Lord, have mercy. He was one of four kids and the only one who lived outside of West Virginia. But when it came to their mother divulging secrets, he always got the weird stuff. Always.

Weighing his words—and her sweet nature—carefully, he said, "Mama, I promise, there's easier ways to meet men than to go um, swinging on a boat. Plus, I don't think you even know what you're talking about." His mother might go around thinking she was a fifty-nine-year-old woman of the world, but he knew better. She was small town and sheltered.

"I'm looking at the brochure, Gunnar. It's fairly easy to understand. Even for a simple, ole country gal like me," she said, sarcasm thick in her voice.

He was still trying to figure out what a "swing cruise" brochure could possibly say. Surely nothing good. Honestly, just thinking about his mother adrift on such a boat gave him the willies.

He needed some support, stat.

"Mama, what about Darcy? Have you spoken to her about your plans?" Darcy was number two in the Law children lineup, and she'd always been the enforcer in the family.

"I haven't told her yet either, Son. Like I said, I just paid the deposit."

He hadn't caught that. But if she'd already paid money, there was a chance she wasn't going to get it back. "Well, maybe you shouldn't tell Darcy about this adventure of yours."

"Why not?"

"Because it's not proper." And because Darcy would have a hissy fit if she found out—and that was putting things mildly.

"It's not a sin, Son."

"Heck yeah, it is."

"Don't say 'heck.'"

"Mom, really?"

"No, don't try to excuse yourself. You've got an impressionable boy at home now. Plus, everyone knows what you're thinking when you say words like that."

Correcting his not-swearing had finally pushed him too far. "Everyone's going to know what you're thinking if you go on some freaking swinger's cruise!"

Jeremy's door opened and he poked his head out. When their eyes met, the boy's bright blue eyes appeared shell-shocked.

And who could blame him?

Gunnar slapped a hand over his face. Honestly, he just couldn't win right now.

On the other end of the line, he heard his mother gasp. Then take a deep breath . . . then burst out laughing.

He held the phone away from his ear, because she never could *not* laugh like a hyena. He waited for a couple of seconds . . . but it still sounded like she couldn't catch her breath. After another few, he started to get irritated. "Mama—"

"Oh, good night. It's not a swinger's cruise, Gunnar. It's a ballroom dancing cruise."

"You said 'swing.'"

"You know, like swing dancing."

"Swing dancing?"

"There's a difference, Son," his mother continued, her voice sounding as stern as all get out. "A fairly big difference. One is dancing the jive and the other is . . . not. You need to remember that."

"Yes, ma'am." His face was probably purple, he was so embarrassed.

"Are we clear now? I want to go on a cruise in the Caribbean Sea, walk around at shops and such during the day, and practice ballroom dance lessons at night."

"Yes, ma'am. I understand."

She was sounding snippy now. "And just for the record, the cha-cha is more my style."

Why had he even picked up when she called? "Gotcha. I . . . I obviously misunderstood."

"I would say so." She giggled. "I swear, just when I think I've heard everything . . . I can't wait to tell Martin, Darcy, and Andrew about this!"

"Please don't."

"Honey, I don't know how I can't. It's . . . it's priceless."

He gritted his teeth. It was mortifying, is what it was.

"Now, honey the actual reason I called is because I heard that there's a really good ballroom studio in Bridgeport, and none other than our very own Shannon Murphy has set up shop there."

Shannon was from their little town of Spartan back in West Virginia, and he knew where her shop was because a couple of his buddies had gone to her recent wedding to Dylan Lange, a cop in town. Growing up, Shannon had lit their little town on fire with her competitions and trophies. They'd all been sure they were going to see her on *Dancing with the Stars* one day. They might have too, if she hadn't gotten hurt.

"I know about her place."

"You do? It's called Dance With Me. Have you been there?"

"To take lessons? No. No, I have not."

"Well, I'm going to. That's why I called, as a matter of fact. I'm going to be taking lessons from none other than Shannon herself next week. Isn't that something?"

He was finally connecting the dots. Ballroom dance lessons plus Shannon Murphy equaled his mother was coming into town within the next seven days.

His mother was coming next week.

"Wait, what?"

"You heard me, Son. I'm driving in on Sunday after church. I should arrive around five or six."

Her voice was bright, belying the information she was throwing out his way. And, just for the record, Sunday was in five days. Not seven.

"Mother, you're coming into town in five days and planning on staying here?"

"Well, yes." Her voice turned hurt. "Why are you talking like this isn't okay?"

"Because you didn't ask me if that was okay."

"I didn't think I had to ask permission to visit you, Gunnar."

"Things are different than how they used to be. Mama, Jeremy is here now."

"Of course I know about Jeremy. We've FaceTimed, remember? I'm planning on spending lots of time with him. I thought I could teach him to play hearts."

It was on the tip of his tongue to point out that he was a grown man who worked two jobs and was trying to develop a relationship with a teenage boy who'd already been through a lot. That Jeremy needed stability, not surprise houseguests. In addition, the boy was fifteen, not half that, which meant that there was a real good chance that Jeremy was not going to want to sit around playing card games with an older woman he didn't know.

But then reality hit him, along with the point that his mother might be a handful, but she was all his and she'd also been through a lot.

No matter what, he loved her and she'd loved him. That was what counted.

Softening his tone, he said, "I'm looking forward to seeing you soon, Mama."

"I'm looking forward to it too, dear. Almost as much as I am looking forward to dancing with you."

"Say again?"

"I can't dance the cha-cha without a partner, silly. We're going to have such a great time."

Boy, he wished she'd called Martin first. "Yes, ma'am."

After speaking for a few more minutes, he hung up and looked around the living room. It was a decent size, but fairly sparse. So was the rest of his house. It was also filled with dust. He cleaned the bathrooms on occasion but hadn't paid for a cleaning service to stop by in months. In addition, the house that had already been filled with his crap now had another layer of teenage-boy crap on top.

He sighed. His mother was going to start cleaning the minute she put her suitcase down on the floor.

Jeremy poked his head out again. When he saw that Gunnar was off the phone, he started forward. "Who were you talking to?"

"My mother."

"Ah. Mrs. Law was nice when FaceTimed."

Deciding to put it out on the line, he added, "She was on good behavior when she did that. By the way, her first name is Willa. You can call her that if you don't want to call her Grandma."

"I'll call her Willa."

"Good call."

Jeremy's eyebrows lifted as he walked closer. "How come you look so worried? Is Willa really mean?"

"Mean? Gosh, no." Hating that he messed everything up, he said. "I promise, she's really nice."

"But?"

He sighed. "But I think we need to have a talk. Come sit down here with me for a spell."

Jeremy sat down on the edge of the couch, but everything in his body language proclaimed that he was not doing that easily.

Gunnar rested his arms on his knees. "I've got some news. My mother is coming for a visit. She gets here on Sunday evening."

"What's wrong with that? Does she not want me here?"

"No, no, no." When Jeremy looked stricken, Gunnar firmly told himself to pull it together. He was messing this all up. "Sorry. What I'm trying to say is that my mom wants you here. Very much so."

"Really?"

"Really. I promise, she's excited about it." Thinking of her game plans, he muttered, "Maybe too excited."

"What does that mean?"

"It means my mother, who is loud, chatty, and all-girl is going to be staying with us for a week. We're going to have to make some adjustments. And clean."

"Okay . . ."

"She's also going to be on you like a tick in June."

Jeremy's lips twitched. "Which means?"

"Get ready to have her not only make you a huge breakfast every morning, but sit with you while you eat it." He held out another finger. "She's also going to try to pick you up from school in the afternoons, and ask you questions all the time." Realizing that those things didn't really come close to describing his mother, Gunnar added, "Actually, my mom's more like a category four hurricane that comes to visit."

His eyes widened. "She sounds like a lot."

"Oh, she is." Wiping a hand over his face, "She's great, but she's a lot. And I know I sound mean, but all of my siblings think the same thing. My youngest brother Andrew has been known to go on two hour runs just to catch a break."

"Wow."

Still thinking hard, he added, "Luckily, she'll be in the guest room in the basement, so you'll have some space. She's been known to suck all the oxygen out of a room."

Jeremy's lips curved up. "She sounds funny."

"She is. But she can cook like a dream and she likes to shop. Expect her to making about a dozen Walmart and Target runs. And . . . she wants to teach you how to play hearts. It's a card game."

"She wants to play cards with me?"

Pleased that the boy didn't look horrified but kind of happy, Gunnar nodded. "Honestly, you got the good end of the deal. She wants to dance with me."

"Huh?"

"Ballroom dancing."

Jeremy grinned, then started laughing. "No way."

"I wouldn't lie about that. She's planning to dance the cha-cha on some swing-dancing cruise ship."

"What's the cha-cha?"

"I have no idea but she's coming here so I can take lessons on how to do it with her."

"You're gonna take cha-cha lessons?"

"Yep." His lips twitched. It wasn't going to be pretty, he knew that. He weighed 240 pounds. Guys like him didn't move lightly on their feet.

As if he was imagining it, the boy laughed harder. Gunnar couldn't blame him. They were going to have quite the time of it, and that was a fact.

But when he found himself chuckling as well, Gunnar realized that it was going to be okay. He had this boy on his side now.

CHAPTER 10

"Joy to the World, the Lord is come.
Let earth receive her King."

Sometimes Kimber thought that the noise and commotion surrounding her old apartment in the center of Manhattan had nothing on her room on the top floor of Dance With Me.

Currently, the building felt filled to the brim and it was as noisy as all get out. She'd woken to Jennifer blaring old school eighties music while she made five dozen cupcakes for one of her clients. Kimber swore if she never heard another Bon Jovi song, it wouldn't be long enough.

Just as Jennifer finished, Shannon had opened the doors for her weekly ballroom class for senior citizens. They were a noisy bunch—especially when Gwen was there.

Gwen, who had recently moved in permanently, was also in the studio. Even though she was only nineteen, she had a way with the seniors that was magical. They all loved her and the good feelings seemed to be mutual. Whenever Gwen entered the room, it reminded Kimber of Norm from that old television show *Cheers.* Choruses of "Hi, Gwen!" rang out like bells.

Gwen was also the birth mother of little baby Bridge, Kimber's sister Traci's son.

About once a week, Gwen also babysat for Traci so Traci could take a long shift at the police department. It all coincided on the same night this week, so Kimber was on baby duty. She and Jennifer were sitting on the floor in the living room with baby Bridge. They'd turned the fire on, Jennifer had made snowball cookies, and Christmas music was floating upstairs from the seniors' class.

All in all, it was exactly the opposite type of evening than those she used to have in New York City. Back then, she and her model roommates were either always getting ready to go out or work the next day. It had been stressful, expensive, and loud.

This was cozy and quiet. Kimber couldn't imagine a better night.

Especially since Bridge was getting so darn cute. The little guy was six months old. He was chunky and happy, and just learning how to crawl. Just being near him relieved Kimber's stress.

She and Jennifer were sitting on opposite sides of a quilt. In the center, Bridge was lying on his back and squealing while he played with some kind of musical contraption. When Bridge lost interest in the sounds and seemed happier to play with a set of plastic containers and a spoon that was next to Jennifer, she looked over at Kimber and smiled. "Does seeing Bridge ever make you wish for a baby of your own?"

Kimber already loved Bridge. Thought he was adorable too. But having one of her own? No way. "Sorry, but no."

"Really?"

"You have Jack and are practically engaged. I am not. I think

I'll worry about getting a boyfriend before I add a baby into the mix."

"Oh, don't be so literal. You don't have to be in a relationship to think that having a baby sounds like fun."

"This is true. But shouldn't a gal *think* that having a baby would be fun. I do not. I can't imagine all the responsibility right now."

"Traci and Matt seem to be doing okay with him."

"I don't disagree." Kimber stretched her legs. "I already love this little guy, though."

As if Bridge had just noticed her, he directed a big, gummy smile her way and crawled toward her.

She picked him up with a laugh. "You sure know how to get around, sport. I didn't know babies could crawl so fast!" Kissing him on the cheek, she cooed, "I'm going to need to keep my feet in sneakers to keep up with you."

Bridge giggled then crawled back to the center of the quilt and started playing with the buttons on the toy again.

Kimber leaned back and stretched out her legs. She might not admit it out loud, but there were moments like this when she thought that *maybe* having a baby one day wouldn't be such a bad thing. Bridge was so cute.

"Hey, Kimber?"

"Hmm?"

Jennifer tilted her head as she studied Kimber more closely. "Do you miss traveling?"

Sitting up, she asked, "You mean traveling for modeling?" When Jennifer nodded, Kimber shook her head. "Not really. I got to visit a lot of amazing places, but it was hard too. I was always on someone else's dime and usually felt like a pin cushion," she joked. "Why do you ask? Are you planning a trip?"

"Oh, no. No offense, but lately, I've thought you seemed restless. Not unhappy, really. But just kind of bored."

Though she was about to deny it, Kimber thought about Jennifer's comment. There definitely was some truth to it. "I guess I am restless. Not today, of course. I love hanging out with you and helping with Bridge. But . . ." She let her voice drift off because she wasn't even sure how to describe how she'd been feeling.

"But?"

"But, my life here in Bridgeport is a lot different than it was before I moved. I'm used to being really busy or making plans. Back in New York, I was working a lot, or trying to get jobs, or planning for one of those trips or for shows. Now I feel like I suddenly have too much time on my hands." Of course, she was also usually worrying about her stalker or disappointing her parents, and about coming to terms with the fact that she wasn't making a bunch of money anymore.

When Jennifer continued to eye her quietly, Kimber shrugged, not wanting to share just how consumed she'd had to be with her looks when she was modeling. She'd worked out all the time and had gotten regular facials, manicures, waxing appointments . . . all sorts of things. Now? Now, she just had a lot of extra time. "I'll get over it though. I'm volunteering at the library, and I like helping all of you when I can."

"If you ever want to just talk, I hope you'll think about talking to me. I mean, if you need someone. I'm a really good listener."

"I'm sure you are." Jennifer was sweet. She had been through a horrific experience and still suffered from agoraphobia. She would never judge another person. "Jen, if there was something to talk about, I'd let you know. But I'm fine, I promise." She shrugged. "I'm just getting through a little midlife crisis. I expected it would happen when I dropped out of modeling and moved to Ohio." When Bridge crawled back to her, she cuddled him close for a few seconds before he squirmed and headed back to Jennifer, who had become quiet.

Kimber felt like she let Jennifer down, but she wasn't sure what to say. How could she complain about her life or her confusion about what to do next when Jennifer had already been through so much?

She'd never been happier to hear her cell phone ring. She connected before even looking at the screen.

"Kimber Klein."

"It's Brett Day, Kimber."

Her agent. Forcing her voice to sound positive and not snippy, she said, "Hey, Brett. How are you?"

"I'm good, darling. Excellent."

"Good to hear it."

"Listen, doll, we need to talk because something's come up. It's exquisite news too."

Exquisite was his top-of-the-world adjective. Using that word, along with his tone, was Brett at his finest—he was about to pressure her to do something. It was certain that he wasn't going to back down easily either.

Realizing that this used to be her life, chills ran down her spine. She'd take slightly bored over these verbal gymnastics any day.

After exchanging hand signals with Jennifer, she walked up the stairs. "There's nothing to say, Brett."

"Just listen. *Women's Weekly* decided to run a special issue and they want you on the cover."

She stopped. "What?"

"Cover. *Women's Weekly*. Special issue. This is big, Kimber. Really big."

For once, Brett wasn't exaggerating. The cover of *Women's Weekly* was a big deal. At one time it had been her ultimate goal.

He continued. "The amount they're talking about is six figures, sweetie."

"Six figures."

"Yep. And, it includes a four-page spread with you modeling clothes from the top four designers that they chose for the year." He paused. "They *only* want you, Kimber." He lowered his voice. "Do you hear what I'm saying? The magazine is going to be highlighting Kimber Klein as much as the clothes."

"They're not hiring a group of women? Just me?" Her voice might have squeaked. This was huge. Bigger than huge. Something every model in the industry worked years to achieve. Something hardly anyone ever achieved.

"At last you're listening." His voice noticeably lifted. "I'm so proud of you, Kimber. You've worked hard and deserve every bit of this success."

"We did this together, Brett."

He chuckled. "I'm feeling pretty jazzed myself. So, is it a yes? Can I call up the publisher and say you're in?"

Even though she was nodding, Kimber found herself hesitating. "Let me call you tomorrow."

He let out a long, drawn-out sigh. "Kimber, they've got no time for this. You can't diva out on *Women's Weekly*."

"I'm not diva-ing. All I'm telling you is that I want to think about it for a time. I'll call you tomorrow."

"You can have twelve hours."

It was five. "I'm not calling you back at five in the morning, Brett. I'll call you at nine."

She could practically hear him grinding his teeth. She felt bad for him too. This was a huge offer and she would be a fool to turn it away. And if he lost the commission on a job like this, it would be really hard.

"Fine. But I'm going to be staring at my phone at nine *on the dot* tomorrow morning. You better call."

"I will. And, um, Brett?"

"What now, Kimber?"

This time she didn't even try to stop herself from smiling. "Thank you for this. I mean it."

"Sure thing, doll." His voice warmed. "And, congratulations, Kimber. You worked hard for this. It's awesome. Really awesome. I'm thrilled for you."

Hanging up, Kimber knew he was correct. Being asked to do this really was awesome.

Just as she was about to go back down to rejoin Jennifer, her phone rang again. This time she checked the screen, and just about fell off her chair.

"Gunnar?"

"Yeah. I hope you don't mind me calling."

"Not at all." He sounded strange. Maybe worried? "So . . . what's up? Is Jeremy okay?"

"He's good." His voice sounded strained. "I called to see if you'd like to get a drink or something."

He was asking her out. "Um, when?"

"Tonight?"

"Tonight?"

He kind of groaned under his breath. "I know. There's probably some kind of dating rule book that says you're supposed to think I'm being rude and disrespectful because I'm not giving you a ton of notice. But that's not the case. I just was hoping you could give me an hour or two. I need to talk with someone."

After looking at her watch again, she realized that the seniors' dance class was finishing up. Gwen and Shannon would be finished and could help with Bridge duty.

"You know what? I can meet you somewhere downtown. I live downtown."

"Really? What part?"

"I live above Dance With Me. Do you know it?" A lot of

people did. It was a remodeled three-story building that was close to a hundred years old. It was now currently decorated with about a million bright-white lights.

It sounded like he was choking. "Please tell me that's not the ballroom dance studio."

"It is. Why? Do you dance?"

"I don't, but someone was just telling me about it. Do you know the gal who owns it?"

"Shannon?"

"Yeah. Shannon Murphy."

"I do, and it's Shannon Lange now. She got married."

"So you know her well."

Kimber was curious why he cared. "Gunnar, I know her even better than that. Shannon is my sister."

"No way." He muttered something under his breath. "Kimber, how about I pick you up there and we'll walk to one of the restaurants or bars nearby? I think we've got a lot to talk about."

Now she was really curious. "Come over in about thirty minutes or so. I'll be here."

"Thanks. See you soon."

When she hung up, she felt like there was something new in his tone, but she couldn't place it. But boy, talk about a crazy thirty minutes! She could hardly wait to find out what the rest of the evening was going to be like.

Walking back into the living room, she found Jennifer and Bridge were no longer alone. Gwen and Shannon had joined them. They were all chuckling about something but stopped when they saw her face.

"Kimber? What's up?"

"I've got a date in thirty minutes. I need to go get ready."

"With who?"

"Gunnar Law."

"You're going out with Gunnar Law?" Shannon's face went slack. "Wow."

"Do you know him?"

Looking amused, she nodded. "You could say that. I grew up with him in Spartan."

Well, at least that explained why he sounded so surprised when she mentioned Shannon was her sister. "Girl, some days, this world is just too small."

"You have a point, but in this case, you're in luck. Gunnar is a great guy."

"He seemed like it, but . . . are you sure?"

"I'm positive. I wouldn't steer you wrong about a man. I promise, he's as down to earth as they come."

"That's high praise coming from you," Jennifer said.

"You know how much I love my hometown. He and I were never in the exact same circles and he was three years ahead of me in school. But I'm friends with guys who are friends with him, and we definitely know each other. Of course, our parents know each other too. When did you say he was going to be here? I want to say hi."

"In a half an hour. And you don't have to say hello tonight," she warned.

Just thinking about the high-pitched southern squeal Shannon was due to bring on and how awkward Kimber was going to feel, since she'd never done any of that southern stuff in her life, made her feel queasy. "You know, this is a first date. It might be better if we kept things low key. None of you need to go near the door at all."

"You might as well let Shannon say hey," Jennifer said. "We're all going to be downstairs anyway."

Kimber threw out a hip and tried to cop an attitude. "You ladies are going to scare him off if you do that." And yes, she was perfectly aware that she'd done the same thing to Shannon and Traci.

"Maybe . . . or maybe you're just worried about *you* getting scared off," Gwen said.

Kimber sighed. "You're on this train too, Gwen?"

"Uh, yeah." Even though she was holding Bridge close, the girl still managed to look kind of full of herself. "Sorry, but I totally have to see the guy who is finally good enough for you to give him the time of day."

That didn't make her sound too good. "I don't act like I'm too good for the men around here."

"I don't think it's men in Bridgeport, I think it's all men," Gwen retorted.

"Hey."

"We're only saying that you have a tendency to be super guarded and standoffish. Even though I sound critical, I'm not trying to be," Shannon added.

"Sorry, but it sure sounds like you are."

Her sister's expression softened. "Come on, Kimberly. You might as well let us invade your space. Otherwise we'll just be sneaking around and Gunnar is sure to notice."

"You really wouldn't do that. Would you?"

"Of course I would. But I'm warning you now, seeing a bunch of women attempting to sneakily spy on you isn't a good look. No doubt it'll make the whole family look bad."

Kimber had been around these women long enough to know when it was time to give in gracefully. "Fine, but everyone, all I'm doing is going out for a drink. Don't make it into something it's not."

"We'd never do that," Shannon said with an *almost* straight face.

"You all are going to embarrass me. I can feel it coming on now."

"Not intentionally," Jennifer murmured.

"Payback can be painful. Remember that," Kimber tossed her hair over her shoulder as she walked up the stairs to her room.

Their giggles didn't give her a lick of comfort.

Instead, all their laughter did was make her feel like they hadn't listened to a single word she said. Or that maybe they'd heard her, but they had no intention of doing what she asked.

Not one bit.

CHAPTER 11

THE SUGAR PLUM FAIRY: *The beautiful fairy who lives and dances in the Kingdom of Sweets.*

What a small world. Gunnar couldn't believe that out of all the women he could have met by chance in Bridgeport, he was interested in one who lived in the building he was trying so hard to avoid. Though he knew it was just a coincidence, it still felt like a weird trick of fate.

And then there was the comment about Shannon Murphy being her sister. Though he remembered Kimber saying she'd been adopted, she didn't look anything like Shannon Murphy. Shannon was at least ten inches shorter than Kimber and her skin was lighter too. It just didn't make sense.

Already regretting his spur of the moment invite, he parked on the street and approached the Dance With Me building with caution.

It was a real sight, that was for sure. Lights were blazing from every floor and the faint sound of music was filtering through. Shannon needed to hire someone to look into that. He'd bet they were paying a fortune in heating bills.

Stewing on that, he rang the doorbell.

Kimber opened the door. "Hey," she said.

He couldn't help but smile. Once again, she looked like a million dollars. Kimber had on dark jeans, a black turtleneck, and a ton of silver jewelry. She wore low-heeled boots, which he appreciated. She was still about an inch shorter than him. He wouldn't have cared if she was taller, but he couldn't deny that his ego liked there being a slight edge to his height.

But none of that mattered, since she was currently looking like he was from the IRS instead of her date for the evening.

Instead of holding his hand out to her, he stuffed his hands in his coat pockets. "Hi. Everything okay?"

"It's great. Grand," she added sarcastically.

"Sorry, but you've lost me. Did I miss something?"

Looking aggrieved, she stepped back. "Come on in and you'll see what's going on."

As soon as he closed the door behind him, he understood. A whole crew of women were standing there, and each one was wearing the type of smile women wore when they had a secret.

"Gunnar Law, look at you," Shannon exclaimed as she approached.

"Shannon Murphy, I can't believe we're both standing here in Bridgeport." He carefully gave her a hug. She was the type of woman who always reminded him of a delicate flower.

She held up her left hand, showing a sparkly diamond. "It's Shannon Lange now."

"Congratulations. I'm real happy for you."

"Thank you." She beamed, then cast a sideways glance at Kimber. "I tell you what, you could have just about knocked me over with a feather, I was so surprised when Kimber told us who was picking her up. I had no idea y'all knew each other."

"I couldn't believe it when I learned y'all were sisters either."

"We just met," Kimber interjected. "Gunnar and I are practically strangers."

"It must have been some first meeting then," a young woman holding a baby said.

"Sometimes it just hits you like a hammer," a golden-haired woman added.

"Don't mind them. They're crazy," Kimber said.

Since she wasn't doing the honors, he took a step toward them. "Hi. I'm Gunnar Law."

"I'm Jennifer Lange," the blond said as she shook his hand. "I'm Shannon's sister-in-law."

"I'm Gwen," the younger woman holding the baby said. "I'm . . . well, I don't know what I am but I'm kind of related. Oh! And this is Bridge."

"It's a pleasure to meet all of y'all," he said as he gently rubbed a finger on Bridge's tiny sock-covered foot.

Gwen beamed as Bridge cooed.

"So . . ." Shannon said, looking like she was ready to invite him in to chat.

"So I think it's time we got on our way." Kimber pulled on her coat before he could help. "I'll explain it all to you when we get out of here. Are you ready?"

"Almost, but give me a sec, babe."

Kimber's eyebrows rose. "Babe?"

He ignored her and Jennifer's giggles. "Hey, Shannon, I need to talk to you about something. See, my mother just called. She wants to learn the cha-cha. And maybe swing dancing too." He could practically feel his face heat up as he remembered that whole swingers cruise convo.

"That Willa. Oh my stars, Gunnar! I should have mentioned that first thing. I talked to her on the phone yesterday. She's just as bubbly as ever."

"She is that. Mom can't wait to take your lessons. She says you've got quite the great reputation."

"She's sweet. Willa's going on a cruise, right?"

"Yep. It's called Swing Cruise, if you can believe that." Please God, he hoped his mother never shared that he'd misunderstood what kind of cruise it was.

"I can believe it. I'm looking forward to seeing her and to seeing you both dance."

"Wait, what?" Kimber asked.

Shannon grinned. "Gunnar is going to be his mama's dancing partner!"

"Guilty." He stuffed his hands in his pockets. "I'm afraid she can talk me into just about anything."

"There's nothing wrong with that. Y'all are going to do great."

"Wait a minute. Gunnar, are you saying that you're going to take dancing lessons from my sister?" Kimber asked.

"I got roped into it." Realizing he sounded like a jerk, he added, "But I'm sure looking forward to your lessons, Shannon."

"We'll have the best time talking about Spartan."

"That we will." He smiled at Shannon again before offering his arm to Kimber. "Ready?"

Looking suddenly shy, she nodded. "Don't you all still be standing here when I get back," she called over her shoulder as they walked out the door.

Bright laughter followed them out.

"They're a kick," Gunnar said as he placed a hand on her back as they walked down the steps.

Though she looked a little grumpy about it, Kimber chuckled.

"That they are. Half the time I feel like I'm living in the middle of a sorority house."

"And the other half?"

"I feel like I must have done something pretty special to deserve them. They're great."

He liked that answer. Walking down the sidewalk by her side, he said, "I thought we could run into Paxton's. Will that work for you?"

She smiled brightly at him. "It will. Absolutely."

Gunnar had planned on asking her about her relationship to Shannon right away. He was curious as to how two such different women were sisters. But he pushed his question to the back shelf. At the moment, he didn't care about a thing except for walking by her side. She looked so pleased, he could practically feel her warmth thawing everything that had been giving him fits over the last two days.

After they entered the cozy bar and restaurant, they were seated in a back corner. Under a strand of multicolored Christmas lights but away from the worst of the noise. It was also out of the main entrance, so they didn't catch the draft that blew through every time the door opened.

The server took their drink order as well as an order for chili-cheese fries.

Kimber rested her elbows on the table. "Now, want to tell me what's been going on with you? How's Jeremy?"

"You know what? Today, we're doing okay."

"You have to add that qualifier? Oh, Gunnar, have things been that rocky between the two of you?"

"No." He held up a hand to emphasize his point. "Not at all. We seem to get along well. That said, I'm always second-guessing myself. Sometimes I get the feeling that Jeremy wishes he was anywhere else."

"I know for a fact that isn't the case," Kimber said.

"For a fact? What did he say?"

"Nothing specific, other than whenever he mentions your name he grins. Plus, I've seen the two of you together, remember? He looks at you like a son looks at his dad."

Her words caused a lump to form in his throat. "If he does that at all, I'll be thankful. No, the main thing that got me rattled was my mother's call that she was coming to town and taking dance lessons with Shannon."

"And, she's staying with you?"

"Yep. She's going to be with us for a whole week. I've always thought I had a good-sized house, but I'm telling you, I think things are going to be cramped around there."

After accepting her glass of club soda from the server, Kimber laughed. "Maybe it won't be that bad. My parents are supposed to be coming here sometime soon too."

"I promise, my visit is going to be more stressful—unless you're folks have dance lessons on the agenda too."

"They don't, but it probably won't go great." She frowned.

"Why's that?"

She leaned back in her chair. "I love them and they love me, but I don't always make them very happy."

"Come on."

"I'm not trying to throw a pity party, but it's true." Looking pensive, she said, "They'll probably grill me because I don't have a job right now."

"How come?" He was confused. He thought she was a model.

"Well, I'm currently having a midlife crisis at twenty-six."

"Sounds challenging."

"It has been. See, I've been modeling for a while, now. I got sick of it, so I quit and I've been taking a break." When the server brought their fries, she smiled at the gooey mess like it was a long-lost friend. "And eating. Actually . . . I've been eating a lot."

"Wow. I don't know much about modeling, but I can't imagine that you've been eating a lot of fries."

She forked a good-sized pile on a plate. "Nope. Though . . . I had a crazy phone call this afternoon myself. Brett, my old agent, called with a job for me. I don't know what to do about that."

"Why? Are you thinking about taking it?"

"Yep. It's for the cover of a magazine plus a featured spread. A lot of money. It would be hard to pass up."

"I bet." He wasn't sure what *a lot of money* was to her, but he figured it would be a *whole lot* to him.

"I haven't made up my mind. I told Brett I'd call him tomorrow morning with my answer."

He was having a hard time imagining saying no to that kind of money. But he supposed paychecks like that weren't everything. "What do your sisters think?"

"I haven't told them. I haven't told anyone . . . but you."

"You can tell me whatever you want . . . but why haven't you told them?"

"I don't know. I mean, Shannon was working and my other sister Traci is working tonight too. She's a cop. But really, I'm afraid they might talk me out of it." She looked down at her plate. "I've complained about both Brett and my job a lot. I feel if I give in, it's going to be like all my griping was just talk."

"Good luck with your decision."

Her eyebrows rose. "That's it?"

"Since I don't reckon you're going to start asking me about building houses and fixing cars, I'm not going to start telling you what to do about modeling."

"I feel like if I say yes, it will be my last hurrah, you know? I can go out on top."

He wondered how far away she actually was from that top.

He was starting to get the feeling she was already there. "It would be cool to see you on a magazine cover."

"It's not that big of a deal."

Heck yeah, it was. Gunnar shook his head, hardly able to imagine it. He was an average-looking guy from a dying town in the middle of West Virginia. He worked with his hands and it showed. Both his hands and his face were a little weathered and worn.

In addition, he'd played sports in high school, but he'd never been the star athlete. He hadn't gone to college, hadn't ever even thought about community college. Instead, he'd just worked hard. Worked hard, prayed a lot, and built himself a business. He'd made himself a good life, but it was never going to be a fancy one. He'd never earned six figures and didn't know if he ever would.

Men like him didn't date fancy New York cover models.

And yet, here he was.

Looking into her eyes, he allowed himself to reveal a little bit more of himself. "'Course, I'd be lying if I didn't think you looked even better sitting right here in front of me."

Her brown eyes warmed in the dim light of the restaurant. "You're a regular smooth talker, Gunnar Law."

"Yeah, that's me." He sipped his beer. "For what it's worth, I already feel better about my mama. She'll enjoy those classes with Shannon. I know she's going to be good with Jeremy too."

"If I'm home when you're over, I'll come down and watch." She gave him a smile that was both parts amused and sexy as all get out.

Which made him really not be in any hurry to embarrass himself. "Don't you dare. I'm sure I'll have two left feet."

"I have those myself. Shannon's trying to help me learn to tap. It's painful how bad I am at it."

"That makes me feel good."

She smiled at him. "I guess we're both going to do okay,

Gunnar. But just in case we aren't, I think I'm going to put you on speed dial."

"I'll look forward to it."

Two hours later, he walked her back. Her hand was in his and he decided he liked it there. Liked it a lot. "I'm sorry I kept you out so late."

"I'm not." Her smile widened. "It was something I didn't know I needed. Really nice."

He loved how she'd phrased that. Good moments were like that, he supposed. Filled with experiences he didn't see coming or hadn't known he needed. He squeezed her hand lightly. "I think so too." It was a lame response, but that was him, he guessed. Full of good intentions but not always the best choices of words or phrases.

When they got to the door of the building, he waited until she found the key. "Good luck tomorrow. I'll text you later to see what you decided."

"Good." She smiled softly at him before unlocking the door. When it opened and he saw that a light was shining on the second-floor landing, she said, "I guess I'm set now."

He didn't know if it was an invitation or not, but he leaned closed and kissed her lightly on the lips. To his satisfaction, she rested her hands on his shoulders and leaned into him. When they pulled apart, her lips were parted slightly.

He covered one of her hands with his own. "Night, Kimber."

"Good night, Gunnar Law," she murmured before walking inside.

After he heard her lock the door, he walked back to his truck, thinking that things might be good in his future after all.

CHAPTER 12

THE CAVALIER: *The handsome partner of the Sugar Plum Fairy*

"Okay, ladies. That's it for tonight," Miss Shannon said. "We had a real good class tonight. Y'all worked real hard. All of you are dismissed."

There was a collective sigh through the whole room. The practice had been really hard.

Practically collapsing on the floor, Bethany waved to two of the other girls who were already on their way out the door. She wasn't that anxious to get out of there, but she was anxious to give her feet a rest. She was pretty sure she had two new blisters on her right foot.

Just as she sat down on the floor to undo the ribbons of her toe shoes, Miss Shannon walked to her side. "Are you okay, Bethany?"

"Yes, ma'am." Pulling off her right shoe, she winced as she

saw that one of those blisters she'd worried about had not only appeared but had started to bleed.

"Uh-oh," Shannon said. "You're going to need to soak that foot tonight."

"I will." Luckily, her mother never gave her lectures about bloody toes, just pulled out her footbath and handed her a towel.

"I'm glad we're the only two people left in here, because I wanted to talk to you about something. Do you have a moment or does your mother need you to rush off?"

"Um, I'm pretty sure I have a moment. But, could I text my mom and tell her I'll be another five minutes?"

Miss Shannon looked pleased, which helped her roaring nerves a lot. "Yes, honey. You do that. Get yourself together and text your mom. When you're ready, I'll be over at my desk."

"Yes, Miss Shannon."

"And Bethany?"

She skidded to a stop. "Yes?"

"Try not to feel so nervous. This is a good thing, I promise."

Smiling weakly, Bethany nodded. Then she quickly did as her teacher suggested, putting on sweatpants, thick socks, and her favorite rubber flip flops that had the Velcro straps across the toes. Finally, she texted her mom that she had to meet with her teacher for a few, tossed her phone in her purse, and hurried over to her teacher's desk.

She looked up like she'd forgotten Bethany was there. "Boy, that was quick."

"I didn't have much to do."

"Goodness, but you look worried." Frowning slightly, Miss Shannon's usually thick accent got even thicker. "Honey, I'm real sorry. I didn't mean to scare you. Like I said, what I wanted to talk to you about is a good thing."

"Yes?" Bethany wished she'd just get on with it.

"I'd like you to take on the part of the Sugar Plum Fairy."

She just about fell over. "You mean the main one?"

Shannon's smile got bigger. "Yep. You've really been working hard and it shows. All of you girls are very talented, and honestly I couldn't decide between two of you, but then today, your pirouettes were incredible. And you're picking up material more quickly than the other girls."

"Thank you."

"You've also become a real leader, dear. You have a good way with the little girls in the cast. They look up to you and I think you'll be a great help to me. In short, I think you'll make everyone proud."

"I don't know what to say." She had been working hard, but she hadn't thought anyone noticed.

"Do you want to think about it? It does mean more practices and more responsibility."

"No." When Miss Shannon blinked, Bethany said in a rush, "I mean, no, I don't need to think about it. I want to be the Sugar Plum Fairy. Thank you!"

"You're very welcome. I'll work on the schedule and talk to you and your mother later this week."

"Yes, ma'am." Anxious to tell her mother, she suddenly thought of something. "Um, is this a secret? I mean, can I tell my mom?"

A warm smile appeared. "It's not a secret at all. Tell whomever you would like, dear."

"Thank you!" she said again before she hurried to the parking lot. A quick scan showed her mom was sitting in her van. Like usual, she had her Kindle open and was reading. She started when Bethany opened the door. "Oh, Bethy. You startled me! Is everything okay?"

"Mom, you'll never guess what happened?"

She turned off her tablet and put it in her purse. "You better tell me quick, then."

"Miss Shannon asked me to be the Sugar Plum Fairy! Mom, the main one!"

"That's incredible!" She reached out and hugged Bethany tight. "Congratulations! My goodness, think of all the years you performed other parts."

"I know! Remember when I was a baker for about two minutes?"

Her mother nodded. "It was so hard for Dad and me to sit through all those dress rehearsals for your fleeting brush with fame."

Just the reminder of how much her parents had done for her was humbling. "You've done so much for me. Thanks."

"Oh, sweetie. This isn't about us. It's about your hard work. You should be very proud to be cast as the Sugar Plum Fairy. It's quite an achievement."

Bethany held out her hand. "When Miss Shannon first asked me to stay late, I was worried that I'd done something wrong. But then she gave me a bunch of compliments and said she wanted me to be the fairy."

"This is so exciting. You deserve it too. You've been working so hard."

"She said I'm going to have to do extra practices." Suddenly thinking about her mother's job as a receptionist at the veterinary hospital, she felt another rush of doubts. "Can I do that?"

"I don't see why not. Dad and I and your brother will figure it out."

Her brother was a senior and driving, but he'd never acted horrible about taking her places when one of their parents couldn't. "Thanks, Mom."

"Now, are you done worrying about everything under the sun?"

"Yes."

"Good." She held up the container that had been sitting in the cup holder. "Because I brought you a shake."

"You did?" she asked, pretending that ice cream wasn't her favorite food in the world. "What kind?"

"It's a vanilla malt from Frank's Frozen Custard. Last I heard, it was your favorite. Any interest?" She picked it up and playfully looked like she was going to take a sip. "Of course, if you don't want it now that you're the main Sugar Plum Fairy, I'll be happy to consume all those calories."

Giggling, Bethany snatched it out of her mother's hand. "Stop. I still want it!"

Her mother laughed as she started driving home.

Taking a sip, she smiled. "These are the best malts in the world. Thanks, Mom."

"Anytime."

As her mother drove with care along the windy roads of Bridgeport, which were partially covered in snow, Bethany thought about the beautiful costume she was going to get to wear and how good it felt to do something well.

And how good it felt to get noticed.

Between that, her mother's sweet treat, and Jeremy finally making a move, it had been a good day. One of the best.

CHAPTER 13

"Away in a manger, no crib for a bed.
The little Lord Jesus laid down his sweet head."

In the end, deciding whether or not to accept the modeling job hadn't been a difficult decision after all. A model's career was a short one, one that Kimber had often compared to a pro athlete's. She had a finite number of years to make good money before everyone moved onto the next "it girl," and she was left behind like yesterday's news. She also couldn't think of another job where she could earn six figures in four or five days.

Put that way, her choice hadn't really been a choice at all. A couple of weeks of watching her figure and a week of being at a photographer's beck and call was nothing compared to the amount of security she'd gain. After all, one never knew what was going to happen in one's future. There might be a time when that extra money would come in handy.

"I'm so relieved, Kimber," Brett said when she'd called to tell him the news. "Last night, I swear I almost drank myself silly worrying about what I was going to say if you told me no."

Sitting on the couch by the fireplace in their loft, Kimber rolled her eyes. "Drinking himself silly" was a constant occurrence in Brett's life.

He didn't need an excuse, it just happened. At one time, she'd worried about him, fearing that he was going down a dark path. Now though, she shrugged it off. She'd come to learn that her agent exaggerated as much as he supposedly drank.

She tucked her legs under her in an attempt to get warm. She never knew when he was being real and when he was heaping on the BS. Deciding to take the high road, she said, "I'm glad you're happy. I'm happy too. Ecstatic. I appreciate you calling me about this job. You didn't have to do that."

"I'd do anything for you, Kimber. You're special to me."

Oh, gag. She'd heard him say the same thing to a dozen other models. "I'm assuming you'll email me with the information?"

"Yep. Expect your flight info in the next day or so."

"Thanks." When Traci and Shannon walked into the kitchen, Shannon wearing slim black leggings and an ugly Christmas sweater emblazoned with JINGLE ALL THE WAY, she felt a sense of relief. Brett might be a great agent, but he still made her uncomfortable. Honestly, he was the exact opposite of her down-to-earth sisters.

Surging to her feet, Kimber said, "Sorry, but I've got to go. Something just came up. Bye." She hung up as he was sputtering questions at her. As far as she was concerned, she'd done what he wanted and he could wait a few more days to ask anything more of her.

"Who was that?" Traci asked as she poured herself some coffee. "Oh, and what is there to eat? Has Jennifer made anything good?"

"Was it Gunnar?" Shannon asked, raising an eyebrow and smiling.

"Not Gunnar. That was Brett—and yes, cherry scones."

Shannon had already gotten herself a cup of coffee and started walking into their living room. Kimber followed and flicked the switch on the gas fireplace.

After standing in front of the fire for a moment with a pleased smile on her face, Shannon took the chair closest to it. "Brett? As in Brett the agent?"

"None other."

Traci brought over both the tin of scones and her cup of coffee. Placing the tin on the coffee table, she grabbed one and sat down next to Shannon. "Any reason why he called?"

"Yep. He called yesterday to offer me a job."

Traci looked at her closely. "And . . ."

"And it was a really good job. One of the best opportunities I've ever had." She waved a hand. "*Women's Weekly* offered me the cover—an inside spread, everything."

"And I guess it pays real well too," Shannon said dryly.

"It does. The whole package was too good to pass up." She still felt self-conscious about her earnings, but she would never lie about the money.

"Where is the photo shoot?" Traci asked. Both her posture and her tone seemed carefully controlled.

"It's just New York. Not far at all. And it's only for a couple of days. It seemed almost too good to be true." Huh. Was she selling the job to them or herself?

Shannon put down her coffee cup. "I'm starting to realize why you're telling us all this. You took the job." Her voice was flat.

"I did. I didn't have a choice."

Traci eyed her over the top rim of her coffee cup. "Sure you did, Kimber. You can always say no."

"You two don't know what it's like. People in my profession don't get asked to do things like this very often. Usually never.

This was a really good offer—and I'll probably never get offered a job like this again."

Shannon got back to her feet and turned to face the fire.

Traci, on the other hand, was staring at her directly. "I'm not saying you were wrong to take it . . . only that you shouldn't pretend you didn't want to."

"Maybe you're right. I don't know." But she was beginning to feel a little annoyed. She didn't expect them to be jumping up and down, but she would have thought they'd at least be a little more gracious about her decision.

"I know I'm right." Traci continued to look at her right in the eye. Kimber had a suspicion Traci used that pointed stare all the time when she arrested folks.

She wasn't a big fan of it being directed at her.

She bit back her irritation and attempted to joke. "You and your confidence, girl."

"It's not being confident if I'm right."

"Whatever."

Shannon turned to face them again. "When is this job?"

"Soon. Maybe in a week or so. Brett's going to email me the details."

Shannon frowned. "But Christmas is right around the corner. You don't think they'll send you there before Christmas, do you?"

"Maybe." It was actually more of a *probably*. Kimber didn't mind if it was though. If she went up to New York before Christmas, then she could relax again. She wouldn't have to be exercising and dieting on Christmas Day.

But for some reason, she just felt worse. "Like I said, I won't be gone for more than a couple of days."

"Well, at least you'll get to see all the decorations and everything," Shannon said. "It's so pretty in New York City at Christmas."

Feeling worse—though she really wasn't sure why—Kimber

blurted, "Hey! Maybe after I get done I could stay and you girls could join me. We could go to a show."

"I'd love to go see the Rockettes again," Shannon mused. "But you know I can't. *The Nutcracker* has taken over my life. I'm practically dreaming about it every night."

Feeling a fresh wave of guilt, Kimber looked down at her shoes. She'd been leading Shannon to believe that she'd be around to help as much as possible. It hadn't been a lie. She absolutely had been planning to help. But what could she do? This was a great opportunity.

Lifting her chin, she tried to come up with the right words to justify what she was doing again. "This came out of the blue. But it's a really good job. I have to go to New York. What about you, Traci, can you get away for a couple of nights?"

Traci looked just as disappointed. "Between my work schedule and Bridge, it's a no go for me too. It would've been fun, though. I've never been to New York."

"We should plan something then." Feeling desperate to make amends, she said, "Hey, maybe we could go in June? The weather's nice then, and I won't be doing a job."

"Yes. Of course. Maybe in June." Shannon grabbed one of the scones. "Well, um, speaking of work, I better get on my way downstairs. My senior steppers are coming in to practice their tap dancing and then my little preschoolers are arriving to learn their dance."

When she turned away, Kimber felt even worse. Shannon had wanted her to tap dance, and she had even bought her a pair of tap shoes. But instead of appreciating her kindness, Kimber had made sure Shannon knew that she hated every minute of it.

She sat down. How come it felt like every single "right" decision she had ever made was suddenly coming back to bite her? She felt bad about everything.

Practically feeling the heat behind Traci's disapproving glare, she said, "I get it. You're disappointed."

Traci raised her eyebrows but murmured, "I'm not anything. Whatever you want to do with your life is your business. I mean, I'm not your mother."

"I know that. And just for the record, my mother's going to be very happy I said yes to this job." Although, technically, Kimber wasn't positive about that. Her mother had wanted her to do something with her brain, not pose in "those tiny outfits."

"I'm sure she's proud of you," Traci said. "I mean, you've made a great career as a model. You're beautiful and famous."

She felt her cheeks heat. Put that way, she was being ungrateful and maybe greedy. "I'm sorry. I don't know what else to say. I said yes. The decision has been made."

Traci stood up, taking the tin with her. "I guess I'm just thinking it's a shame that all the reasons you quit don't seem to matter anymore. You sounded so sure, but I guess you weren't. Or maybe you changed your mind."

There was only so much recrimination she was willing to put up with. "For the record, I'm thinking it's a shame that you can't be happy for something I've worked so hard for. I don't know a single model in my profession who would have said no to this."

"I guess that's what counts, then." She smiled tightly. "I'm going to go say hi to Gwen before I get on home. Matt is with Bridge but he's got to run in to see a patient this afternoon. Kimber, I'll see you around."

"Yeah. See you, Traci." Why did that feel like they were suddenly talking to each other like strangers?

Reaching for another scone, Kimber came up empty.

Traci had taken that darn tin with her! That little gesture ticked her off, because she knew that Traci had done it on purpose. Maybe she hadn't done it out of spite. Maybe Traci had taken it since she knew that Kimber was going to be back to watching what she ate, which meant no scone binging.

She wouldn't have been wrong.

But . . . Kimber still felt those yummy Christmas treats' loss. Almost as much as her sisters' presence.

She picked up her phone, ready to text Gunnar, but inevitably decided against it. If he was disappointed in her too, she would feel even worse.

And if she started feeling even worse about herself, Kimber didn't know what she would do. She couldn't take much more of this.

CHAPTER 14

"There's a song in the air!"
—JOSIAH G. HOLLAND, "CHRISTMAS"

After spending most of the last hour not doing much except looking out the window and pacing, Gunnar suddenly muttered under his breath.

Jeremy was beyond glad about that. It had been the longest morning in the world—especially since Gunnar had kept making him clean the same stuff over and over. Jeremy was sure the kitchen countertops had never been as shiny as they were now.

"That's her?" Jeremy walked to his side and stared at the sporty red SUV that had just pulled into their driveway.

"Yep." Looking like he was about to head into battle, Gunnar pulled on his jacket. "Grab a coat, Jeremy. Let's go help my mother unload. If she's true to form, she's going to have a ton of stuff."

Jeremy did as Gunnar asked, but he was confused. "I thought you liked your mom."

A line formed between Gunnar's eyebrows. "Oh, I do. She's great. I love her a lot."

"Then why are you acting so freaked out?" Gunnar was acting weirder than when Melanie was there, and that said a lot.

"It's just that . . . Well, you'll understand in a minute or two."

When he saw that Mrs. Law was still fussing and hadn't opened her door yet, Jeremy paused. He wanted to see what the big guy's mother looked like. Gunnar was acting too weird, so Jeremy figured he had better be prepared for anything.

But then he had to laugh when he saw her get out. Why, she was just a little thing. And, she looked pretty normal too, dressed as she was in jeans, a lavender sweater, and gold flats. She had shoulder length hair that was pulled into a ponytail. From a distance, she didn't look much older than thirty or so.

"She looks nice, Gunnar."

"She is. But get ready, buddy. My mom—well, my mother can be a lot." Gunnar straightened his shoulders and walked down the steps. "Hey, Mama!"

"Oh, Gunnar. Gunnar Alexander, look at you!" she exclaimed before hugging him tight. Then she even patted Gunnar on the arm, which was hysterical, since Mrs. Law only reached his collarbone.

Feeling better, he slowly walked down the steps. He'd say hello and then go to his room.

Yeah. That sounded like the right thing to do . . .

"Jeremy!"

Caught off guard, he froze. Then, feeling awkward, he smiled, raised his hand, and waved awkwardly. "Hi, Mrs. Law."

"No, no, no. I don't want a wave," she said as she waved him over. "Come give your new grandma a hug."

His new grandma? He barely had time to give Gunnar a "help me" look before she pulled him into a fierce hug. "Oh, Jeremy. Aren't you wonderful?"

Raising his hands, he kind of circled them around her and hung on, because she didn't seem in any hurry to let him go. He was aware of the scent of sugar cookies and lemon and some kind of flowery perfume. The whole combination was intense, but not awful.

She was, well, a lot. Gunnar had described his mother to a T, that was for sure.

Just as Jeremy tried to crane his neck to look over at Gunnar in the hopes that he'd rescue him at last, Mrs. Law dropped her hands and stepped back.

He exhaled.

She might have been giving him space, but she was still staring at him like he was Santa Claus and the Easter Bunny rolled into one. "Oh, but you are so handsome," she said. "Gunnar didn't tell me that."

"Thanks?"

"No need for thanks there. God gave you those looks, right?"

"Right." He didn't know what else to say, so he just stood there and hoped he could move out of her reach soon.

"Mama, I think you're starting to scare the boy. Relax, would you?"

She chuckled. "Sorry. Now, don't worry. We'll get to know each other real well soon. It's going to be so wonderful."

"Yes, ma'am."

"Now, go help your dad bring in my suitcases. Can you do that?"

"Yes, ma'am."

Mrs. Law looked around the yard. "Gunnar, you don't have a dog yet, do you?"

"No, ma'am."

"Good to know," she said as she sailed right into the house.

When the screen door closed with a snap behind her, Jeremy looked over at Gunnar. "Is she like that all the time?"

"Nope. She gets quiet when she sleeps."

Jeremy couldn't help it. He cracked up as he reached down and grabbed the handle on a giant purple roller bag. "I can't believe you two are so different."

"I never needed to talk when she was around." Picking up a tote bag and the handle on the other bag, he grunted. "Lord, but this is heavy. Be careful now."

"I've got it." But the thing had to weigh over fifty pounds.

"My mom tends to overpack. Always has, always will. My father used to say traveling with her was like bringing Kmart Supercenter on vacation. She seems to need everything on earth."

Jeremy slowly wheeled the bag toward the house, listening raptly to Gunnar. "What was your dad like?"

"Quiet, like me. He loved her so much though. Always said she kept him on his toes. I promise, you'll get used to her. She's a lot, but she'll grow on you."

"What did she mean about a dog?"

Gunnar opened the door. "That, Jeremy, is a topic for another day."

"Are you sure about that?" He was thinking if he and Gunnar were a permanent thing, a dog added to the mix would be awesome.

"I promise. You have no idea."

* * *

Jeremy had expected Mrs. Law to be waiting for them in the entry way, but she wasn't. "Where did she go?" he whispered, half-afraid she was going to bound out of a corner and hug him again.

But this time, instead of looking pained, Gunnar grinned.

"She's in the kitchen. Come on, boy. This is going to knock your socks off."

Jeremy was too curious to even give him grief about the old-fashioned expression. He followed Gunnar through the living room, past the dining room, and then started smiling too. Because there was Mrs. Law with an apron on, already rooting around the pantry. And she had out a bag of chocolate chips.

"Do you like chocolate chip cookies, Jeremy?" she asked as she pulled out the sugar.

"Yes, ma'am." Didn't everyone?

She looked pleased. "I was hoping you would say that. I knew Gunnar wouldn't have any chips so I brought a bag with me."

"You travel with chocolate chips?"

"Only on special occasions."

Gunnar was at the cupboard. "Want a glass of water, Jeremy? You might as well have a seat too. My mother is going to want to chat while she bakes."

"Gunnar, I swear sometimes you make me sound crazy. All I'm doing is trying to get to know Jeremy here."

"Yes, ma'am," he said.

Jeremy hopped on one of the barstools that lines the island and watched Mrs. Law pull out ingredients he had no idea were in the cupboards.

Gunnar handed him a glass of water, then curved a hand around Jeremy's shoulder. "I'm gonna go take a shower. You keep my mom company, okay?"

He was getting left alone with her? "All right."

"Take it easy on Jeremy, Mama. He's new to you and to be honest, he's looking a little afraid."

Mrs. Law turned to face him. "Are you afraid of me?"

"No."

Her slight frown turned into a bright smile again. "See,

Jeremy's going to be just fine. Go shower, Son. When you get out, we'll discuss dinner and my first dance class."

"Yes, ma'am."

After he disappeared down the hall, Mrs. Law chuckled. "Jeremy, that Gunnar is kind of a pistol."

This was news to him. "He is?"

"Oh, yes. He always says yes, ma'am, sweet as you please, then darts off and does his own thing. You should remember that."

"I will."

She pulled out an electric mixer, started beating butter and brown sugar and some eggs. Jeremy watched. His mother hadn't really been around much and she hadn't been one for cooking. But sitting here, sipping water, he was thinking that simply watching Gunnar's mom wasn't too bad. "Do you always start cooking the minute you get here?"

"No, dear. I just . . . well, I like to be busy sometimes. And I've been looking forward to baking you cookies since I woke up this morning."

"Oh. That's, um, real nice of you."

After she poured in the flour and a couple of teaspoons of some other stuff, she opened up the bag of chocolate chips. Then her voice softened. "Gunnar told me that you've had a time of it."

"Yeah." His dad had never been around and his mother had never been around all that much either, and then she'd died. And then had come the series of foster homes. None of them had been horrible, but until Gunnar, he'd never really been too happy with any of them.

After putting a cookie sheet in the oven, she poured herself a cup of coffee that he hadn't even realized she'd brewed. "Do you drink coffee?"

"Not really."

"That's probably good. It's my vice. I love it." When she sat down next to him, she said, "So, Gunnar was one of four kids. I had them all close together and sometimes felt like I was a cop on crowd control instead of their mother. My husband, you see, was always working so the kids would have shoes and such. Then, when he was around, he was a softie. Those kids could get away with murder."

Jeremy grinned. "Gunnar too?"

"Gunnar . . . Gunnar was number three out of four. I don't know how he managed it, but he became the most easygoing of them all. My eldest, Martin?" She waved a hand. "He loved getting his way. Still does, if you want to know the truth."

"Who's second?"

"Darcy. Darcy was our star pupil. We never had a lick of trouble with her. Now, she's a physician's assistant and is married out in Denver. She already has two kids and a nanny."

"Wow." He'd never met anyone who had a nanny.

"I know! I told her that she was acting pretty fancy for a girl from Spartan, but she told me to stop my fussing."

"Then there is Gunnar."

"Yep, and you know all about him. He's as steady as can be." She sighed. "And then there's Andrew."

"What's wrong with him?"

"Oh, nothing much."

"Much?" That didn't sound too good.

"Don't fret, child. He's fine. He just doesn't want to grow up. One day, though . . ."

"Don't listen to my mom," Gunnar said as he joined them, now clad in a thick pair of black fleece sweatpants and an old T-shirt. "Andrew is a sergeant in the Army and is stationed out in Colorado Springs. I promise, he's plenty grown up."

"He's far from home. But every time I say that, he says that he could be farther." She walked to the oven, slipped on a mitt, and pulled out a tray of perfectly baked cookies. Looking pleased, she glanced his way. "Do you like warm cookies, child?"

"I do."

"Good. I'll get you a plate and a glass of milk." She gave him a hard look. "Don't fuss about drinking milk."

"I won't." If Gunnar hadn't been there, he would have told her that Gunnar made him drink milk too.

As he watched Mrs. Law do just what she said, Gunnar poured himself a cup of coffee too.

"Sounds like Mom has been filling you in on everyone."

"Yep."

"I hope she told you the truth. How I'm the best of the lot."

"She said you were steady."

Gunnar didn't look too impressed. "Gee, thanks, Mom."

"Oh, stop. I gave you a compliment, and you know it. I'm real proud of you. Always have been, but don't you go tell the other kids that I said that," Mrs. Law said as she handed Jeremy a plate of five cookies.

"No, ma'am."

"Now, what do y'all think about chicken and rice casserole?"

"It sounds good, but we should probably have it another time. It's already getting late and I don't want to run to the grocery store. The boy needs to eat soon."

"It's already made. I'll pop it in the oven. Okay?"

Jeremy gaped at her. "You came with casseroles and chocolate chips?"

"She's kind of like Mary Poppins that way, Jeremy. It's easiest if you just kind of go with the flow."

"I can do that." Popping a second warm cookie in his mouth, he was kind of thinking that he'd put up with a lot of Mrs. Law craziness for food like that.

Gunnar laughed. "I thought I'd keep her culinary skills a surprise for you. She's a great cook."

Mrs. Law shook her head. "You make it sound like I'm doing something special. I'm not. Well, not for most people."

"I never got the hang of cooking," Gunnar supplied.

"How that can be, I don't know. You can rebuild an engine but you can't seem to follow the most basic directions in a cookbook."

"It's harder than it looks."

"Jeremy, do you see what I have to put up with? Now, I not only have to find a good woman for Gunnar, but one who can cook too."

"I don't know if Kimber cooks, Gunnar," he said before he realized that he probably should have kept his mouth shut.

Because Mrs. Law zeroed in on Gunnar like Jeremy didn't even exist. "Kimber?"

Gunnar's expression became a blank slate. "We don't need to talk about Kimber right now."

"Sure, we do. You know there's no time like the present." She looked at the clock. "We've got thirty-five minutes before supper is ready."

"Because I don't want to be grilled before you've even gotten settled in your room. Don't you want to go do that?"

"Not especially." Turning to Jeremy again, she said, "I guess you've met this woman?"

He stuffed a cookie into his mouth so he wouldn't have to talk. But he went ahead and nodded.

"You've already brought her around the boy? It must be real serious."

"For your information, Jeremy met Kimber before me."

Mrs. Law looked his way. "How did that happen? Is this Kimber the mother of one of your friends?"

"No. She's a volunteer at the elementary school library. I'm doing my community service credits there."

She smiled at him encouragingly. "And you liked her so much that you introduced her to Gunnar?"

Feeling like he'd just swallowed a truth serum, he kept talking. "Um, not exactly. Kimber had car trouble one day after school. When Gunnar came to pick me up, he noticed that she needed some help. He helped her get a tow."

"That was nice of you boys."

"It was a little more involved than that, Ma," Gunnar said. "In any case, we're seeing each other a little bit, but it's nothing serious yet."

"She must be sweet if she's a volunteer librarian."

"She . . . is."

"Is she pretty? And I'm only asking because I'm curious. But we both know that looks aren't everything, boy. Do you remember me telling you that?"

"Yes, ma'am." But he couldn't keep his lips from twitching.

"You know what? I shouldn't have even asked. I'm sure she's real nice, no matter what she looks like.

Jeremy couldn't help it, he started laughing.

Mrs. Law raised her eyebrows. "Jeremy, what is so amusing?"

"Nothing, Mrs. Law."

She put her hands on her hips. "I not only raised four children, I can spot a lie a mile away. Try answering me again, if you please."

"It's nothing . . . except that she's a model."

"Say again?"

"Kimber's a model," Gunnar said. "She's flat-out gorgeous . . . and she's famous ."

"How famous?"

"Famous enough to be on the cover of more than one magazine."

She turned back to him. "Jeremy, is he pulling my leg?"

"No, ma'am."

Jeremy watched as Mrs. Law blinked. Blinked again. Then looked right at her son. "And she's dating you?"

Then, he couldn't help it. He started laughing so loud, the noise felt like it filled the whole house.

But to his surprise, Gunnar just walked over and rested a hand on his shoulder and laughed too.

CHAPTER 15

*"Happy, happy Christmas, that can win us back to the
delusions of our childish days; that can recall to the old
man the pleasures of his youth; that can transport the
sailor and the traveler, thousands of miles away, back
to his own fireside and his quiet home."*

—CHARLES DICKENS, "THE PICKWICK PAPERS"

He was going to do it. At least, Bethany was pretty sure he was.
Ever since he'd first offered to walk her home, she'd been sure that
Jeremy was going to ask her to the Christmas dance. She'd been
listening intently, ready to hear what he had to say.

But so far, he hadn't said much of anything.

All he'd done was talk about how much he had eaten at lunch.

And about the weather. Jeremy had talked for almost five full
minutes about how it was really cold and supposed to snow again.
She hadn't known what she was supposed to say to that.

When Jeremy had finally taken a breath, he groaned.
"So I guess I've been sounding like an idiot for the last ten
minutes, huh?"

"Not an idiot." *Not exactly . . .*

He ran a hand through his short dark hair. "Only like a guy who eats a lot and watches the weather channel obsessively?"

She giggled. "Maybe. But it's okay if that's what you like to do."

"It isn't."

He looked so aggravated with himself, she teased him a little bit. "Are you sure? Because it's okay if you are fixated on weather patterns."

"I'm positive. I promise, I'm a lot more interesting than that." He winced. "But there's nothing wrong with it. You know . . . if you like watching the Weather Channel."

"Actually, I've never watched that channel, Jeremy." She barely stopped herself from giggling when he slapped a hand over his eyes and groaned.

"Sorry. I promise I don't usually talk about the weather." He frowned. "Or food."

"What *do* you usually talk about?"

He winced. "I don't know." He shrugged. "Nothing all that important, I guess."

She let that sink in as they walked a little more. He was making her nervous.

Actually, Bethany was starting to wonder if she even wanted to go to the dance with him. What if Jeremy acted weird and awkward the whole time? What if he only talked about weather and food to all of her friends?

She could totally see how they would react to that too. They'd egg him on and then share glances when they didn't think he was looking. But of course he would notice, and then it would be awful. By the end of the night, everyone would be making fun of him.

And, maybe of her, too, because she was his date. Though it made her feel shallow, Bethany was old enough to realize that she wouldn't care too much if people made fun of her if she believed in Jeremy and what he was about. But so far, she didn't know him all that well. She only had a hunch that there was something about him that she really liked.

But that wasn't enough.

Thinking that maybe she needed to take over the conversation, she decided to go big. "Hey, Jeremy?"

He cast her a sideways look. "Yeah?"

"Hey, can I ask you something that's kind of serious? You don't need to answer if you don't want."

He looked relieved that she was taking charge. "You can ask me anything. Promise."

"All right. Um, what's going to happen to you next year? Will you still live here in Bridgeport?"

His eyes clouded. "I think so. I mean, Gunnar is going to adopt me."

That seemed really good, but maybe it wasn't? "You don't seem that happy. What's wrong? Do you not want him to adopt you?"

"I do. I get a choice. The social workers and the judge and everyone makes sure of that. And there's nothing wrong with Gunnar. He's great."

"Oh."

He sighed. "I don't know what's wrong with me, to be honest. My parents weren't great. My father was never around, and my mother was nice enough, but she wasn't exactly what you'd call hands-on. Then she got shot at an ATM."

"That's horrible. I'm so sorry."

"It was bad. She'd left me home alone, so when the police came to tell me, it was hard." He took a deep breath. "But even though my mother wasn't like some TV mom or anything, she tried her best. Now, sometimes I feel like . . . if I get adopted, it will mean that I'm getting rid of all traces of her."

Bethany nodded.

"Some days I think that maybe she doesn't deserve that, you know?" Before she could answer, he shook his head again. "Forget it. I know I'm not making any sense."

"You are. I don't think what you're saying is wrong, Jeremy. I never thought about getting adopted from that perspective."

"I hadn't either until a couple of nights ago." He looked down at his feet, then said, "Before I was at Gunnar's house, I was with another couple of foster families. Some were fine, but there was one couple that was really special. The Robinsons were great."

"They were nice?"

"Yeah. But they were older, in their fifties. They were some kind of super foster family—they've been taking in kids for years. I went there right after my mom was murdered, so I was kind of a wreck."

She couldn't even imagine losing both her parents suddenly then being forced to live with strangers. "How long were you there?"

"Six months. That was their limit, I guess." He sighed. "They did a lot for me and got me through a lot of sleepless nights and a couple of bad moments when I was freaking out."

"Freaking out?"

"I kept saying stuff like 'Why me?' and then getting mad because there wasn't an answer."

"I would've been thinking the same things. I mean, how could you not?"

"A couple of days before I was due to leave, another kid showed up. A kid a few years younger than me. He was nine or ten." Jeremy's voice lowered. "He'd been forcibly removed from his house."

"Because his parents were abusive?"

"Yeah. They'd screwed him up bad." He stared at her. "But it had happened years ago, Bethany. He'd been floating around from home to home, pretty much acting up and being a little, uh, jerk. He came to the Robinsons' as kind of a last resort."

"Wow."

"After being around him an hour, I kept my distance. The kid was twisted. But then one night after dinner, Mr. Robinson knocked on my door and asked to talk to me for a minute."

"What did he say?"

"He told me how they felt that God meant for them to foster kids and not adopt them. But if things were different they would want to adopt me."

"Wow." Feeling like she was about to cry, Bethany attempted to control herself. But, it was hard, because she felt like that had been a cruel thing for them to say. None of what had happened was Jeremy's fault.

Jeremy smiled. "Hey, it's okay, Bethany. You look like you're about to go hit someone."

"But weren't you upset? I mean, it sounds like kind of a mean thing to say."

"I was kind of bummed, but what Mr. Robinson said next mattered more. He said something like it's a waste of time wondering why things happen. That there's nothing you can do about the past, only the future. He said that I was lucky because I lived most of my life with a decent woman and they'd heard that the couple I was getting sent to live with next was decent too."

"And were they?"

"Yeah. They were fine. All the families were fine." He brightened. "But then one day Melanie showed up and told me that she found someone for me, and that he was really different from everyone else I'd been with. He was doing it because he wanted to help a kid and one day adopt."

"And that was Gunnar?"

"Yeah." He smiled. After they walked a little bit more, he said, "I can't believe I just told you all that. Sorry."

"Don't be. I'm glad you told me some more about what

happened to you." She smiled up at him. "I'd rather hear about that instead of the weather."

He chuckled. "I bet." He released a ragged sigh. "Bethany, I'm going to be honest. I've been afraid that if you found out about my past, you wouldn't want anything to do with me. But then I started thinking that maybe it's better you knew. In case . . ."

His voice drifted off.

"Jeremy, in case what?"

"In case I finally ever get the nerve to ask if you'd go to the Christmas dance with me." Looking horrified, Jeremy stared at her for a long minute before looking down at his feet again.

He'd asked her! Elation filled her insides like she'd been deflated and she hadn't even known what had been missing.

All Bethany *did know* now was that there was something about Jeremy that she really liked. She didn't care how his mother died or that he was a foster kid. She didn't even care that he was kind of shy and unsure of himself. She liked that. It was different. He was different in a lot of ways—ways that counted.

Though her palms were sweating a little, she said, "Jeremy, maybe you should go ahead and ask me."

His chin popped back up and his blue eyes were bright. "You think?"

She pointed to the red-brick house with black shutters that was just up the road. "Well, yeah, since we're almost at my house."

He stared at her house, seemed to kind of shake his head, then collected himself again. "Bethany, will you go to the Christmas dance with me? I promise I won't bore you with foster kid stories the whole time."

"Yes."

"Yes?" He looked kind of stunned, which was really cute.

"I don't even care if you tell me a bunch of foster kid stories either." She kind of liked them, but she didn't want to tell him that. She was pretty sure he'd think that was weird.

"I won't. But thanks."

Glad that he'd asked her at last, relieved that she knew more about him, and so happy about a lot of things, she giggled. "I better warn you—you're going to have to meet my parents before the dance. They don't let me go out with anyone before meeting them first."

"Yeah, that's fine." He frowned at her home like he expected her mother to come running out the door. "You've got a really big house."

"It's not that big."

"It looks like it to me."

Embarrassed now, she shrugged. "I've lived there all my life. I guess I don't think about it much. And don't worry about my parents. You don't have to meet them today."

"Good. I don't know if I could take it."

She giggled again as they walked to the foot of her driveway. "Well, um, I guess I better go inside. Thanks for walking me home."

"Wait. Can I have your number?"

At last! She called out the numbers when he pulled out his cell, feeling a strange sense of satisfaction as she watched him punch her phone number in. A couple of seconds later she heard her own cell beep.

"I just texted you so you'll know my number too."

"Thanks." She wondered if he was going to text her later. She kind of hoped he would.

He smiled at her. "Okay. I'll see you later."

"Bye, Jeremy." She smiled at him before walking up her driveway. Even though she didn't dare look back, she was pretty sure he didn't move until she was almost at her front door. It was strange, but she was glad that he did that. He was so different from any of the other boys she knew. None of the other guys she'd dated had ever acted like she was anything special to them.

Unable to help herself, she started humming some song they'd been practicing in choir. She hadn't really liked it at the time, but now it seemed like it was the only thing that could sum up her feelings.

"Who was that?" her mother asked the moment she tossed her backpack on the floor inside. "He watched you until you were halfway up the drive."

Bethany was feeling so happy she didn't even care that her mother had watched her out the window. At least she hadn't opened the door or anything. "That was Jeremy Widmer."

Her mother folded her arms across the front of her gray sweater. "Jeremy Widmer? I don't remember you mentioning him before."

"I haven't mentioned him because he's new."

"And he walked you home? Maybe you'd better tell me something about him."

Oh, her mother and her twenty questions! "Mom, there isn't much to tell." Which was a lie, of course. There was a ton to tell but she wasn't going to share it.

"How about some basic facts, then. What grade is he in?"

"He's a junior like me."

"He looks pretty cute."

"Jeremy is cute. And . . . he just asked me to the Christmas dance."

Her mom raised her eyebrows before smiling. "What did you say?"

"Yes."

Her smiled wavered. "Even though you just met him?"

"Jeremy is really nice, Mom. I promise. And he's different from all the other boys."

"Different? That's kind of a funny way to describe someone you like."

118

She figured her mother had a point but she wasn't going to explain what she meant. "Don't worry. I already told Jeremy that he's going to have to meet you and Dad, and he said that was fine."

"I see. Now, there's about a dozen questions in my head but I'm going to give you a break and not ask any of them."

"Thanks, because I've got to go get ready to go to the Upchurchs' house in an hour." There was also a pretty good chance that she wouldn't have answered any of her mom's questions anyway. No way did she want her mom to start classifying Jeremy into some kind of neat little box.

"Are you watching kids or dogs?"

"Both." Even though she didn't really mind, she frowned.

As she'd hoped, her mother flew into action. "Three kids and four dogs? How many hours?"

"Three. Just until Mr. Upchurch gets home from a late meeting."

"Oh, Bethany, I better go fix you a snack. You're going to need it if you're going to be over there for so long."

"Thanks, Mom," she said, even though Mrs. Upchurch always left her the best snacks. "I'm going to run upstairs and change." And check her phone. Maybe Jeremy had already texted her. Then, of course, she was going to have to tell all her friends. Karyn and Jules were going to be beyond jealous. Jeremy might be kind of awkward but he was nice—and so cute.

She was pretty sure that tomorrow she was going to be the most envied girl in the junior class.

CHAPTER 16

"Glory to God in the highest, and on earth peace,
good will toward men."
—LUKE 2:14

Gunnar was sitting on the stoop when Jeremy got home twenty minutes after saying goodbye to Bethany. As usual, Gunnar was wearing faded jeans, scuffed brown Timberlands, a flannel shirt, his black Gor-Tex jacket, and a ball cap. He was also wearing a frown.

That was kind of new.

When he saw his foster parent's expression, all the huge, optimistic feelings that had been spinning around inside him died. The guy was pissed.

Really pissed. Jeremy knew why too. He'd ignored Gunnar's text when he was talking to Bethany and then had forgotten about it. It was like Bethany was all that mattered to him anymore.

Of course, that wasn't true. But it was pretty hard to think of anyone but Bethany right now. Her saying yes to the dance made him feel like he'd accomplished something pretty big.

But now he had to face the fact that while he might have gotten Bethany to say yes, he'd also managed to make Gunnar mad. With his luck, Gunnar would probably be so mad that he'd ground him from the dance or something.

His steps slowed as he tried to think of something to say. But even though he tried his best, his mind went blank. He honestly couldn't think of a thing to say. Gunnar hadn't given him a ton of rules to follow, but the main one was to always let him know when he wasn't going to follow his usual schedule.

Since he'd ignored that rule big time and he didn't have any sort of decent-sounding excuse, Jeremy decided to just stand there and let Gunnar have his say. As he tried to look anywhere but at Gunnar, the cold air seeped into his clothes.

Funny, it was the first time in hours that he'd noticed just how cold the temperature actually was.

After another minute passed—which felt close to an hour— Gunnar stood up, his hazel eyes cool under the brim of his ball cap. "Looks like you took your time getting home today."

He swallowed. "I know."

"You know?" A line formed between his brows. "I gave you a cell phone for a reason, Jeremy Widmer. Is it working . . . ? Or did it break for some reason and you didn't think to tell me?"

Oh, boy. "It's not broken. I mean, it's working just fine." It had sure worked fine a couple of minutes ago when he'd texted Bethany and she'd texted him right back.

"We had some rules we agreed to." His voice deepened. "Did you forget what they were?"

"No, sir. I didn't forget."

Gunnar's expression became even more confused. "I'm trying

121

to keep my patience here, but you're starting to make it real diffi-cult. You going to give me a reason for being late and not calling? Maybe even apologize for making me worry? Because I'm begin-ning to get pretty tired of hearing your short, pat answers to my questions."

"I'm sorry."

Gunnar still didn't look impressed. "Is that it?"

"I mean it. I really am sorry I didn't call."

He cracked his knuckles. "I'm waiting, boy."

It didn't look like Gunnar was getting ready to hit him or anything, but he did look like he was barely holding it together.

Okay. It was time to start talking even though he might really regret sharing so much. "First, I thought you were going to still be at that house working. I didn't think you'd notice if I came home on time or not."

When he saw Gunnar's expression tighten further, he winced. That had absolutely not been the right thing to say. Like, at all. "I mean—"

"Boy, if I've been staying there working, it was because I trusted you to be here. Part of me even thought you might need some time to relax and watch TV or whatever without me watch-ing over you like you were a little kid."

Jeremy had never thought about it like that. "Um . . ."

Gunnar cut him off again. Looking at him directly in the eye, he blurted, "Have I been wrong? Have you been doing this a lot?"

"This?"

"Going out after school?" He waved a hand. "Have you been doing your own thing and lying to me?"

"What? No." When Gunnar's eyes narrowed, Jeremy tacked on another word. "I mean, no, sir. This was the first time. I prom-ise it was . . . and I had a good reason. I really did."

He sighed. "I sure hope so." Gunnar stuffed his hands in the pockets of his down vest, as if he'd suddenly noticed the temperature outside. "You know what? Come on in. Let's go sit down. I'm too old for twenty questions and it's getting real cold out here."

The sun had started slipping down and the wind had picked up. He was no weatherman, but it sure looked like more snow was on the way. Jeremy followed Gunnar inside, closing the door behind him and kicking off his tennis shoes. Gunnar had gone into the living room and lit the fireplace. When the flame roared to life, he stood for a moment facing it, warming his hands in front of the fire.

Watching him, Jeremy thought about how Gunnar did a lot of things like that. He did a lot of things in an adept, concise way, without a lot of fuss or worry. He also did a lot of them for Jeremy's sake, so he would feel secure and happy. Yep, what had used to feel foreign and new was now expected. He'd begun to take a lot of Gunnar's mannerisms and habits for granted.

Which was kind of amazing.

Glad of the few moments' reprieve, Jeremy sat down on the couch. He wondered if he should try to think of something to say but elected to stay quiet.

At last, Gunnar broke the silence. "Jeremy, this is where you start talking, yeah?" He turned at last. "And don't even think about giving me a bunch of 'I don't knows.' That's not going to cut it."

"Fine. I was walking Bethany Seevers home."

Gunnar blinked and he looked kind of taken aback. Then his eyes lit up. "Huh. I guess you can tell I'm surprised. I don't know why, though." He rubbed a hand over the stubble on his cheeks. "I guess I should've realized there was a girl involved."

Figuring he might as well get the rest of his news over with, he said, "I walked Bethany home because it took me all that time to work up the nerve to ask her to go to the Christmas dance with me."

"You're already going to take a girl to a dance? You're moving fast, buddy."

Gunnar was sounding a whole lot nicer. "Not that fast. All the guys were asking. It's in a couple of weeks. On December twenty-third."

He slowly smiled. "You don't mess around."

"I'm not really doing anything different than anyone else. All the guys I know are asking girls to the dance now. Phillip told me that if you wait too long all the girls like Bethany get asked up."

"Girls like Bethany?"

"You know, the special girls."

"So . . . don't keep me in suspense. What did she say?"

"Yes." Unable to help himself, Jeremy grinned.

"She did, huh?"

"Gunnar, it was so great, because Bethany didn't even make me wait. All she did say was that I was going to have to meet her parents before that night."

"Sounds like she's got parents who care."

"Yeah. I hope it goes okay."

"It will. Don't you worry about that." He chuckled. "Well, I'm real pleased for you, Jeremy. That's great news. I've had my share of asking-out-girls horror stories."

"No way."

"Yeah. Well, not every girl I liked felt the same way. A couple weren't shy about letting me know that either."

Jeremy didn't even want to think about that. "I was nervous, Gunnar. I didn't know what I was doing, and some guys were going all out, making banners and putting bouquets of flowers on girls' cars and shit."

"Don't say *shit*."

"Fine. But they were doing a lot, and I wasn't doing any of that. And Bethany's really pretty. She could have been asked out by any guy in the school."

"But she said yes to you. Maybe she didn't need all that other stuff."

"Phillip said that she liked me. He could've been messing with me, though."

"If she said yes, he might have been right."

"Maybe. That's why I asked her out today. I couldn't do it at school though. I mean, if she told me no, then everyone would know and I'd have to deal with it all day. It would have been embarrassing."

Gunnar nodded. "I reckon that would be bad."

"I asked her if I could walk her home and finally asked her when we were standing in front of her house."

"Even though you should've let me know what you were doing, that sounds like a good way to go. I'm glad she said yes."

Suddenly, a thought rushed forth. "Hey, I am going to be here at Christmas, aren't I?"

Gunnar frowned. "Jeremy, we filled out the papers together. I mean, you sat there with me when I did."

"I know, but . . ." His voice dropped off. How could he say what he was thinking without sounding dumber than he already felt?

Gunnar turned to face him more fully. "Look, we still have our rules to talk about, but this is more important. Are you really thinking that I would change my mind after working on that paperwork together . . . and that I'd do it right before Christmas?"

He shrugged. What could he say? He'd learned from a couple of those foster kids that foster parents could do a lot of stuff that didn't make sense.

"Jeremy, I know this is hard, but if we're going to have a partnership, then we need to be able to tell each other things. So come on now. Talk to me. Do you want to wait longer to finish the paperwork? Have you changed your mind about living here with me?" He paused. "Or, maybe you aren't ready to have me as your 'real' dad?"

"No! I mean, that's not it at all."

"Okay, then what are you thinking?"

"I thought maybe if you were mad at me you might have changed your mind."

His eyebrows rose again. "You mean because of me being upset about you coming home late tonight?"

'Well, yeah."

"I'm not going to change my mind."

"Okay."

Gunnar shook his head. "Boy, this is normal stuff that all adults and kids go through. Kids sometimes bend or break rules and parents have to figure out how to make sure the kids know that they're loved but that they still have to mind." He shook his head. "Shoot. That sounded like a jumbled mess, didn't it? My mom and dad made it all sound so good. I guess all I'm trying to say is that if we've got problems and we're talking about it, then I think it's kind of a good sign. It means we're moving forward."

Jeremy smiled. "It's like we've moved into a new phase of our relationship or something."

Gunnar chuckled. "I'd say that too."

"Hey, that's great." He grinned.

"I think so too, kid. I mean . . . it would be . . . if you would've called or texted to tell me that you were going to be late."

"Yes, sir. I really am sorry."

"Good." He paused. "I'm new to parenting and all, but I believe this is where you tell me that you won't do that anymore."

"I won't." He was so relieved, he smiled. "I promise."

"Good." He slapped his hands on his thighs as he stood up. "Now that's settled, I'm going to go see about our supper. My sister Darcy sent me a foolproof recipe for chicken and rice soup.

I'm going to give it a try and surprise my mom. She's been out running errands for hours."

Jeremy stood up too. But the shock of what had just happened held him still. "Wait. That's it?" Gunnar was just going to go make soup?

Gunnar turned back around. "I think so. Why? Do you want it to be something more?"

"No, I just thought you were going to ground me or something."

"For forgetting to call because you were fixated on asking a girl to a Christmas dance? I think that would be pretty harsh. Don't you?"

"Yeah. I guess. I mean, I think it would be really harsh." Especially since he didn't want to be grounded.

Gunnar chuckled. "I tell you what, boy. I don't know what I would've done if you hadn't come into my life. You make things good."

The warm feeling of acceptance settled inside Jeremy, catching him off guard. "I'm glad," he said just as he realized that Gunnar probably hadn't expected an answer.

His feeling was confirmed when Gunnar chuckled again.

The sound was good.

It was almost as good as the sound of the text he received four hours later from Bethany, telling him that he could walk her home again on Friday.

CHAPTER 17

"Christ was born on Christmas Day,
Wreathe the holly, twine the bay."
—THOMAS HELMORE

Gunnar had really hoped that his siblings would never find out about these dance lessons. Unfortunately, he was fairly sure that their mother had already told the world about them across various forms of social media.

If he wasn't feeling so trapped by her will, he'd have been real impressed. His mother was a perfect combination of old-school comfort and cutting-edge technology. She could post pictures on Instagram and tweet about them to her thousands of followers quicker than he could pull out his phone from a back pocket.

As he pulled up to the front of Dance With Me, his mother gasped.

"My goodness, isn't this pretty!"

He completely agreed. As good as the place had looked the

night he'd picked up Kimber for their drink, it looked even more spectacular now. The entire front of the building was festooned with white lights and two beautifully decorated Christmas trees shone brightly through the front windows.

In addition, there were two large wooden soldiers near the front holding a sign emblazoned with The Nutcracker, December 23!

"They're going to be performing *The Nutcracker* in a couple of weeks?"

"Looks like it, Mama," he said as she pulled out her phone and snapped a picture of the sign.

"I just love that ballet." She frowned slightly. "It's such a shame that I won't be here to see it."

"It is a real shame," he said, though he was secretly cheering. If she had been staying that long, he knew he'd be taking her to the ballet, and he drew the line at sitting through three-hour ballets starring dozens of children.

"You'll have to tell me all about it."

He winced, hoping it looked legitimate. "I'm not sure if I'm going to be able to go."

"Really? But I thought that girl that Jeremy liked so much was in it."

"You mean Bethany, the girl he's taking to the dance?"

"Well, yes. He doesn't have any other girls around, does he?"

"No, ma'am. At least, I don't believe he does." When she raised one eyebrow, he inwardly groaned. Honestly, his mother was like some kind of super sleuth. She'd been in their house all of three days and she already knew more about Jeremy's crush than he did. "How do you know about Bethany being in this ballet?"

She released a long-suffering sigh. The same type of one she'd released since he'd been born. "I talk to the boy, Son. It sounds like you need to do some talking with him as well."

"I do talk to Jeremy."

"Good. Then sooner or later he's going to tell you all about her performing in this ballet, and I'm sure you'll offer to go see her shine."

Boy, she was laying it on thick. "It's time we went inside."

"Of course." She put her hand on the door handle. "Now, are you ready to cha-cha?"

"Absolutely. Stay there and I'll come around for you. I don't want you to slip on the ice." Luckily, she didn't argue once and stayed put until he was at her door.

When she reached up to take his hand, she beamed. "Gunnar, dear, I do appreciate you doing this with me. I promise, I do."

"I'm glad to be able to help, Mama." He escorted her up the steps and opened the door for her.

And then was surrounded by Christmas music, the scent of cinnamon, teenage girls in black leotards, pink tights, and some kind of flowy skirts . . . and Kimber.

She had a clipboard and looked to be getting information from the girls. It also looked like she had some kind of ribbon around her neck.

"What are you doing here?"

She raised one perfect eyebrow. "I told you I lived here. Did you forget?"

"Not at all. I didn't think you danced though."

"I don't. I'm helping Shannon corral her *Nutcracker* dancers." She smiled at the girls who were now staring at him. "Ladies, please meet Gunnar. Gunnar, please meet Macey, Autumn, Bethany, and Grace, four of our Sugar Plum fairies."

All four girls raised their hands and waved. One of them smiled shyly.

"Hi. It's nice to meet y'all." Realizing that he'd forgotten that his mother was standing there, he added, "This is my mother, Willa Law. Willa, please meet Kimber and the um, Sugar Plum girls."

All the girls giggled.

Kimber rolled her eyes. "They're Sugar Plum *fairies*, Gunnar Law. There's a difference."

"Don't mind Gunnar, honey. He's not the best at remembering girly things. He never was." She held out a hand. "I've heard so much about you, Kimber. I'm delighted to know you."

After darting an amused glance his way, Kimber shook his mother's hand. "I'm delighted as well, Mrs. Law."

"Please call me Willa."

"Willa." After she smiled at him mom again, Kimber looked his way. "Any special reason you two have stopped by?"

"Yes. We've got a ballroom dance class with Shannon."

Kimber eyes widened before she pulled in her surprise. "She didn't tell me about that. Huh."

"It's supposed to start right now. Where are those classes held?"

One of the girls pointed to the open door. "In there. That's the studio."

"Great. Thanks."

Then, before he could shuttle his mother to the studio, she turned to one of the girls. The one with the shy smile. "Are you by chance Bethany who knows Jeremy?"

While the rest of the girls giggled, she blushed bright red. "Um, yes?"

"It's nice to meet you. Jeremy told me you're a dancer. Good luck with your performance, dear."

"Thank you?"

Gunnar thought about introducing himself to Bethany as well, but he decided to wait. The girl seemed shy, and his mother was enough for anyone to take at one time. "Mama, let's get started."

"Oh! Yes!"

Kimber was still standing there, looking amused. "Are you two learning any dance in particular?"

"He's helping me with the cha-cha," his mother supplied.

When Kimber's eyes lit up, Gunnar knew that he didn't just have to worry about his siblings. No, he was going to get teased about this by Kimber Klein.

And he hadn't even attempted a single step.

* * *

Kimber wasn't really proud of her motives, but there was no way she was going to *not* watch Gunnar dance the cha-cha with his mom. Deciding that she'd promised to help Shannon write a letter to parents about their schedule, she entered the room, ignored Gunnar's stunned expression, and sat down in the back of the room.

Shannon, in full teaching mode, looked as beautiful as ever. She was wearing another one of her flattering wrap-style dresses, this one in steel gray. Her hair was in a ponytail and she had on her three-inch black heels that she claimed were more comfortable than a new pair of Nikes.

Mrs. Law was wearing a pretty navy pantsuit that looked both matronly and adorable at the same time.

And Gunnar? He was in a pair of jeans, boots, a T-shirt, and a black sweater. He already looked like he was dying of heat.

He also wasn't moving all that well. He looked kind of like the tin man out of the *Wizard of Oz*—like moving too fast could cause him some serious pain.

Shannon, who had the patience of a saint, was coaxing him to relax.

"If you just try to feel the music, it gets easier. I promise. Forward, side, cha-cha-cha."

"I'm trying," he said.

"Gunnar, you haven't looked into my eyes yet. Lift your head."

"I can't. I'm afraid of stepping on your feet."

"I'll worry about my feet. Look into my eyes."

"Mama, I'm real sorry, but your eyes are right around the middle of my chest. I can't count, watch my feet, and listen to Shannon all while bending down to see you. Trust me on this."

"I'm looking up."

Shannon sighed. "Let's try this again. This time with music." She walked to her iPad, threw Kimber a pained expression, and then tapped a few more things.

Seconds later, Marc Anthony's "I Need to Know" came on.

"Oh! I love this song," Mrs. Law gushed.

Gunnar looked like he was biting the inside of his lip bloody.

"Come on now, feel the music," Shannon coaxed. "And here we go. One, two, cha-cha-cha. One, two cha-cha-cha."

Kimber stopped even pretending that she was filing papers and watched. And when Marc Anthony called out "Tell me, baby girl, 'cause I need to know," and Gunnar looked like he was about to throw up, she started laughing.

Which, unfortunately, caused the three other people in the room to skid to a stop.

"What, exactly, is so funny, Kimber?" Shannon asked, her tone testy.

"Nothing. I mean, nothing other than the fact that Gunnar looks kind of green, dancing to that song with his mom."

"And what is wrong with it?"

Oh, boy. Shannon was in full schoolteacher mode. "Nothing. It's just that it's , um . . . romantic and sexy."

"It's just a song, Kimber."

"You're right. I'm so sorry." Just as she was about to go back to filing, Gunnar spoke up.

"Have you danced the cha-cha before, Kimber?"

"No. I tried tap, though."

Shannon, obviously still in a snit, popped a hand on her hip. "Kimber isn't much of a tap dancer."

Kimber would've been offended if Shannon hadn't spoken the truth.

"Why don't you give the cha-cha a try?" Willa asked.

This was getting uncomfortable, and it was no less than she deserved. "I really am sorry. I think I'll just go ahead and get on out of here."

"No, dear. I'd love to see you dance with Gunnar." Willa fanned her face. "I kind of need a break anyway."

"What do you say?" Gunnar asked. "Are you ready to show me how it's done?"

She had no choice. Gunnar was giving her no choice, and even if she decided not take him up on that offer, if she refused, Shannon would never let it go. "Fine. But, I don't have any shoes."

"Yes, you do. You left those under my desk the other day."

Her beautiful Jimmy Choos. "Fine." Stepping over in her skinny jeans, she toed off her flats and slipped on her Choos.

Gunnar looked at them like they were a pair of stilts. "Can you even walk in those things?"

"Honey, one day I'm going to make you watch an old tape of me on a runway show. You wouldn't believe the things that I've had to do in high heels."

"I can't wait to see it," he murmured as she stood in front of him.

"You two stop talking and listen," Shannon admonished. "Now, let's review." Quickly she reminded Gunnar of where to put his hands and went over the steps once again.

Kimber stopped joking and concentrated. Gunnar looked marginally more relaxed.

"It's easier because you're a lot taller than my mom, but I wish I hadn't worn these boots. I really don't want to hurt you."

"With me you don't have to worry. I've got tough feet. Honestly, you should be more worried about me landing on your foot with one of my spiky heels."

"I wasn't going to say anything, but those do look pretty lethal."

After going over the steps two more times, Shannon smiled. "Let's try it to music. And in honor of Kimber, I'll put on something else." With a few more clicks, Credence Clearwater Revival's "I Heard it Through the Grapevine" filled the room.

"Here we go," Shannon said. "One, two, cha—"

Kimber was pretty sure Shannon was still counting and ordering them around, but all she was aware of was the way Gunnar was holding her and the beat of the song.

"You two . . . you two look really good!" Shannon called out. And yes, she sounded surprised.

"You feel good," Gunnar murmured. "I love that you're so tall."

It was true. She was five feet, ten inches barefoot. Now, in her heels, she was at least an inch over six feet. Almost Gunnar's height.

"You feel good too," she teased.

"Turn now!" Shannon called out.

He twirled her, then she stepped back into his arms. And they picked up where they'd left off. For the first time in her life, she was forgetting about all the stuff that took up her time and energy and everything that hurt her.

She was forgetting about her stalker, about Brett, her career, her weight, her sisters, her future . . .

All she was aware of was moving with Gunnar. Of the way his eyes were gleaming with approval. Of the scent of his sandalwood cologne, of the way she felt pretty. Pretty in a girl-meets-a-cute-boy-who-likes-her way.

Pretty like she didn't think she'd ever felt in her life.

And then it stopped.

Gunnar dropped his hands. She gaped at him. Both were breathing hard.

And both Shannon and Mrs. Law were looking at the two of them with something that could only be described as triumph in their eyes.

CHAPTER 18

"Sitting under the mistletoe
(Pale-green, fairy mistletoe),
One last candle burning low,
All the sleeping dancers gone,
Just one candle burning on,
Shadows lurking everywhere:
Someone came, and kissed me there."
—WALTER DE LA MARE, "MISTLETOE"

"I think y'all have got those steps down now," Shannon announced, effectively breaking the tension between him and Kimber. "So you can stop . . . if, you know, you two would like to take a break."

Still holding Kimber close, he stared down into her eyes. She blinked, looking just as confused as he felt by the directions.

But then his mother giggled and reality hit him in the face.

Embarrassed, he dropped his hands and took a full step back. What had he just done? He was here to learn the cha-cha with his mother, not get lost in some make-believe world with Kimber!

Making himself ignore the fact that Kimber was still frozen in front of him, he cleared his throat. "Mom, are you ready to practice?"

"Well, actually . . . I've decided to come back tomorrow night to Shannon's senior class."

He turned to face her. "What? Why?"

"Well, I was talking with Gwen here while Shannon was working with you and Kimber and she was telling me how much fun the senior class was." Her voice was as chipper as usual, but there also seemed to be something else underlying there. Like she had a really good secret that she wasn't interested in sharing with him. "Plus, those folks know a lot of the dances, so I can work on improving, not just learning basic steps like you are."

"Oh. I guess that does make sense."

"I think it does. The senior class is going to be a better fit for me, I think . . . for several reasons." She smiled over at Shannon. "I'm delighted to have gotten to watch you teach though. You did a good job."

Gunnar looked back at Kimber. She'd moved a little bit away, but she didn't look like her usual assertive self. Actually, she seemed to be feeling just as confused as he was. "I guess you learned to cha-cha for no reason," he said to her. "I'm sorry to waste your time."

"You didn't waste it." Gesturing toward her sister, she said, "Shannon's been after me to learn something new." She smiled tightly. "Tonight I did."

"Ballroom dancing just might be your thing," Shannon said, her voice all business. "You did a lot better cha-chaing than you did at ballet or tap."

"Ballet was extremely painful, though I did better than Traci."

"Only marginally so," Shannon said.

His mother chuckled. "I find that hard to believe, dear. You look like you can do a lot of things well."

"Not as many as one would hope." Looking adorably flustered, she walked over to his mom. "I'm glad we got to meet. How long are you in town for?"

"Only about a week or so. Although these classes were a good excuse, I really wanted to meet Jeremy before I go on my Christmas cruise."

"He's a good kid."

Right before his eyes, his mom turned into a grandmother. "He's a wonderful boy."

"Thanks, Mom," he said.

Shannon gave his mother a card. "Here's all the details about tomorrow night's class. I'm delighted you'll be there."

"Thank you. I never imagined liking something new so much, but I do. I'm starting to realize that there are a whole group of people out there my age who like to dance. I'm really excited about my new hobby . . . and the cruise, of course."

His mother looked so excited, Gunnar explained about how her cruise was a dancing themed one.

"I would love to go on one of those," Shannon said.

"You should work on one of the dancing cruises, dear. They would pay your fare. I bet your husband's too. I bet it would be great fun."

"Dylan probably won't want to dance, but he would love to go on a vacation. I'll have to ask Dylan what he thinks about that. It would be perfect, especially if it was free."

Worried about staying too long, Gunnar said, "Well, we should probably get going. It's been a long day."

"Do you need to go this minute?" Shannon asked. "We were just about to go upstairs and have some red velvet cake. Would you like some?"

"Did you make red velvet?" his mother asked.

"Oh, gosh no," Shannon said. "I don't cook."

"Kimber?"

"I'm afraid I'm not the chef either. It's Shannon's sister-in-law, Jennifer. She lives with me and Gwen and makes an amazing array of things."

"I haven't eaten so well since I lived at home," Shannon said.

"What do you say, Mom? Want some cake?"

Her eyes lit up with interest. "I hate to impose."

"You won't be imposing one bit," Kimber said. "Jennifer has been trying out cakes all week. She's thinking of offering them to some of her customers that she cooks for."

"We have cake coming out of our ears," Gwen said. "I promise, you'd be doing us a favor, Mrs. Law."

"Would we be able to maybe take a piece home to Jeremy?"

"Of course," Kimber said. "Come on up and join us."

His mother beamed and followed Shannon up, talking a mile a minute to both her and Gwen.

Gunnar waited for Kimber to remove her shoes and then walked by her side. "How are you?"

"I'm pretty good. You?"

"Better now." When she arched an eyebrow, he explained. "I've been kind of dreading this lesson for days. I can't believe I got so lucky with you being here."

Her cheeks pinkened a bit but she shook her head. "I didn't really do much."

"You did." He couldn't put into words how she'd helped him out. It was probably too personal for where they were, but he knew that holding her so close had felt amazing.

"Your mom is nice." She smiled. "Chatty too."

"You got that right. My brothers and I used to say that it's surprising that we ever learned to speak."

She laughed. "I've got a mom like that too."

"I guess we've got that in common."

"I guess we do."

When they entered the kitchen, he found Shannon, Gwen, and his mother already sitting at the table nearby. The other blond in the room was slicing a thick wedge of red velvet cake.

She smiled at them. "Hi Gunnar. It's good to see you again."

"Likewise. Thanks for the cake."

"I've already put your son's slice in a plastic container."

"Thanks. Jeremy's going to love it." Picking up his piece, he glanced at Kimber. "Are you having any?"

"Nope. I'll have some tea and sit with everyone, though."

"Do you not care for red velvet cake, dear?" his mom asked.

"I do like it, but I'm afraid cake isn't in the cards for me right now."

"She has a modeling job next week," Shannon explained.

"As soon as I get back, Jennifer better look out, though. I'll probably be tasting everything she makes."

"How did you get started modeling?"

"It's kind of a funny story. I was out shopping with my mom at one of the big department stores in Manhattan, and a person who worked there asked if I'd like to help out with their runway show that afternoon. I didn't want to, but my mom thought it sounded like fun for me—especially when they offered to give me one of the items from the show for fifty percent off."

Gunnar leaned closer. He was as interested as his mother.

"I got there early and was nervous about what to do, but one of the real models just said to have a good time since I wasn't a professional or anything," Kimber continued. "So that's what I did. I think I did everything I wasn't supposed to. But it must have been enough, because next thing I knew I was signed up with a modeling agency and had two shows booked."

"And the rest is history?" his mother asked.

"Yes. Well, pretty much. I guess I was in the right place at the right time."

Shannon looked at her fondly. "Kimber's far too modest. I have a feeling she built a career out of tenaciousness and hard work. She's pretty special."

"Not that she's biased or anything," Kimber joked.

His mother looked positively smitten. "Well, I'm going to have to go see if I can google some of your magazine covers. I can't wait to tell everyone back home that our Gunnar is dating a real, live cover model."

Gunnar groaned. "Ma, stop."

Kimber laughed. "You're making me feel good, but I'm not just being modest. Whatever success I've had is really due to a whole lot of luck. I was blessed with good genes, I happen to photograph well, and was at the right place at the right time."

From the other side of the table, Shannon raised her eyebrows at Gunnar.

He winked. Kimber could deny it until the cows came home, but he was pretty sure there was a whole lot more to her successful career than luck.

Looking even more flustered, Kimber asked, "Can we please talk about something else now? How's that cake?"

"Amazing," Shannon said. "I swear, sometimes I think Jennifer could make a gourmet meal out of any five things in this house. I see nothing. She sees possibilities."

"I'm just glad that I have all of you to experiment on," she quipped.

"You know, I do think Shannon did make a good point," his mother said. "That's how life is. It's all about who sees nothing and who sees possibilities." Smiling at Kimber, she said, "I've always been fond of the possibility side of life, myself."

Reaching for his mom's hand, Gunnar gently squeezed. "Me too, Mama."

CHAPTER 19

*"Yes, Virginia, there is a Santa Claus. He exists as
certainly as love and generosity and devotion exist."*

—FROM AN EDITORIAL IN *THE NEW YORK SUN*, 1897

She was three days away from her trip to New York. Almost unconsciously, Kimber had fallen back into her former routine, preparing for the upcoming days like an athlete might prepare for a sporting event.

She'd begun sleeping as much as she could, following a strict diet, and drinking lots of her favorite Vitamin Water. After a day of protest, her body had accepted the changes and seemed to be taking it all in stride.

Ironically, it was the rest of her life that she was having a difficult time getting back on track. The fact was, ever since she'd accepted the job, her quiet Bridgeport life had turned on its side. Her model friends had come back out of the woodwork and were reaching out to make plans. Brett was texting constant updates, and both the designer and the merchandiser had called for more information. Even one of the seamstresses had emailed to make sure her measurements hadn't changed in the last three months. She'd experienced a moment of panic when she'd asked Gwen to help with the measuring tape.

All of the attention and stress wasn't a surprise, and part of it actually made her feel good. It was nice to know that she was still wanted and that she had been missed.

For a few hours, Kimber had actually contemplated what her life would be like if she started saying yes to Brett again.

But on the heels of all that satisfaction came a curiously empty feeling. The money and the stress and her former life wasn't what she wanted anymore.

It was just too bad that she was feeling like a woman in limbo. She wasn't excited about her chosen profession, and she was at a loss about what to do with her future.

Feeling like she was going to crawl out of her skin or she start screaming, Kimber went downstairs to Shannon's dance studio.

Twelve little girls, all dressed up in black leotards, pink tights, and pink ballet slippers were lined up against the wall. Shannon was standing in front of them holding up a small white tulle tutu and talking very seriously.

Boy, they were adorable. After smiling at them for a moment, Kimber scanned the rest of the room. And had to stifle a gasp.

The whole area by Shannon's storage closet was covered in small wooden nutcrackers. There had to be at least two dozen of them spilling out of the closet and onto the floor. She shook her head. Shannon was one beautiful dancer and one heck of a mess.

Unable to help herself, she walked over and picked one up. It was a beautiful thing, all gold and white and adorned with fake jewels and goose down. One of his shiny black boots had been scratched, though. Placing him carefully against the wall, Kimber sighed. These tiny works of art should have been wrapped in tissue paper and carefully stored in boxes. Not tossed into a sack like yesterday's trash.

At least her mood had brightened. Now she had a plan for the day—to save those poor little guys and find a far better way to store them.

"Who are you?" a little voice asked.

She turned and felt herself blush as all the girls as well as Shannon were staring at her. She straightened. "I'm Kimber. Who are you?"

"Erin."

Erin was wearing a shiny pink little skirt around her black leotard. She was also staring at Kimber expectantly.

Feeling a little whimsical, Kimber half-curtsied. "Miss Erin, it's nice to meet you."

Erin smiled big enough to show that she was missing a front tooth.

"I'm Alison," a little dark-haired girl next to Erin declared.

Kimber curtseyed again. "Pleased to meet you, Miss Alison."

She smiled at the rest, the majority of whom were wiggling like it was killing them that they hadn't spoken to her. "You all look very pretty."

As she'd hoped, all the girls smiled back at her. One kind of fluffed her tutu, which made Kimber stifle a laugh.

Then she heard a loud clearing of a throat. The girls froze.

And Kimber lifted her eyes to see Shannon staring back of her like Kimber had just been caught with her hand in a cookie jar. "Sorry for interrupting, Shannon."

"I should hope so," Shannon huffed. The little girls giggled.

"I was just walking by and saw this . . ."

Shannon raised her eyebrows. "Mess?"

"Yes. This mess." She picked up one forlorn-looking red-and-black nutcracker. "These poor little guys need to be cared for better, girl."

"I know." Looking uncomfortable, she added, "We had a hard time trying to find the right costume."

"I'm a snowflake!" Alison piped up.

"Are you? Like in *Frozen*?" She was pretty sure there were talking snowflakes in that movie. But maybe they were fairies?

All the girls erupted in laughter. Shannon too. "I guess you ladies are not dancing in *Frozen*?"

"They're snowflakes," Shannon said importantly. When Kimber continued to gape at her, she added, "They live in the Land of Snow in *The Nutcracker*."

"Ah." Kimber held up one of the wooden guys littering the floor. "It's all making sense now."

"Want to see us?" little Erin piped up. "Can we show her our dance, Miss Shannon?"

"I don't see why not." Walking to her iPad, Shannon said, "All right, snowflakes. Let's see if you can get into position."

The little girls went tearing around, giggling and whispering to each other. Five seconds, then ten passed.

"Now, who's ready?"

They each raised a hand. Well, except for Erin, who was smiling at Kimber.

"Erin, I need you to be a snowflake right now, if you please."

The little girl immediately straightened and carefully curved her arms just like the others.

Still holding one of the wayward nutcrackers, Kimber leaned against the back wall as the music started and the little girls all tried to perfectly mimic Shannon who was dancing the steps directly in front of them.

Their dance was imperfect. Okay, it wasn't very good. Most of them were late on Shannon's counts. One simply twirled a lot, another kept looking like she would rather be running through a field instead of concentrating, and little Alison got her feet tangled when Shannon called out pas de deux and almost fell.

But not a bit of that mattered. What did was the look of delight

145

on their faces, their extreme adorableness, and the almost angelic expression that had appeared on Shannon's face as the little girls' parts were done. As if to celebrate, Kimber's beautiful sister began to pirouette like she was a ballerina in the middle of a music box.

She looked so beautiful.

Shannon loved dancing. She loved teaching dance. And because of that, it all showed brightly through each cell in her body. Kimber could watch her every day, just seeing that look of bliss on her sister's face made everything a little bit brighter.

And right on the heels of that realization was that knowledge that Kimber wanted some of that too. She wanted it bad.

When the music ended and all the girls curtseyed, following Shannon's graceful example, Kimber clapped. "Bravo!"

They grinned at her then sobered as they looked at their teacher. Shannon wasn't smiling.

"Snowflakes, we have some work to do before our performance. A lot of work," she said in a sober tone. "If you cannot start dancing in a straight line and moving in sync, I'm afraid we're going to have to have extra practices."

One of the little girls frowned. "But, Miss Shannon—"

She shook her head. "No, I'm afraid there is no good excuse here. We must dance our best, even in front of ladies like Kimber." She rang a little bell. "Go take a water break and come back in five minutes. We'll go over the middle section one more time, and then try it to music again. Off you go."

They scattered like wildflowers in a summer wind.

Walking to her side, Kimber frowned at her. "Boy, that was kind of harsh, teach."

"I have to be. Once I smile at their cute antics, they'll try do the same things again and again. Trust me on this."

"I do. But they were sure cute, though."

Shannon smiled. "Oh. My. Word. They were so cute. I dream

about these little girls, they make me so happy. But they are currently some sorry-looking snowflakes."

"I guess I can't argue with that."

"So, you haven't told me why you're here. Did you need something?"

"No. I was . . ." How could she admit that she was feeling kind of *blah* about her work situation? "I guess I had a little bit of time on my hands so I decided to come down to see if you needed help cleaning."

"As much as I need your help with those nutcrackers, I need help teaching even more. Want to help?"

"No. You know I don't know a thing about dancing."

"You can listen though, and help me keep an eye on twelve busy six-year-olds."

"I don't know—"

"Here they come." She lowered her voice. "It's easy. I promise, even you can catch on. Just watch me and try to help the girls do the same thing. Thanks!"

And with that, Shannon clapped her hands and told the girls to get back in line. "Miss Kimber has agreed to help me teach this class today, ladies. She's going to help me correct your mistakes."

Little Erin smiled at her again.

Kimber smiled back, fearing that hers looked far less sure.

But there was no time to lose as Shannon called out, "Watch me ladies. I'm going to do this once by myself, then we're all going to do it together. Plié, revelé, chassé to the right." She paused. "Ready?"

"Yes, Miss Shannon!" they chorused.

"Let's go then. Kimber, you watch the six closest to you."

"Yes, Miss Shannon," she answered.

And then she had no time to even smile at the girls. All she could do was keep up and arrange little girls' arms and positions.

Fifteen minutes later, she stood back against the wall and

watched them dance. And . . . they were better! When they curt-sied, she clapped and clapped.

And when Shannon smiled brightly and called out, "Well done, snowflakes!" Kimber felt like she'd done something good too.

"Thank you Miss Kimber," Erin said as she gave her a hug at the end of class. "I hope you help us all the time."

"I'm sure I'll come back. I had a good time, sweetie."

She waved to her again when she was at her mother's side. Then waved to a few other girls who told her goodbye. And then, at last, they were gone and it was just her, Shannon, and a bunch of fallen nutcrackers.

The room felt strangely silent.

"Did you have a good time?"

To her surprise, she had. "I did. It certainly cured whatever was ailing me."

"I find the same thing happens to me with them. Every class has its own personality. But I can't deny it. These little girls have my heart."

Ten minutes later, another group of ballet students entered the studio. Shannon greeted the older girls and instructed them to warm up.

Kimber was just about to ask if Shannon wanted her to help out some more when her cell phone rang. Surprised—she'd forgotten it was even in her back pocket—she swiped the screen to connect. "Hello?"

"Kimber, why haven't you answered my letters?"

It was Peter Mohler. Her skin crawled. "How did you get this number?"

"How did you think? I'm still watching you."

"You need to stop." Hurrying to the corner of the room, she whispered, "I have a restraining order against you."

"Did you think that would keep me away? You're mine."

Rattled and seriously creeped out, she disconnected, then turned off her phone for good measure. She knew she should be contacting the police, but they would probably just either think she was exaggerating or ask her why, if she was so scared, hadn't she gone to see them when she first moved to Bridgeport.

And what would she say then? That she'd wanted to pretend he was going to simply fade out of her life?

"Kimber?"

She looked up at Shannon. "Yes?"

Shannon's expression went from curious to worried. "You look like you're about to faint. Are you okay?"

"Sure. I'm fine." She smiled weakly.

Not seeming to care that the little girls were inching out of their formations and a few brave ones had even started to giggle, Shannon stepped closer. "Who was on the phone?"

"Nobody. It was just the wrong number."

"The wrong number got you that shaken up?"

"Don't worry about it. I'm fine."

Just as Shannon was about to speak again, two girls peeked in the room.

"Can we come in, Miss Shannon?"

"Of course, Diana. Warm up and I'll be with you in a few minutes." After a pause, Shannon reached for Kimber's hand. "These girls are the angels. They're all about seven and eight. Would you mind staying for this class too?"

Did she want to help little girls or go sit alone and worry about her stalker? There was no choice. "Of course. I'm happy to help."

Ten minutes later, when Shannon put the music on and started counting, Kimber walked over to one of the girls who'd been making the most mistakes and seemed to be near tears. "I promise that you'll get it, honey. Just take your time and stop worrying so much."

"I'm having a hard time."

"I know you are, but things will get better. I promise."

The little girl stared at her before awkwardly lifting her right arm when Shannon called out the directions.

"That's right," Kimber whispered. "You're doing real well."

"Thanks." She smiled.

And so it continued. She smiled and encouraged and redirected. Peter Mohler's voice echoing in her head all the while.

CHAPTER 20

"A good conscience is a continual Christmas."
—BENJAMIN FRANKLIN

"I'm sorry, but I just can't," Kimber said. "I leave for New York tomorrow."

Gunnar was disappointed but he knew he was a fool to think that she would have arranged her day with his schedule so they could see each other. "I understand. So, ah, when will you get back?"

"I'm not sure yet. Either Friday or Sunday"—she paused—"or maybe Monday."

"The job is that up in the air?" He would have thought they would be on a pretty tight schedule.

"Oh, no. Those days are set in stone. I'm trying to coordinate plans with my parents. I'm still waiting to see if they have time to see me."

"They don't know if they can fit you in?" He knew he sounded incredulous, but he couldn't help it. He would've thought her parents would've moved heaven and earth to see her.

"It sounds worse than it is. My father's dad is sick and my mom's job is crazy right now. Plus, they don't really like going into the city."

"I would have thought seeing you would be their priority."

"Like I said, I'm making it sound like they're uncaring, but they're not." She sighed. "Honestly, everything with them and me is kind of complicated."

"Sorry, it's none of my business."

"I kind of think it is," she said, surprising him. "I don't want you thinking that I'm being evasive on purpose."

"I didn't think that." Realizing that she had enough stress in her life, he changed the topic. "So are you ready for your big trip?"

"I hope so. I haven't gotten up the nerve to get on the scale, but I think I'm good. My measurements were fine last week." She laughed softly. "And, Lord knows I've done enough crunches over the last three weeks."

Glad she couldn't see his look of incredulousness, he shook his head. She had already been really thin and toned, at least it had seemed that way to him. "I know you're going to be busy and all, but text when you can, okay? I'll be worried about you."

"I will, but I promise that New York City isn't as scary as you think."

"Believe it or not, I've been to New York. I'm not worried about you in the city. I'll be worried about you."

Her voice softened. "Thanks. Gunnar, I'll be thinking about you too."

"You better."

She laughed. "I'll see you soon."

"You will." Deciding it was time to press a bit, he asked, "Hey, is anyone already planning to pick you up at the airport?"

"No . . ."

"Count on me doing that then."

"Don't forget, I'm not exactly sure . . ."

"Let me know and I'll be there. I want to be there, Kimber."

"Wow. Um, okay."

She sounded cute and flustered, and he figured that was enough for now. He liked that he was able to break through her exterior from time to time. It gave him hope that one day she'd let him in all the time.

Five minutes later they hung up. He set down his phone, thinking that even though they weren't going to see each other for a while, something new had happened between them. Maybe they were making progress after all?

He was still stewing on their conversation a while later when he went into the kitchen to make him and Jeremy some supper.

He found Jeremy at the stove heating up some ramen noodles. As usual, the boy wore cut-off sweatpants, an old T-shirt, and had bare feet. When he'd first moved in, Gunnar had worried that he would get cold, but Jeremy had looked as surprised as he'd used to act when his mother had asked him such things.

What was new was that there were two schoolbooks spread out on the kitchen counter. It looked like he was reading while he was stirring a pot on the stove.

"Hey, ah, what are you doing?"

Jeremy frowned. "I'm studying while I'm cooking noodles. Why?"

"No reason." This was another one of those weird no-man's-land moments. Was he supposed to say something about how it would be better to study when he was sitting down or leave it alone because the boy was actually doing his homework?

"Uh, do you want some?" Jeremy asked when Gunnar continued to stare into space. "I could put in another package in the water, if you'd like."

"You know what? Thanks."

Jeremy grinned as he opened another orange package and crumbled the noodles into the water. "I make a mean batch of noodles. Just you wait."

"I didn't know it was your specialty."

"It pretty much is. I started making it back when I was eleven or twelve." He lowered his voice. "The trick is to boil them an extra five minutes and then pour a little soy sauce on top."

"That sounds great. I can't wait to try them."

When Jeremy grinned again as he leaned back over his book, Gunnar took a step back.

Yeah, he probably should be looking into the refrigerator to make the kid something halfway decent, but he decided to hold off from bringing it up. The last thing he wanted to do was make Jeremy feel bad.

Honestly, it was good to see the boy looking so pleased with himself.

He grabbed a beer and sat down. Popping the top, he exhaled, pleased to take a five-minute break. He'd worked on a remodeling job today and while it was going well, he was sore as all get out.

"You're going to just sit here and watch?"

"Pretty much. It's been a long day and you're cooking. I decided things can't get much better than that."

Jeremy shrugged. "All righty."

Taking a first sip, he watched the boy go back to reading textbooks and stirring noodles. "I thought most of your books were on your computer now."

"They are, but I asked for copies too. I like the real books."

"Gotcha. Of course, back when I was in school, we didn't have a choice about such things, but I would've picked the books too."

"Were you good in school?"

"Yeah." He'd actually done real well in school. Well enough

to have gotten a scholarship to college to study something fancy. He hadn't had the nerve to take the opportunity, though. He was small town enough to be intimidated by the thought of going to a big university. Then, there were his three younger siblings. He would have missed them, and his parents.

So instead, he'd done what had been expected of him and continued his job at the auto shop. He'd ended up going into construction in the summers because he'd wanted to learn something new. It had all turned out fine. He had a good life, so maybe his choice had been the right path after all.

He stopped his musing long enough to realize that Jeremy was staring at him. Whether it was because he was waiting for Gunnar to talk some more or he was confused, he didn't know.

He was prevented from asking when there was a rap at the door.

"I'll get it," Jeremy said.

Gunnar leaned back and had another sip then just about choked when the boy walked back into the kitchen, Melanie right on his heels.

Dressed in gray wool pants, black suede boots, and a chunky black turtleneck, the social worker looked more dressed up and polished than usual.

She also seemed to be just as alert as ever. She didn't seem to miss a thing. Not him sitting and drinking beer at six in the evening. Not how Jeremy was wearing shorts, a T-shirt, and had bare feet while he was boiling noodles on the stove.

No, she didn't even miss the kid's books laid out on the counter. She smiled. "Hello, Gunnar."

He surged to his feet. "Hey, Melanie. I didn't know you were coming. Did I miss a call or did I just forget it or something?"

"You didn't miss a thing." Glancing at Jeremy, who had taken his place next to the stove again, she added, "This is one of my surprise home visits."

155

She was speaking like they'd just run into each other at the store or something, but there was a sharper look on her face that let him know that she wasn't missing a thing.

"Can I get you some ah . . . tea? Coffee, maybe?" He wished he could hide his beer but it was obvious that there was nothing he could do about that. "I'd be happy to make you coffee."

"You know what? Coffee sounds wonderful."

Glad that she hadn't asked if he had decaf, he hustled to get on it. "Coming right up."

While he was measuring coffee grounds, she turned to Jeremy. "So, what's for dinner?"

"Ramen noodles."

Her eyebrows rose. "Is that right?"

"It's chicken too. That's my favorite. I make great ramen." Tossing a grin his way, Jeremy added, "I'm making some for Gunnar too."

Even though his face was probably beet red, he said, "I was about to make us something but he had already started on it."

"I see."

Yes, he bet she saw that real good. This visit was getting worse and worse. After pouring water into the machine, he stood there and watched the coffee drip down into the carafe. Anything to not face her.

But she wasn't looking at him anyway. She was standing next to Jeremy. "Looks like you're working on your homework at the same time."

"Yeah, it's better than doing nothing while it cooks."

"I bet you're right. I hate watching noodles boil."

Jeremy grinned at her.

Gunnar had never felt more unworthy. "The coffee will be ready in a few. Want to have a seat, Melanie?"

"If you don't mind, I think I'll go take a look around. Jeremy, are you still in the same room?"

"Yeah."

"Great. I'll be right back."

After she disappeared down the hall, Gunnar closed his eyes and tried not to panic. He couldn't remember the last time he'd vacuumed in there. Maybe it had been a week?

Had it been longer?

"What's wrong?"

He opened his eyes. "Nothing. I'm good."

"You aren't," Jeremy said. "You're acting worried or something. What's wrong?"

"I just wish I was making a better impression." Realizing that he hadn't cleaned the boy's room in days, he said, "How bad does your room look?"

He stopped to consider. "Not bad."

"Not bad" could mean anything. "Is there laundry all over your floor?"

He shrugged. "Maybe. I don't know. It's no worse than usual."

He bit back a curse. The kid probably had half his dirty clothes strewn all over the floor and Melanie was going to think that he not only didn't cook or supervise the boy's homework, he was too lazy to run the washing machine too.

When he heard Melanie approach again, he reached for a mug and poured her a cup. "Do you take cream and sugar?"

"Nope. I like it black." Reaching for it, she took a tentative sip and smiled. "Thanks. This hits the spot."

"You're welcome." He got himself a cup too. "So I was just asking Jeremy how bad his dirty clothes situation was. Were you able to walk inside the room?"

She chuckled. "I managed. It wasn't that bad." She sat down and unzipped the tote bag he hadn't noticed she'd been carrying around. "Do you have some time to talk right now?"

"I do." When she pulled out her tablet and clicked a button at the top, followed by slipping on a pair of glasses, he gazed at her warily. "Is everything all right?"

"I think so, but we need to go over some things right now, if you don't mind."

"Do you want me to go over it too?" Jeremy asked.

"Of course," she replied. "This affects you, Jeremy."

Jeremy clicked off the stove and joined them at the table.

Watching Melanie open up her laptop, Gunnar worried that everything he'd been sure about was on the verge of blowing up in his face.

What was he going to do if he lost this boy? He could hardly think about it.

CHAPTER 21

"When they saw the star, they rejoiced
with exceedingly great joy!"
—MATTHEW 2:10

Gunnar looked like he was about to lose it.

Sitting in between him and Melanie at the kitchen table, Jeremy was starting to feel uneasy. He'd been in enough foster homes to not have been all that shocked about the social worker's surprise visit. That was what they did, and because they were so overworked, they usually didn't come around all that much.

This was all new to Gunnar though. He looked like he'd just had the worst scare in his life. And now, the way that his voice had a thicker twang than usual?

Well that was a sure sign that he was freaking out. Big time.

After visibly trying to get himself under control, Gunnar said, "Melanie, I feel like you caught me at my worst tonight, and I honestly don't know how to make things better."

She'd been sorting papers and writing notes. But after glancing his way, she put her ball point pen down. "Forgive me, but I'm not following you. You're going to have to be more specific about what you're worried about."

Oh boy. Gunnar now looked even worse, like he had a killer migraine coming on.

Hoping to help him out, Jeremy said, "I think he's worried about—"

Gunnar cut him off. "Thanks, but I can speak for myself, boy." He shifted, then blurted. "I know what it must have looked like when you got here. Me sipping a beer while Jeremy here was cooking at the stove. I promise, it's not usually like that."

"All right . . ."

"And, um, the way he was doing his homework. Usually he does it in his bedroom. There's a desk in there. Usually he can get to it too. You know, when it's not covered with old towels and laundry."

"I saw the desk, Gunnar." She smiled at Jeremy.

He smiled back, knowing what her smile meant, even if Gunnar didn't. Melanie had been with him in a lot worse situations than this. And this wasn't even bad.

He tried again to save his foster dad from himself. "Gunnar, if—"

"Jeremy, let me finish, yeah?"

"All right." He leaned back and hoped that Gunnar would get a handle on his verbal diarrhea real soon.

After kind of straightening his shoulders, he spoke again, this time his voice gravelly. "I don't know a lot about parenting, but I'm trying my best. I usually do cook something. I don't usually sit around here and drink in front of him either." He inhaled. "No, what I'm trying to say is I don't drink that much. I don't sneak alcohol either. I promise, I don't have a drinking problem."

"Um, Gunnar?" Melanie said.

But it was like the guy's mouth was on autopilot. "And we've even talked about maybe getting him some more help with his schoolwork, you know, for things like chemistry, which I don't really remember all that good. See, it's been a real—"

"Mr. Law," Melanie interrupted again, this time her voice firmer.

"Ah, yes?"

She smiled softly. "Take a deep breath. Everything's okay." She pointed to the papers and her open old-fashioned calendar. "I didn't just come over here to see how Jeremy is. I have some good news."

"Yes?"

Her smile got bigger. "Gunnar, we have a tentative court date set. We have a couple more hoops to jump through, but things are looking very positive. I know your lawyer should be telling you this news, but I asked everyone if I could do the honors since Jeremy and I have been through so much . . ."

"I'm sorry, but what?"

"Your application for adoption has been tentatively accepted." Her smile got bigger. "Though I need to schedule another formal interview with Jeremy and some people at his school, I was able to pull some strings and get you on the judge's calendar."

"What date is it?" Jeremy asked.

Melanie looked down at her calendar. "Right now, it's set for January seventeenth."

Jeremy couldn't believe the news. It was really going to happen. "Man."

Gunnar glanced his way. "January seventeenth is our date? Jeremy, does that sound good to you?"

He had a lump in his throat and he felt like crying, but he was going to hold it together. "Yeah. You?"

Gunnar exhaled and then he leaned his head back against the chair and closed his eyes.

Worried, Jeremy looked over at Melanie. Smiling, she reached out and gripped his hand.

When Gunnar looked at them both again, tears were in his eyes. "This . . . honestly, I can't think of another moment in my life that can come close to this. I'm real happy, Jeremy," he said in a hoarse drawl. "I already think of you as my son. I couldn't love you more if you'd been mine since birth. I can't wait for the rest of the world to know that too."

Gunnar loved him. Loved him like a son. Jeremy couldn't help it. He started crying.

Gunnar stood up, wrapped his arms around him, and pressed one of his heavy palms in the middle of his back.

And that pressure, that touch? Well, it was all Jeremy needed to believe that his life was finally getting better. He wasn't going to be "that foster kid" anymore. He wasn't going to be switching houses, switching schools, just getting by.

Taking a deep breath, he said, "January seventeenth sounds like a real fine day to become Jeremy Law."

Melanie, who had gotten to her feet too, folded her arms across her chest. "I'll most likely be back in touch after the New Year. That's when I'll be able to officially let you boys know that we're all set. Sound okay?"

"Yes, ma'am," Gunnar said.

"Me too," Jeremy said with a grin.

* * *

Even though an hour had passed since Melanie left, Gunnar still looked shaken. They'd cleaned up the kitchen together, Mrs. Law had called to say she was going to be late because she was going out with her new dancing friends for dessert and coffee. Jeremy had finished up the last of his homework and texted back Phillip and Bethany.

The whole time, he'd been kind of waiting for Gunnar to say something more, but he'd been quiet.

Figuring Gunnar didn't want to say anything about it after all, Jeremy started for his room.

"Jeremy, wait."

He turned. "Yeah?"

"Are you hungry?"

Jeremy shook his head.

"Oh. Okay. Well, um, come sit down in the living room."

He followed Gunnar into the room, stepping around their monster ugly tree that they'd chopped down a couple of weeks ago. Gunnar had turned on the fireplace and the room was warm and looked good.

Jeremy sat down on the couch and waited.

Gunnar ran a hand down his face in the way he always did when he was feeling a lot of emotion. Then he rested his elbows on his knees and kind of shook his head. "What a night, huh?" Making a face, he said, "Did I really start talking and never stop until Melanie made me?"

"Uh, pretty much."

His blue eyes darted back to him. "You sure you're going to be okay with a guy like me?"

"A guy who sometimes lets me cook ramen for supper, doesn't nag me all the time about the clothes on the floor, and tells the social worker and me that today is one of the best days of his life? Yeah."

A reluctant smile appeared. "All we needed was my mother to come in and start talking a mile a minute."

Jeremy grinned. "At least when she did, Melanie knew you came by all that talking naturally."

Gunnar laughed. "No kidding. So we should celebrate or something. Do you want to go out to eat tomorrow?"

Jeremy thought about it, then shook his head. "Let's wait until January seventeenth."

"I can do that. Get ready, though, 'cause I'm going to start telling everyone about the seventeenth. I reckon Martin, Darcy, and Andrew are all going to come here. All our friends here in Bridgeport too. Expect presents."

"I can do that."

"Good." After another second passed, he started laughing again. "Oh, Jeremy, I . . . I was so scared. I was freaking out."

Jeremy laughed too. "I liked the part how you told Melanie that you didn't have a drinking problem!"

"Do me a favor and don't tell my friends I said that, okay?"

"I won't tell a soul." After all, they were almost official now. Some things . . . well, they needed to remain in the family.

Their family.

CHAPTER 22

"Love the giver more than the gift."
—BRIGHAM YOUNG

Staring at the rehearsal schedule that she'd just received from Miss Shannon, Bethany felt sick to her stomach. How could something she'd wanted so badly also be the same thing that could break her heart?

The first full rehearsal of *The Nutcracker* was the same night as the Christmas dance. And, on the cast members' schedule was an additional note about that specific rehearsal. Miss Shannon stated that if a cast member couldn't make the rehearsal, they would be forfeiting their part. No exceptions.

She was either going to have to miss the dance or quit the ballet. To make matters worse, her parents had already bought both her dress for the dance *and* her Sugar Plum Fairy costume. In addition, they'd also paid for her extra lessons, a new pair of toe shoes, and shoes and a purse to go with her dress for the dance. All of it had cost a ton of money. And even though neither her mom nor her dad had said much, she knew both expenses at Christmas had been a lot for them to take.

With a feeling of dread, she took the paper she'd just printed out and searched for her mom. Bethany found her in the laundry room folding sheets.

She looked up when Bethany peeked in. "I'm so glad to see you. Grab all your laundry and take it to your room."

"I will. But I need to talk to you about something first."

"It sounds serious."

"It is."

Looking concerned now, her mother finished folding the sheet and placed it on top of the dryer. "Where do you want to talk?"

"Here's fine." Ready to get it over with, she held up the Nutcracker schedule. "Miss Shannon emailed everyone the rehearsal schedule for the ballet."

"Good. We've been waiting for it. What's the problem?"

"The first full company dress rehearsal is next Saturday night."

"On a Saturday night?"

"Something about it was the only time that week that she could have the theater for four hours."

Her mom groaned. "Four hours. You know it's going to get stretched out until five. Those things never end on time." She sighed. "Well, I guess we'll make the best of it, right?"

"Mom, next Saturday night is the dance! The Christmas dance!"

"Oh dear."

Oh dear was right. Placing the schedule on the dryer, she pointed to her teacher's note. "Look at what she wrote."

"All performers have to attend. No excuses . . ." She sighed. "Students who miss will be cut from the cast . . ." She whistled softly. "This is pretty harsh for a bunch of kids, don't you think?"

"Yes." Then, remembering just how many people tried to get out of stuff, Bethany added, "I guess she doesn't have a choice, though. I mean, otherwise, half the cast would be gone. The other day before class I overheard a mother tell Shannon that they had a special shopping trip planned so her daughter was going to miss practice."

"I feel for both the mom and Miss Shannon. Christmas is a tough time to have a dance recital. But I have to side with your teacher on this one. It's impossible to fine tune dances when people are missing."

"Yeah." Bethany hated even agreeing that much.

Looking worried, she said, "I think you know what you have to do."

"I have to call Jeremy and tell him that I can't go to the dance."

"I'm sorry, but I'm afraid so. You've made a commitment and you have a role that you've been working hard for, for years. You can't ignore that."

"I know."

"Plus, we've already bought the costume. It wasn't cheap, Bethy."

"I know. I guess we can return the dress. The tags are still on it."

Her mother nodded slowly. "That would probably be best . . . though maybe you could try to do both?"

"How could I?"

"Meet Jeremy at the dance? You'd be late, but better late than never, right?"

As good as that sounded, she couldn't imagine that being okay with him. "Mom, that means he wouldn't be able to ask anyone else and he'd have to show up there by himself. He's not going to want to do that."

"You don't know that for sure, dear. He might. You should ask him."

Ask him if he'd want to do all that for her? "I don't know.

167

You don't understand, Mom. He's really cute. Half the girls in the junior class probably have a crush on him."

"He asked you. Maybe he has a crush on you."

Her mother always made everything seem like a Disney movie—with everyone's problems vanishing by the end of the night. "I don't know about that."

"You need to be positive! Try to think that way when you talk to your teacher tonight too."

"Mom, I don't have anything to talk to Miss Shannon about."

"Believe it or not, she was once a high school girl taking dance classes herself. I know you have to be at the practice, but maybe she'll work with you so you can leave a little early."

"I don't think she'll do that."

"You won't know until you ask."

"Fine. But first I have to talk to Jeremy. I'm not going to ask to leave if he wants to take someone else."

Her mother looked pointedly at the clock. "You have an hour before we leave for your class. You better go give him a call."

Picking up the sheet of paper, she turned around.

"Bethany, get your laundry too."

She turned on her heel, grabbed her laundry basket, tossed the schedule on top, and headed back to her room. This was horrible. Why did everything good always have to happen at the same time?

By the time she put away half her laundry she felt better and knew that she couldn't put it off any longer. She picked up her phone and, with a shaking hand, called Jeremy.

He answered on the second ring. "Bethany?"

"Yes, it's me." Boy that was stupid! She cleared her throat. "Um, sorry. Is this a bad time to call?"

"No. What's up?"

"I have some bad news."

"What happened?"

She loved that there was so much concern in his voice. She was pretty sure that he really did care about her. "Um, there's no other way to say this, but I don't think I can go to the dance with you after all."

"You're backing out?"

"No! I mean, it's not like that. I'm in *The Nutcracker* and one of the big rehearsals is the same night as the dance. I can't skip it."

He didn't respond for a full two seconds. "That's why you're canceling? For a dance rehearsal?"

"I don't have much choice. If I skip one of the dress rehearsals then I'm kicked out of the ballet. She means it too."

"Oh."

But everything in his tone said that he didn't believe her and that he didn't understand. She felt like crying. "I'm so sorry. I just found out about an hour ago. I went and talked to my mom but she agreed that there wasn't any way I could get out of the rehearsal."

"Okay. Well, bye."

She opened her mouth, ready to tell them her mother's plan about how she could go late and meet him there. But . . . what was the point?

"Bye," she said softly. When she heard him disconnect, she threw her phone on the bed.

He was mad at her. She didn't even think he believed her when she'd told him her reason. He probably thought she was blowing him off or something.

Or . . . did he have somebody else in mind and so he couldn't wait to go ask her?

What was she going to do if he took someone else while she was sitting around at that dumb rehearsal all night?

With a sigh, she knew exactly what she was going to do. She'd pretend like she couldn't care less . . . and then she'd go home and cry.

Kind of like she was doing now.

CHAPTER 23

*"God gave us our memories so that we might
have roses in December."*
—J. M. BARRIE

Bethany had blown him off and made him feel like a loser. Worse, everyone was going to know that she'd said yes and then changed her mind.

They'd all think that something was wrong with him, because there sure wasn't anything wrong with her.

Looking around his room, he ignored the laundry and the towels that Gunnar was always griping about and stared at the stuff that he'd first stared at when Gunnar had shown him the room for the very first time.

The full-size bed with the frame made out of black steel that a buddy of Gunnar's had made for him. The flat-screen television on the wall, the sturdy oak desk, and the black leather chair with wheels that Jeremy secretly loved. Gunnar had even painted one of the walls a dark gray and had hung up a cool photo of the mountains in Colorado.

It was a great room. A grown-up room for a kid who had money and security.

The first time he'd gone to sleep in that bed, he hadn't wanted to close his eyes, sure when he woke up that he was going to be back in one of his other homes. Sleeping on a bed that dozens of kids had slept on before he'd gotten there.

A couple of days later, he'd told Gunnar that he thought the room was too nice for him. But Gunnar had shaken his head and said it was perfect. That the room with all the fancy stuff was a good fit for him.

Now, months later, Jeremy had started to believe it too.

But, maybe there really was something wrong with him and Bethany had seen it before Gunnar had.

After all, he was the one who'd had the messed-up life, not her. Maybe he'd said or done something that took her off guard. Going back to his desk, he sat down at the chair and tried to think of their last couple of conversations. Unfortunately, nothing came to mind.

Looking back at his stack of homework, he flipped to the easiest to accomplish—a worksheet based on the lab they'd done in biology that morning. Scanning through his notes, he was able to fill out the sheet without any trouble. Closing that notebook, he put it on his bed. At least he'd have one class where he wasn't feeling like he was completely lost.

Moving onto the next subject, he opened his planner and groaned. He had to write an essay on *Julius Caesar*. Like he cared about Shakespeare right now. Flipping through the play, he found the correct act and scene and read the question again. *How did Marc Antony feel about the plans for battle?*

He didn't know.

When Gunnar knocked on his door twenty minutes later, Jeremy was still glaring at the open book and stewing about Bethany.

"Hey, you almost done?" Gunnar asked when he poked his head in.

"Nope."

He released his hold on the door and walked in. "What are you having trouble with . . . Oh, Shakespeare?" He grimaced.

"Don't worry. I'll figure it out." But he wasn't really thinking about the play at all. No, he was trying to figure out what was wrong with him.

Gunnar sat down on the end of Jeremy's unmade bed. "What's wrong? Are you having trouble in school?"

"No more than usual. I'm not great at school, Gunnar."

"I don't need you to be great. But, I do need you to talk to me if you need help. That's something we agreed to do when you moved in, right?"

"Right. I will ask if I need help. But I don't." All he needed was for the guy to leave so he could stew in peace.

Gunnar looked like he was about to stand up, but then he paused. "Everything else good?"

"No." Now why had he even said that? "Never mind."

Gunnar stared at him for a moment then seemed to make up his mind. "Okay, I'm thinking that it's time for us to have a talk. Get up, grab your books, and come on into the kitchen. We're going to work on your homework—and whatever has been bothering you at the same time—all while eating the dinner I just brought home from the Works."

"I told you I don't need your help."

"Well, I'm telling you now that I didn't just ask you to do this." His voice hardened. "Now, listen up. I'm telling you to do this, and I don't expect you to argue. Got it?"

Jeremy blinked. Gunnar was usually so laid back, it was hard to come to terms with the fact that this was the same guy.

"Got it."

"Good." He turned and walked down the hall.

Even though Gunnar hadn't looked back at him, Jeremy did as he asked. Picking up his books, he headed down the hall after him.

He wasn't real smart, but he was learning that there were some things a guy didn't argue with. Gunnar, when he was aggravated with him? Well, that was one of them.

When he got into the kitchen, he found Gunnar at the sink and his head was lowered. He didn't move when Jeremy put his stuff on the table.

There was already a pizza box, a container of salad, and a glass of milk on the table. On another time, Jeremy would grin about it. No matter how many times he told his foster father that he wasn't a kid, Gunnar still did things like that.

Carefully, he pushed the containers to one side and set his books down. He paused, waiting for Gunnar to acknowledge him. When he didn't, Jeremy decided to continue on his homework.

He'd just flipped back to *Julius Caesar* when Gunnar turned to face him. The silence felt like a brick to his chest as he approached. Jeremy wasn't sure where to look so he stared at the pages. The words on the page blurred.

"Jeremy, are you not going to look at me?"

He popped his head up. "I'm looking." But what he saw didn't make him feel any better. Gunnar looked like he'd just been hit on the head or something. "What's wrong?"

He sucked in a breath. "What's wrong?" He laughed softly. "Boy, do you really not expect better from me?"

"I don't know what you're talking about."

"I lost my patience with you in there. I was being a jerk. Not the person you needed me to be. Not the dad I wanted to be for you."

"I keep trying to tell you that I'm not a little kid. You don't need to act like I'm going to fall apart all the time."

"One day, when you're older. When you're old, that is . . . I'm going to remind you of what you said." He half-smiled. "Maybe then you'll understand how I feel right now. Anyway, for what it's worth . . . I'm sorry."

"It's all right."

He nodded. "Okay then." He reached over to the kitchen counter, grabbed a pair of plates and some silverware that were sitting out, and placed them on the table. "Grab something to eat and we'll talk."

Jeremy took two pieces of pizza and put a handful of the salad on his plate. Then, while Gunnar was doing the same, he drank about half the glass of milk. That was his peace offering.

Gunnar didn't say anything, but his lips twitched.

Finally it was time to just put it out there. "Bethany called me this afternoon. She backed out of the dance."

"I don't understand."

"She said that she just got the rehearsal schedule for *The Nutcracker* thing and the first big all cast rehearsal was the night of the dance. Her teacher said she couldn't miss it."

"Shannon said that? Huh."

"Is that her teacher? Wait, do you know her?"

"She is and yes, I do. We grew up together in West Virginia."

Relief flared in him. "So you can fix it, right?"

Gunnar had just taken a bite of pizza and he looked thoughtful while he chewed. "Um, I don't think so."

"You don't want to try either?"

"What do you mean by either?"

"Bethany said that she wouldn't even talk to her teacher about it.

She said it wouldn't be right." When Gunnar looked like he was going to say something, Jeremy spoke faster. "But you know, that doesn't make sense. I mean, I bet Shannon doesn't even know about the dance. And if she did, she'd let Bethany go. Then everything would be good. Unless—" He stopped himself before he shared his fear.

But of course Gunnar didn't let him off that easy. "Unless, what?"

"Unless . . . she was just looking for an excuse to not go with me."

"You acted like the two of you had a good thing going. Why would she want to back out?"

"Because maybe she doesn't want to be seen with me or something . . ."

"You've got to be kidding."

He glared. "Do you think I'd be telling you all this if I was kidding?"

"Hey, now. Settle down."

"No, just forget about it." He scooted back in his chair.

"Oh, no. You're not going anywhere, and I'm not going to forget anything. Furthermore, I'm trying to talk to you so, let me tell you a couple of things. You eat your pizza and just listen for a sec. First, and most importantly, you've got nothing to be embarrassed about. You are a nice guy. A good guy. Plus, you're cool."

Jeez. "Gunnar—"

"No, listen to me. The way I see it, God put a whole lot of people on this earth who are all different. Some guys are destined for all kinds of great things but maybe they're not exactly the coolest cats in high school, you know?"

"Coolest cats?"

"Shut up. Okay, I admit that sounds lame, but you know what I mean. Anyway, that's all good, but that's not you. You made friends right away. You kept those friends. They like you and want to be your friend. Okay?"

"Okay. Fine."

"Good. Now that we've got that settled, let's talk about girls."

He could only imagine where this tangent was going, and it wasn't going to be good. "Um, let's not."

"Oh stop. I'm not talking about sex. Listen, Jeremy."

"I am."

"Here's what I know about dating. Girls like Bethany? Girls who are sweet and pretty and have a lot going for them like she does? Well, she can pretty much pick whoever she wants to see. She wouldn't have said yes to you if she didn't want to."

"But"

"You said you told her about you and me. You did, right?"

Jeremy nodded.

"Then she's not all of a sudden going to change her mind. If you coming from a couple of crappy parents bothered her, she would have never said yes to the dance."

"You think?"

"No. I know. Girls like her are pretty special and pretty much every guy is going to think that. I have a feeling she could have had her pick of dates, but she wanted to go with you. Do you hear what I'm saying?"

He nodded slowly. "Yes."

"Good." Still looking like he was stewing, Gunnar drummed his fingers on the table. "Now, let's move onto Bethany's dance rehearsal. Just for a second, pretend that you were playing football and the dance was the night before the biggest game. Like for the state title or something."

"Okay . . ."

"Now, say you had a prime position. You were the running back. Quarterback. Coach wants to go through one more set of plays. Are you going to tell him that you can't make it because you've got a date to a dance?"

Gunnar made a good point. "No."

"Sure?" He raised an eyebrow. "Well, how about this? Want to have your dad or better yet, your girl's dad go talk to the coach so he'll understand?"

"No way. I'd be a laughingstock."

"Then why do you think things are different for her?"

"They're not."

Gunnar's expression softened. "Say again?"

"They're not. Bethany can't skip the practice and expect everyone to be fine with it."

"No, buddy. She sure can't. She likes you. She's upset, but she doesn't have a choice."

What he did then hit him like a bag of bricks. "I pretty much hung up on her."

"Ouch. Hmm. Well, it sounds to me like you're going to have to call her back and apologize."

"Do you think I need to do that tonight? Like, right now?"

"Not right this minute. You've got to drink your milk first."

Jeremy felt like smiling for the first time all night, which was saying something, since just a few minutes before all he'd wanted to do was fume.

Without another word, he picked up that glass of milk and started drinking.

CHAPTER 24

"Christmas is a season for kindling the fire for
hospitality in the hall, the genial flame
of charity in the heart."
—WASHINGTON IRVING

Sitting in his room, staring at his phone, Jeremy tried to think of the right way to apologize. But just saying he was sorry seemed lame. Bethany was probably really mad at him and would expect him to do something big and special before she'd forgive him. Phillip had said that was what girls expected.

He wasn't sure if Phillip was right, but he figured there was a good chance he wasn't wrong. The only problem was that he had no idea what he could do that was big and special enough for her.

If he had money, he would send her some flowers. Even *he* knew that all girls liked flowers. But he didn't have any money, so that was a no-go.

Finally, after watching the clock tick for another three

minutes, Jeremy knew he couldn't put it off anymore. He needed to call and say his piece. Then, their relationship—such that it was—was in her hands. If Bethany wasn't going to forgive him, then she wasn't going to. He would be disappointed, but he would stop worrying about it.

Well, he hoped he would one day stop worrying about it.

Before he lost his nerve again, Jeremy clicked on her name and called.

It rang three times. Each ring felt like a jab to his heart. Hating how emotional he was getting, he pulled the phone away from his ear, ready to tap the icon and hang up.

And then he heard her voice. "Jeremy?"

"Yeah. Hi."

After a pause, she spoke again. "What do you want?"

Ouch. He was going to need to start talking, and it was going to need to be fast. "I called to tell you that I'm sorry."

She didn't say anything for a couple of seconds. "For what?"

He wasn't sure if this was a test, or she really didn't know. Deciding to play it safe, he said, "Everything. I shouldn't have hung up on you. I should've understood about your ballet schedule. I really shouldn't have jumped to a bunch of conclusions. It wasn't fair."

"Do you really mean that?"

Her voice sounded softer. Maybe something he'd said had actually made sense. "Of course I do." Deciding at this point he couldn't say enough, he added, "If you knew how nervous I've been to call, you'd know how bad I feel."

She chuckled. "I'm glad you called. I've been kind of upset."

"I've been upset too." He closed his eyes and told himself not to sound so stilted. "I, well, I ended up talking to Gunnar. He told me I was being an idiot."

She laughed softly. "You weren't an idiot."

"I was close. I should have understood that you couldn't just blow off that rehearsal. I should have thought about things from your point of view instead of just mine."

"I wish I could get out of it, but I can't, Jeremy. I mean, I already bought a dress and everything."

She had? Why hadn't he let her talk more? "So, um, I was thinking that maybe we could do something after your rehearsal."

"You don't want to get another date?"

"No."

"Oh." Her tone softened. "What do you want to do after my rehearsal?"

"I don't know. Go get ice cream or something?" There was a Graeter's ice cream shop in the middle of downtown. Gunnar could drop him off at the dance studio and then he could walk her over to Graeter's.

"I had an idea. If you don't mind, maybe you could go to the dance without me and I could come as soon as I finish rehearsal."

"Do you think that would work?"

"Maybe. My mom said I could ask Miss Shannon if I could leave as soon as the main practice is over. I think she might be okay with that."

"Really?"

"I hope so. I mean, she was a teenager once. I could ask and let you know what she says."

"Yeah. That sounds good."

"Are you sure? If you want to go ahead ask someone else, you can. I'll understand."

"I'm not going to ask anyone else, Bethany. That's not going to happen."

She giggled again. "Then I guess I'd better make it work."

"I have a feeling you'll be able to. You're pretty good at getting things to work out."

"I have dance class tomorrow after school. I'll ask Miss Shannon then."

He was totally grinning. "That sounds good. So, I guess I'll see you tomorrow at school?"

"Yes."

"See you then, Bethany."

When she hung up, he felt like he'd just won the Super Bowl or something. Walking out into the living room, he saw Gunnar sitting with his mom. Both looked his way.

"Everything okay, Jeremy?" Gunnar asked.

"Yeah. I just wanted you to know that I called Bethany like you suggested."

"And?"

"And she was glad I called and isn't mad at me. I mean, not anymore."

"That's good, yeah?"

Jeremy nodded. "She's going to ask Miss Shannon if she can leave the rehearsal a little early. She said like as soon as the 'main' rehearsal is over, whatever that means."

"It might work out after all, huh?" Gunnar asked, smiling.

"I think so."

Gunnar's mom shook her head. "I can't believe I missed such a big night."

"It's okay, everything worked out."

"It sure did." She brightened. "Oh! If you'd like me to teach you some dance steps, I can. I can do a mean fox trot now."

"I don't think this is that kind of dance, but thanks anyway." Looking at Gunnar, he added, "I'm going to go get some ice cream. I'm starving."

"Sounds good." He winked. "Get a couple scoops and some hot fudge sauce too. You've got something to celebrate."

Walking into the kitchen, Jeremy realized he really did have a lot to celebrate. Not just about the dance and Bethany either. He had Gunnar now, and it looked like, no matter what, Gunnar was always going to have his back.

CHAPTER 25

"Ring out the old, ring in the new,
Ring, happy bells, across the snow."
—ALFRED, LORD TENNYSON,
"RING OUT, WILD BELLS"

Kimber was back in the city. But this time, instead being crammed into her tiny apartment with her girlfriends, she'd been put up in the penthouse suite at the Lexington Hotel. Instead of taking the subway like she always had, a black town car and driver were parked nearby, waiting to take her wherever she wanted to go.

In addition, there had been champagne and flowers in her suite when she'd arrived, along with a note from the general manager that pretty much stated that the whole staff would be delighted to move heaven and earth in order to make her happy.

The first few minutes that she'd been in the room, Kimber had wandered around the suite, nibbled on grapes, and simply beamed. This was the life she'd always hoped for when she'd started her career.

But now, after a very long day posing in ball gowns and getting pricked and prodded by a half-dozen people for six hours? She was simply tired.

She could care less about all the over the top extravagances. The suite was beautiful and the attention was appreciated, but it felt strange. She was now used to living in a cluttered room in the middle of Ohio. She was used to wearing old sweatpants and hanging out in the kitchen and helping old ladies and little kids learn to dance.

She was used to thinking about Gunnar and his snug-fitting shirts and his gruff ways. And his love for Jeremy.

She'd become a Bridgeport gal.

After checking in with all the girls and texting Gunnar back, Kimber had taken Brett's call . . . and set her mind to playing this game one more time.

Which was why she'd said yes to his dinner invite. It had been the right thing to do, but it was awkward. Because, here she was with a full face of makeup, a clingy emerald green dress that she'd borrowed from the designer, and four-inch heels, sitting at a table near the front of Gotham Grill across from Brett.

From the time she'd met him there, he'd been either on his phone or holding court with everyone who walked by. He'd also been drinking some kind of frou-frou rye concoction. He was on his third already.

She was nursing the same vodka tonic that she'd ordered almost an hour ago. After bypassing most of the choices on the menu and sticking with a piece of grilled fish and some veggies, she was eager to get out of the restaurant and call her sisters.

"Kimmy, what's wrong? Is the fish not done to your liking?"

She really hated it when he called her Kimmy. "It's exquisite, but Robert's ball gowns show every bump."

"You don't have any bumps to worry about, darling. I know,

because I asked Robert to show me a couple of the proofs. You're as perfectly gorgeous as ever."

"Why did you do that?"

"You know why." He carved off another two-inch piece of his steak. "You've been down in Ohio. No telling what you've been doing. I didn't want there to be any surprises."

Surprises? She was a professional. "I don't need you checking up on me."

"Oh, don't be sensitive, Kimmy. It's my job to make sure my little star is still at the top of her game. That's all I was doing." He popped the piece in his mouth and started chomping. "Now, I think we ought to start talking about your next steps."

He was driving her crazy, and that was putting it nicely. "My next steps involve going back home."

"That's great news." His eyes brightened. "Was your loft still available?"

"I'm going back to Ohio, Brett."

"For how long?"

"For as long as I can. I'm done."

"Don't be that way. Kimber, I promise, princess, you've got at least another year."

The way everyone she'd once been so close to kept reminding her about her age was starting to really grate on her. What was wrong with them all? They were making an inordinately big deal about her age—even for people in the industry. "I have a lot of years left," she bit out. And yes, she probably sounded defensive.

Some of the gloss left his tone. "To do what? No offense, but if you're not going to model, what will you do?"

"I don't know." She waved a hand. "Something. Everything."

"Well, that's hopeful." Stirring his drink with its little cock-tail straw, Brett smirked. "You know, you've never told me what, exactly, you were leaving me for."

It was weird how he was making her decision so personal. "I'm not leaving *you*, Brett. Just this career. And I'll figure something out. I've got time." He, of all people, knew how much money she'd made over the years.

His expression turned hard. "You're making a huge mistake. You're going to regret this. I know it."

"Life isn't all about work, Brett. I'm connecting with my sisters. Making friends." Staring down at her very fancy, very expensive plate of food that she'd only been able to pick at, she smiled slightly. "Eating . . ."

"Eating what in the middle of Ohio? The blue plate special at the Bob Evans?"

"Sarcasm doesn't serve you well."

"Neither did living in the middle of the rust belt." He drained his glass. "You forget that I grew up with those people. They're going to grate on you sooner or later. Mark my words."

Those people were her sisters. And Gunnar. Boy, just imagining how her construction worker would react to Brett's pretty boy disdain, she couldn't help but smile. Gunnar would have chewed him up by now.

"I see you smiling, girl. Don't laugh at me." Just as he drew in a breath of air, obviously in order to spew more advice, he smiled at the couple approaching.

None other than Esme and some older man who she was clinging to.

"Tommy! Esme!" After shaking the older man's hand, Brett turned and kissed Esme on the lips. "Darling, you look gorgeous."

Tommy stiffened while Esme laughed.

The whole thing felt icky. In no hurry to enter the conversation, Kimber stood up far more slowly. "Esme, hey."

Esme hugged her. "Kimber, I know I said I'd call as soon as you flew in, but I've just been swamped."

"Don't worry about it. I'm going to be heading back soon anyway."

"Oh? Your job ended that fast?"

"It was a quick one." She shrugged. There was no way she was going to mention the job she was on. Esme was cutthroat competitive.

"Kimber is here for the *Women's Weekly* gig," Brett said. "They've rolled out the red carpet for her too. It's been fantastic."

Esme's warm expression pinched. "Is that right?"

Oh, this was about to go down in a bad way. Hoping to circumnavigate the storm that was about to erupt, Kimber held out her hand to the man who was patiently standing next to Esme. "Hi. I'm Kimber Klein."

He shook her hand politely. "Tommy August. So, you're a model too?"

"Kind of."

"She told everyone she was retiring, but I guess that was a lie," Esme said.

"It wasn't. Brett talked me into something. Like I said, I'm heading back to Ohio real soon."

"*Women's Weekly* wanted Kimber bad. They offered her quite a deal."

"Is that right? How big a deal was it?"

There was no way she was going to go there. "Look, we better sit down. We were just finishing up our meal."

Tommy August's expression warmed, showing that he was on the same page that she was. "Don't let us keep you." He wrapped an arm around Esme's tiny waist. "It was a pleasure to meet you, Kimber."

"You too. See you, Esme."

Esme smiled brightly at her, though her eyes were cold. "I hope so, Kimmy."

And, there it was. Esme was not pleased with her. Not one bit.

After they were escorted toward the back of the restaurant, Brett sat back down with a broad grin. "Looks like you've got a little bit of competition there. Esme was not pleased."

"You spun her up."

He shrugged. "Nothing wrong with competition. Esme needs to not take so much for granted."

He didn't deny it. She realized then that there was also a very good chance that he had probably set it up. Having had more than enough, she placed her napkin to the left of her plate and stood up. "Thank you for the meal but I'm going to get out of here."

"Kimber, don't you go anywhere. I'll take you back to the hotel. We need to discuss a few things anyway."

"I'll grab a taxi."

Brett looked torn between standing up with her and pulling her back down by his side. "What is going on?"

"I have an early call in the morning. I need my sleep, since I'm so old and all."

"We'll talk about this next week. Maybe Tuesday, after you've calmed down."

"We won't. I'm catching a flight out tomorrow night. We're done."

"You aren't. I have some people who want to meet you. They're planning on it."

"You'll have to call them back, Brett."

He stood up. "Kimber, you're making a big mistake." His voice was as cold as she'd ever heard it.

"I don't think so." She smiled brightly before walking to the front and asking for her coat. Luckily, the hostess brought her black cashmere coat right away. After slipping it on, along with her gloves and scarf, Kimber stepped out into the dark.

Immediately, she was surrounded by the cacophony of horns

and sirens that was New York. Bypassing the waiting taxi, she started walking. Breathed in the fresh air that was tinged with a thousand smells that Shannon would probably find abhorrent.

When her phone rang, she glanced at it, just in case it was about tomorrow's job.

But it was Gunnar.

She clicked on immediately. "Gunnar. Hey."

"Hey, yourself."

"It's nice to hear from you. Is everything all right?"

"Everything is fine. Listen, I know you don't need me to fuss but I was worried about you. So will you humor me and let me know that you're all good?"

It didn't make her feel very independent, but she didn't care. "For your information, New York City is as safe as anywhere. It's probably safer than a lot of other cities half its size."

"No, baby, I was worried about you and the job and your crazy agent. And you eating."

In spite of the frigid temps, she got warm all over. "You don't need to worry so much. It's been going all right."

"Sorry, but you don't sound very convincing."

Sidestepping a couple standing in the middle of the sidewalk, she smiled. "That's probably because I don't feel very convincing. It's been a long day."

"I hear a bunch of background noise. Where are you?"

"Walking back to my hotel from the longest dinner ever."

"By yourself?"

"Yes, but don't worry. I'm okay. I'll probably take a taxi soon."

"Probably? It's dark, cold, and you're a beautiful woman walking alone. Kimber, get a taxi."

"I just needed a moment. Now, how are you?"

"Stressed."

"I hope I'm not the reason for it."

"Only a little bit of it." He sighed. "Actually, I called for some advice, but now I realize I should've left you alone. The last thing you need is my problems on your shoulders."

"What's going on? And no, I don't want to be left alone. Actually, I think concentrating on you is going to make my life easier. I need to concentrate on something besides myself right now."

"Are you sure?"

"Positive. Talk."

"Fine. Two days ago, we had a surprise home visit from the social worker."

"You and Jeremy?"

"Yeah. Kimber, when she walked in, I was sitting at the table sipping a beer while Jeremy was cooking us both ramen noodles for supper. His schoolbooks were spread out on the counter too. That's where he was studying."

"What's wrong with that? I thought you told me that he made good grades."

"He does, but shouldn't he be sitting at his own little desk or something?"

"Maybe if he was seven." This guy! His worries were so cute it was almost aggravating. "Gunnar, I'm sure it was fine."

"It ended up being fine, but I have to admit that I was freaked out there for a minute or two."

Waiting for the crosswalk, she smiled. "Only for a couple of minutes?"

"Yeah, because after I made a fool of myself, she gave us some excellent news. Kimber, we have a court date for adoption."

"Well, don't keep me in suspense. When is it?" she asked as she turned down a far quieter side street.

"January seventeenth."

She was now grinning ear to ear. "That's excellent. Wonderful!"

"It really is."

She could practically see him grinning too. "So other than that, how's Jeremy?"

"He's good. He asked a girl to the Christmas dance and she said yes. I don't think anything would have bothered him after that. It's all he wanted to talk about with Melanie."

Kimber smiled. That boy sounded so cute. "See? It's all good." She stopped, then started walking a little faster. It was probably her imagination, but she thought she'd heard footsteps behind her.

"I think Bethany and him are all good. I just hope nothing happens to make Melanie change her mind or anything."

Reminding herself that Gunnar was overthinking because he loved the boy and didn't want to jeopardize their future together, she said, "We'll just have to stay positive."

"And hope nothing happens between now and January seventeenth." He took a deep breath. "I know I keep worrying about the same stuff, but . . ."

Gunnar started talking about some work issues, and some things at Jeremy's school. Kimber tried to listen but she was now distracted.

Half-certain she heard something crackle nearby, she quickly glanced behind her. But beyond a pair of men walking half a block back, she didn't see anything. Still unable to shake the feeling that she was being followed, she picked up her pace.

"So what do you think, Kimber? Should I be worried about that?"

She had no idea to what he was referring. Feeling even more uneasy, she said, "I think I better get off the phone."

"You okay? You sound a little out of breath."

"I'm okay, it's just that I took a shortcut, but things don't seem quite right." Her voice drifted off. She not only didn't want to worry him, but she was afraid to give voice to the fears that were threatening to overtake her.

"What do you mean by that? Are you in trouble? Is someone bothering you?"

"I don't know. I mean, probably not."

"I'm not letting you get off the phone if you're scared." His tone turned even more serious. "When can you get back to a busier street?"

"In about a half a block."

"Then you'll hail a cab?"

She didn't appreciate his bossiness but she knew it stemmed from concern. "Yes." Still practically running, she said, "Hold on, I'm almost there." She rushed to the intersection, practically cheering when she saw all the people. "I'm okay now."

"I wish I was there with you."

Thinking about the dinner with Brett, she murmured, "I wish you were too. I had a heck of a dinner. It was awful."

"I'll take you out to dinner when you get back."

She smiled. "You're quite the sweetheart. First you volunteer to pick me up, now you're promising to feed me too."

"Stick with me, sugar. I'll spoil you rotten."

She laughed. She knew he was joking, but what he didn't realize was that those things counted for her. She'd dated so many men who either only wanted to be seen with her or wanted to talk about themselves. Gunnar Law was reminding her that all men weren't like that.

After checking her surroundings again and finding nothing but a whole lot of uninterested New Yorkers, she said, "When you say things like that, I wonder how all the women in West Virginia let you slip through their fingers."

"I guess I was saving myself for a certain woman in Bridgeport," he teased, warming her insides. "So where are you now? Are you about to grab a cab?"

Noticing that every taxi that passed was occupied, she knew

that wasn't about to happen anytime soon. But there was no way Gunnar needed to know that. "Yeah, probably in a sec or two—" Her words cut off as she felt someone pull her arm. With a gasp, she turned, her phone clattering to the ground.

But all she could see was the quickest glimpse of a meaty hand reaching out for her with a stream of profanities.

Before she could get her bearings, she was thrown to the ground. Then kicked.

And then she wasn't aware of much at all.

Except for the faint echo of Gunnar Law's voice through the speaker of her phone. Over and over again he called her name.

CHAPTER 26

"Late lies the wintry sun a-bed,
A frosty, fiery sleepy-head;
Blinks but an hour or two; and then,
A blood-red orange, sets again."
—ROBERT LOUIS STEVENSON,
"WINTER TIME"

Never had he wanted to both throw his phone and hold it close at the same time. It was serving as his lifeline to Kimber, but it was currently giving him close to nothing.

Nothing except a ton of background noise and a heart attack.

"Kimber?" Gunnar yelled yet again. "Kimber? Kimber!" But all he heard was a clatter of feet, then a couple of exclamations. Hoping that someone had stopped to take care of her, he called out her name again. "Kimber? Kimber, can you answer me, honey?"

After he heard another set of clattering, he heard a rustle of a jacket.

"Ah, hello?"

It was an unfamiliar voice with a New York accent. "Yeah. Hi. This is my girlfriend's cell. Are you standing next to her?"

"Yeah. I was about a block away and saw her go down. Some guy hit her good. I couldn't believe it! I yelled at the guy but he took off."

Gunnar had never been so freaked out. "Wait. Is she okay?"

"I don't know. She was moving a second ago. Hey, what's her name? Oh, hold on!"

"Wait—"

"Miss? Miss, someone called the police and an ambulance," the man said in a gentle voice. "There's someone on this phone for you. What do you want . . . ? Oh! Okay. Here you go."

"Gunnar?" Kimber's voice was weak and she sounded out of it.

He closed his eyes. Lord have mercy, but he was about to lose it. "Yeah, it's me. I'm so glad you're talking."

"I . . . I don't feel good."

"Kimber, baby. Hang in there. They said the ambulance is on the way. Hang in there for a little longer, okay?"

"'Kay."

Her voice was starting to slur. Gunnar was pretty sure she was about to pass out. Hating how hopeless he felt, he did the only thing he could think of—he tried to keep her talking. "Kimber, baby, where are you staying?"

"Hmm?"

"Honey, what hotel? Tell me quick, because I'm flying out there as soon as I can."

"Lexington. It's the Lexington . . ." The last of her words were drowned out by the sound of sirens.

He wasn't sure if she could hear him, but he said, "I'll be there soon. Tomorrow. You remember that. I'm going to be praying for you too."

When she disconnected, he rested his head against the back of the couch and tried to get his bearings. Then he realized that he needed to figure out what to do about Jeremy.

SHELLEY SHEPARD GRAY

Getting to his feet, he started pacing, thinking about work and Kimber and realized he needed to call Shannon and then Ace.

First he tried the main phone number for Dance With Me but only got a recording. Next, he called the main number for the police department and asked for Traci Lucky. To his amazement, he was put right through.

"This is Lucky."

"Hi, Traci? This is Gunnar Law. I've been dating your sister Kimber?"

"She's mentioned you," she replied, her voice sounding much more guarded. "What's going on?"

Briefly he told her about his phone call with Kimber. "As soon as I find a place for Jeremy, I'm going to book a flight out there."

"To New York?"

"It's a quick flight, right?"

"Yes, but . . . are you sure? I'm sure Shannon or I can go."

"You need to do what you need to do, but I can't be here if Kimber's hurt or in danger."

"Sorry, I thought you two had just started seeing each other."

"That's true, but she's already become important to me."

"How about if I talk to Shannon first? Then we'll give you a call—"

"Sorry, but I didn't call for permission. I called to let you know about Kimber. As soon as I see her tomorrow I'll check in again."

"Hold on. Give me your name again. And your phone number."

After he rattled off his information, he said, "I've got to go. I've got to find a place for my boy and book a flight."

"Thanks for calling. Now listen, I'll be expecting to hear from you tomorrow." Her voice had a new thread of iron in it.

But he was in no hurry to enter into some pissing match with her. He was the one who had called her with news, not the other way around. "Yeah, you will," he replied before hanging up.

Just as he was searching through his contacts, Jeremy approached. "What's going on?"

"I think Kimber got mugged or something in New York City."

"No way. Is she okay?"

"I don't know. She wasn't real coherent. All I know is her hotel and that an ambulance had just arrived for her."

The boy's eyes widened. "What are you going to do?"

He forced himself to speak as calmly as he could. "I'm going to call Ace to see if you can stay with him for a day or two."

"Why?"

"I'm flying out there, Jeremy. She's alone and it's freaking me out." Looking him in the eye, he said, "I know this isn't the best situation, but she needs someone right now."

"I like Ace all right. I'll be fine."

"I wouldn't do this if it wasn't so important."

"You don't need to explain. I'm not a kid."

Just as Gunnar was about to tell him that he actually was, he thought about it again. Maybe Jeremy was right and he was wrong. Jeremy had dealt with a lot and now he was being pretty agreeable and not arguing about going to Ace's house at all.

"You're right. You're practically a man. Thanks for understanding."

Jeremy nodded before wandering into the kitchen and opening the refrigerator.

Pleased that the boy was thinking about food, Gunnar called Ace. He answered immediately, and even offered to come get Jeremy as soon as Gunnar made plans.

Buoyed by that, he got online and booked a ticket. There was a flight out at six in the morning and he was going to be on it.

He just hoped he was going to be able to find her after he arrived.

197

CHAPTER 27

"For unto us a child is born."
—ISAIAH 9:6

Kimber had a pounding headache and was pretty much covered in bruises and scrapes. She also had a sneaking suspicion that she'd somehow managed to get a cold while she was passed out on the pavement.

But as she shifted uncomfortably in her hospital bed, all she wanted to do was give thanks that she was all right. More than one nurse and doctor had told her that she was lucky not to be hurt worse—and by *worse* they meant *dead*.

No way was she going to complain about a couple of small injuries.

She was, however, not feeling especially grateful to the cop who had set up shop in the chair next to her bed and was acting a little too full of himself.

"What I don't understand, Miss Klein, is that if you've really been having so many problems with this stalker—"

"I have been. I have proof."

"If you do have proof, and you were so worried, why were you still walking in the dark by yourself? It doesn't sound very smart."

Boy, he was a jerk. "You know where I was attacked. It's a nice area." And, yes, he was probably right that she'd been stupid, but she was a victim, not an idiot!

The cop folded his hands over his rotund middle. "For that matter, why did you even come to New York? I'm sure that even a woman like you would be aware of the dangers you were putting yourself in."

"What do you mean by a *woman like me?*"

"That's not the point of this conversation."

"I'm afraid it is, since I fail to understand what constitutes a *woman like me.*"

"You know." He waved a hand. "A woman in your occupation. A model." He smiled. "No offense, but models aren't always known for making the best decisions."

What was this? 1972? She briefly considered arguing with him about his stereotypes, but she decided to keep that to herself. "Instead of worrying about my reputation, I'd appreciate it if you would focus on the person who attacked me."

"It's been my experience that a lot of these attacks don't happen randomly. Because of that, we need to go over your history once again."

Just as she was about to answer, two of the best faces in her world peeked in the doorway. Gunnar Law and her sister, Traci. Ignoring the cop's latest irritating comment, she smiled at them both. "Gunnar! Traci! I can't believe it. What are you two doing here?"

Gunnar came right to her side. "Did you really think I would be anywhere else?" He bent down and kissed her lightly on the lips. "There's no way I was going to let you be alone another day." Reaching for her hand, he tucked it in between his. "No way."

"You didn't need to do this, but I'm so glad to see you." Reaching out her other hand, she said, "You too, Trace."

Traci walked to Kimber's side, sidling in the space between her bed and the cop. "That's what sisters are for, right?" she asked, carefully holding her hand around her sister's IV tube.

And . . . now she was choked up. "Right," she murmured. "Thanks for being here."

"Don't thank me. You okay?"

"I don't know."

"Excuse me," the cop said. "I need to know who you both are . . . and then you can leave. I'm asking some questions here."

"I want them here," Kimber said. "This is my sister and my . . . my boyfriend."

The cop's expression didn't soften one bit. "Where were you both last night?"

Traci turned on him like a Doberman. "We were both back in Ohio. Why? Do you really think that either of us had anything to do with Kimber's attack?"

"Watch your tone, Miss."

"And you need to watch your attitude, Officer . . ."

"Benson."

Kimber felt like closing her eyes. Even though she couldn't see Traci's expression, she knew by her tone that she was fighting mad. She looked over at Gunnar and raised her eyebrows.

He did too, just as Traci went on a new tirade. "I'm a cop myself, Officer Benson."

"In your small town?" His voice oozed with sarcasm.

"Yep. When I'm not saving kittens I'm serving the public just like you are. And what we both know is that your victim has been hospitalized and needs rest. Not you interrogating her or her family. You're going to have to come back tomorrow."

"We are not done."

This time Gunnar stood up. "Yeah, we are. My girl here can hardly keep her eyes open. Sorry, but you're going to have to come back when she has her lawyer."

Officer Benson got to his feet. "You two are making a mistake."

"I was about to tell you the same thing." Gunnar's voice was calm and low-key but had the same amount of ice in it as Traci's.

"I'll be in touch, Miss Klein," Officer Benson said before walking out of the room.

Traci closed Kimber's door and then turned back to her. "How long was he here?"

"I don't know. Fifteen minutes?"

"Fifteen minutes too long, I think." She took a deep breath and stared at her sister hard. "So . . . for being such a pretty thing, you currently look like crap."

"Thanks."

"Were you done with your fancy photo shoot?"

Kimber loved Traci for getting right down to business. "For the most part. I was supposed to go back today but obviously that couldn't happen. Brett called them and explained why."

"Brett, your agent? Gunnar asked.

"Yes."

"What else has he done? Has he been by?" Gunnar asked.

"No." Not wanting to talk about Brett, she said, "How did you two find me?"

"It wasn't easy," Gunnar replied. "At first we went to the Lexington. You told me you were staying there when you were lying on the sidewalk."

"But they wouldn't have known . . ."

"That's where my profession helped us out. I called a buddy

in NYPD. After a couple minutes of checking, he found out you were here."

Gunnar sighed. "I just wish we got here before that cop arrived."

"Don't worry about that. I was fine."

"Now, how are you?" he asked. "Traci and I tried to talk to someone on our way in here but the nurses wouldn't give us any information other than your doc was going to be coming back around here within the hour."

After filling them in on her injuries, Kimber frowned. "The nurse told me that she has a feeling that they're going to make me stay one more night."

"Good," Traci and Gunnar said, practically in unison.

"You two are bossy."

Traci pushed a lock of hair off her cheek. "Yep."

Kimber might have argued about their heavy-handed ways but she was too tired. She leaned back against the pillows and closed her eyes.

Gunnar immediately rearranged the sheets around her. "Are you warm enough, honey?"

"Yes. I'm okay. Just resting my eyes for a moment. How did you two end up coming in here together?"

"I called her to get information and filled her in."

"After we spoke, I decided that I had to come out too. Shannon and Jennifer said to tell you that they were sorry they couldn't make it."

"I'm glad they didn't come. I'm sorry you spent the money."

"Don't say things like that," Traci said.

"Do you have a place to stay?"

Gunnar shook his head. "Not yet. Don't worry about that none. We'll find someplace."

"Kimber!"

Recognizing that voice anywhere, Kimber jerked and felt a combination of alarm and happiness. "Get ready, you two. The hospital called my parents."

Traci turned to the doorway and then her face went slack.

On her other side, Gunnar sucked in a breath.

"Kimber, look at you!" her mother exclaimed as she strode to her like a steam engine. After kissing her brow, she moved aside for her dad to enfold her in a bear hug.

"Kimber Jean," he murmured.

Even though she'd often felt like she'd disappointed them, in the past, Kimber knew they loved her and she loved them back. She took a moment to appreciate their presence.

When they stepped away with another couple of pats, she smiled at them. "Hi, Mom. Hey, Dad. I can't believe you both came."

"I can't believe you'd think we'd be anyplace else," her father said. "You're my sweet girl."

"Thank you, Dad."

She wasn't sure if he heard her or not, because he'd already turned to stare at the other two occupants in the room. "Now, who are you two?"

"I don't think we've met. Have we?" her mother asked on her dad's heels.

Taking a deep breath, Kimber performed the introductions— all while silently praying that everything wasn't about to get even weirder. "Mom, Dad, this is Traci, my sister. And, this is Gunnar Law, my boyfriend." And she wouldn't have guessed it, but calling him that was feeling almost easy. Easier than introducing Traci as her sister to her parents.

"Your sister?" her mother gasped.

She looked kind of spellbound. Worried for Traci, Kimber said, "I know I've mentioned Traci and Shannon, Mom."

Traci held out a hand. And yes, it was awkward. "Hi—"

"I can't believe it. Look at you!" she exclaimed as she hurried to Traci's side and embraced her in a fierce hug. Seconds later, she stepped back, smiled wider, then hugged her again.

When her mom released Traci at last, Traci reached for the edge of the bed to steady herself.

Kimber didn't blame their reactions one bit. Her parents were larger than life and seemed to suck the life out of any room.

"Dad?" Kimber prodded. He was currently eyeing Gunnar like he didn't trust him and Traci like he couldn't believe she was real.

"Real glad to know you," he said quietly to Gunnar.

"You too, sir," Gunnar said as they shook hands.

"When did you two arrive?"

"A couple of hours ago," Gunnar replied. "We got the first flight out of Cincinnati."

"Shannon wanted to come but we decided that the two of us might be enough," Traci added.

"You are a sight for sore eyes, girl," Dad said to Traci as he reached for her hands. "I'm looking forward to getting to know you. You're the sister who's a cop, right?"

"Right." After sneaking a glance at Kimber, Traci smiled at Kimber's dad. "It's real good to meet you, Mr. Klein."

"It's Charlie and that's Jennifer. We're Charlie and Jennifer to you."

"All right. Thank you," Traci said quietly.

While Kimber's parents had been scaring poor Traci to death, Gunnar had been edging his way back to Kimber's side. She reached out and took hold of his hand. He steadied her and she was so grateful for it.

"You hanging in there?" he whispered.

"I am. I might even be doing better than that," she added. "I'm really glad you're here."

Leaning down, he brushed a kiss on her cheek. "Me too, sweetheart."

Just then she realized that her parents and Traci were all staring at them. Though part of her felt like she was fourteen and getting caught holding a boy's hand, Kimber kept ahold of Gunnar. She might be lying in a bed, but he was helping to center her, and that was the truth.

"Maybe we should bring in some more chairs so we can get caught up," her dad said. "It looks like we've got a lot of things to discuss."

"I don't know if now is the best time, Dad."

Eying their linked hands, her father shook his head. "Actually, I can't think of a better time than right this second. Gunnar, how about you and I go find two more chairs?"

"I'd be happy to." He squeezed Kimber's hand lightly. "I'll be right back. I promise."

Even though she hurt, looked awful, and was a nervous wreck, she smiled. She knew Gunnar wasn't going to go back on that promise. Not a chance.

CHAPTER 28

"At Christmas, all roads lead home."
—MARJORIE HOLMES

Jeremy hadn't been worried about spending the night at Ace's house. Despite the guy looking like he was part of a motorcycle gang or something, Gunnar's boss was easygoing and really nice. His wife, Meredith, was sweet and kind of shy, and their son, Finn, was pretty much the most popular kid at Bridgeport High.

He was the star quarterback on the football team, had a dog and a girlfriend, and also happened to be one of the coolest guys Jeremy had ever met. Finn Vance was laid back and never acted like he was anything special.

Jeremy had worried that he'd have to share a room with Finn, but Meredith had their spare room all tricked out with a queen-size inflatable bed and a TV on a cart. She was worried that he would be upset about the bed, but Jeremy assured her he was just fine. He was glad she had no idea about some of the rooms and beds he'd had to sleep in over the years.

Now, though, Jeremy was sitting with Henry, Finn's dog, on the couch watching the family's big television in their basement. He was also staring at the screen of his cell phone. He'd just texted Gunnar, to see what was going on in New York, and Bethany, because that was what they did now.

Finn came in and sat down on the opposite side of the couch. Henry inched closer to him, obviously pleased to be by his favorite person. "What are you watching, Jeremy?" he asked.

"Nothing really. I've been flipping channels." He handed Finn the remote. "Here."

"Thanks." He clicked on ESPN. "I'm hoping to get my fantasy football lineup set for the week. Do you have a team?"

"Nah." He not only didn't have the money for it, but it wasn't like a kid in foster care had gotten a lot of chances to watch cable or follow players and teams. He wouldn't know who to put on his team.

"I'm in the same league as my dad. Since Gunnar works with him, maybe you could be in it next year."

"Yeah. Maybe."

Finn blinked like he was taken off guard. "Are you not into football? I mean, it's cool if you're not."

"I'm into it." He grinned. "I mean, not like you or anything. Is it true you're going to have your pick of colleges next year?"

Finn shook his head. "A couple of scouts are taking an interest in me, but it's not like everyone is making it sound."

"Oh." When his phone buzzed, he looked down at the screen. It was Gunnar, saying that he wasn't going to be back until probably Sunday but that he'd call later.

Jeremy frowned at it.

"What's wrong?"

"That was my foster—I mean, Gunnar. He said that he wasn't going to be back until Sunday now. His girlfriend, Kimber, must be bad off."

"Wow. That's too bad."

"Yeah." Suddenly feeling like he was in the way, he said, "Sorry I'm going to be here so long."

Finn gave him that same look again. "I don't care how long you're here. It's good to have the company."

Comments like that were probably why everyone liked Finn Vance so much. He not only was cool, he was nice. Way more chill than most seniors. Feeling like maybe he could trust him to not make fun of him, Jeremy said, "Are you going to the Christmas dance?"

"Yep. I don't really care if I go or not, but Allison likes that stuff."

"You two have been going out a while, huh?"

Finn nodded. "About a year or so." He grinned. "She lives next door."

"Next door, huh? Boy, I hope you don't break up." Of course, the moment he said the words, he wished he could take them back. "Sorry. That was pretty rude."

"Nah, it's the truth." Finn shrugged. "I hope we don't break up too, though I doubt it would make a difference as far as us living next door to each other. She graduated in December. So I'm dating a college girl now."

"Wow. Are you going to go to the same college?"

"Doubt it. Allison is attending community college this spring and then maybe Miami or OU. All the coaches who've been looking at me are in other states."

"That's hard."

"Yeah, but Allison is cool with that. She's really into her plans and I want to play ball as long as I can, so we agreed to not try to hold each other back."

Finn had his life together. All of it. And, here Jeremy was, still just trying to believe that the adoption was actually going to go through.

Reaching out to pet Henry, Finn said, "What about you?"

"Me?"

"Yeah. Are you going to the dance?"

Jeremy nodded. " I asked Bethany Seevers. Do you know her?"

"I know who she is. Bethany's real cute."

"She is. She's a dancer."

"That's cool."

Jeremy still couldn't believe that she liked him so much, since she could have anyone she wanted. "Does everyone get their dates corsages?" Even though she was going to meet him after rehearsal, he wanted to make sure she got a corsage if all the other girls had them.

"Pretty much. But don't worry about dinner. My folks are hosting a big dinner here. You and Bethany should come over."

"Thanks, but I'm going to have to meet her at the dance." He briefly explained about her ballet rehearsal.

"That sucks, but you should still come."

"I don't know."

"Sure you do. You're new and you don't want to walk into the dance by yourself, do you? That's the worst."

That would be awful. Thinking how much better it would be to arrive with a whole group of people, he said, "Are you sure parents won't mind if I show up?" Of course, what he was really worried about was if Finn minded.

"Nah. Allison's parents are putting it on too. Plus, there's already going to be like thirty of us. One more won't make a difference. And don't worry about being the only one without a date. There's about five or six who are going to the dance in a group."

Finn made it all sound so easy. "Thanks," he said. "That's really cool of you."

"It's no big deal. Oh, wait. I've got to see this," he said as a new graphic listing players appeared on the screen.

When Finn started watching the updates intently, Jeremy texted Bethany and told her about Finn's dinner idea.

> Would you mind if I went?

He had no idea if she would be mad about that. She texted back right away.

> Of course not.

> Okay, good. I think I'm going to do it then.

> I'll get there as soon as I can. At least Miss Shannon said I didn't have to stay after we went through the ballet one full time. I bet I'll get there by 8:30!

> 8:30 is good.

> We're going to have so much fun.

> Yep.

His finger hovered over his phone's screen. He should probably text something else, but he had no idea what to add. Before he could come up with anything, Bethany had already responded.

I never asked, but you like to dance, right?

Yeah. I like it fine.

But the truth was he didn't really like it. Well, he didn't really know how to dance. He had no idea what she was going to think when she saw just how bad he was.

"Want to grab some lunch?" Finn asked. He pointed to his cell phone's screen. "My dad just told me that the taco truck is parked downtown."

Glad Gunnar had given him some spending money, Jeremy got to his feet. "Sure. Tacos sound great."

Finn grinned. "Cool. I'll put Henry on a leash and let's get out of here."

Standing up, Jeremy followed Finn and his dog. Henry's tail was wagging like crazy, he was so happy to be included in the outing.

Jeremy thought he knew how the dog felt.

CHAPTER 29

*"I will honor Christmas in my heart,
and try to keep it all the year."*
—CHARLES DICKENS

"Is everything okay?" Kimber asked.

Gunnar stopped staring at his phone. "Yes. Why?"

"No reason. You've just been frowning at your phone for the last five minutes."

Realizing she was right, he set it on the small table next to her hospital bed. "I'm sorry. It was Jeremy." He shook his head. "It's the craziest thing—sometimes I feel like I have to pry the words out of that kid. But when it comes to texting, he turns into a chatterbox."

"Maybe he feels safer communicating that way." Shoot, she knew some adults who felt that way.

"Maybe so."

He still looked worried. After reaching for the button that

adjusted her sitting position, she adjusted herself so she could see him better. "Is everything okay? Do you need to leave and go be with him?"

He reached for her hand. "No, no. It's nothing like that. Don't worry."

"You know I'm going to worry. I'm grateful that you're here, but I still feel terrible about you giving up so much to sit here in this hospital room with me."

He shook his head, as if he was amused by her logic. "Baby, work is fine. Ace completely understood why I had to hop on the first flight out. Shoot, he probably would've kicked my rear if I told him I was staying in Bridgeport while my girlfriend had been attacked in New York City."

She winced. "You make it sound—"

"I made your attack sound as bad as it was," he said, once again correcting her attempt to downplay what happened. "Now, stop worrying about me. I'm good. 'Kay?"

"Okay."

"Good." He picked up her plastic glass that was filled with water and ice. "Now, how about some more water?"

"Thanks." She carefully placed her lips around the straw and sipped slowly.

Watching Kimber put in so much effort to get a sip of water, Gunnar felt like he'd been kicked in the gut. No matter what she said, he thought she looked pretty bad. She seemed so small in the middle of the bed. All he wanted to do was protect her.

"Gunnar, now what's wrong?" She took another sip, but this time studying him through half-closed lids.

And just like that, his whole mindset shifted. Instead of looking at her bruises, he started trying not to notice just how perfect those lips were—or how it had felt to finally kiss her the other night.

All he'd done since he'd arrived was kiss her chastely. It wasn't like he wanted to do more, she was in a hospital bed—but he would be lying to himself he didn't admit that he was looking forward to the day when she was feeling better and they could move things forward.

When she held the cup for him to take, Gunnar knew he had to get a handle on himself. "So when are your parents coming back?"

"In an hour or so. They wanted to take Traci out to lunch." She frowned. "I hope they aren't driving her crazy. They've probably asked her a hundred questions."

"They've been sweet, Kimber. They're good people." He wasn't lying either. Though, they were certainly a handful. Kimber, so wary and reserved, was the exact opposite of them. They seemed to speak only with exclamation points.

"They *are* good people, I'm not denying that. But they can be overwhelming."

"Ah, have you met Traci? I only just met her but I can already tell that she's not the type of woman to let people run ragged over her."

"I guess you're right." She pressed a palm flat against the mattress. He'd learned over the last twenty-four hours that she did that when she was worried about something.

"When did you start doing that?" he asked, gesturing to her palm.

"Pressing the mattress like that?" She tucked her hand under one of her many blankets. "I don't know. Back when I realized that I couldn't afford to bite my lip or crack my knuckles, I guess."

"How come you couldn't do that? Would your parents get that upset?"

"Oh, no. It was my career. When I was first starting out, I was so insecure, I felt that any little flaw would put me at a disadvantage. Even something as small as swollen knuckles."

Kimber didn't usually talk about her modeling life. But when she did share details, he always felt a little humbled. "You've sure made me rethink a model's life. I thought you just had to sit there and look pretty."

She smiled at him. "There's plenty of that. But there are a lot of pretty girls out there. For someone like me, who looks a little different, it was a reason to worry."

"You don't have to worry now." He stopped himself from reminding her that she was supposed to be retired. If she'd stuck to her decision, she would have never been in New York in the first place, and therefore wouldn't be sitting in a hospital bed right now.

Looking up at him, her eyes filled with tears. "It's not over, Gunnar. I know it's not."

"All right then, how about this? No matter if it's over or not, you're not alone in this. You've got your sisters and me and your parents."

She looked shell-shocked. "I appreciate that, but we need to keep my parents out of this."

As far as he was concerned, they were already involved. "What are you talking about? I saw how they were looking at you. They love you, Kimber."

"Oh, I know that." She hesitated for a moment, then added, "But they aren't going to want to see that part of me."

"What part?" When she shifted uncomfortably, he knew he should probably let his concerns slide. She was still injured and no doubt feeling badly. Plus, he was no counselor and it wasn't like he didn't have his own issues with his parents from time to time.

Gentling his voice, he added, "We don't have to talk about this anymore, but I've only seen beauty when I look at you. And I'm not talking about the outside either. I'm talking about what's inside—your heart and your mind. You're a pretty special woman, at least to me."

She reached for his hand. "I don't know how I got so lucky finding you. You really are just the nicest guy."

"I'm nice to you."

"That's enough for me."

He brought her hand to his lips. "Good, because I want you to keep me around for a while." He realized then that while he'd tried to show her with his actions how much she meant to him, he hadn't actually said the words. No, all he'd done was skirt around it, but he didn't actually come out and say any of the words that a woman would be looking for.

When he thought about it that way, it felt wrong. Weak, even. And he was a lot of things, but he didn't like to think that weak was one of them.

He scooted his plastic chair a little closer. "You know, Kimber, I've been looking for the right time to talk to you about how I've been feeling, but I guess that was silly."

One eyebrow rose. "Silly?"

He guessed she had a point. He couldn't ever recall a time when he'd used that word to describe himself. "Um, how about wrong?" He thought some more, then went back to his original descriptor. "Weak?"

This time, both of her eyebrows rose. "Weak? Gunnar, whatever you're describing isn't close to how I've been thinking of you. You're gonna have to be a little clearer because I have no idea what you're talking about."

"Okay. What I'm trying to say, and not very well, is that I care about you. A lot."

Her whole expression softened. "I care about you too, silly."

He chuckled. "Uh-oh. I'm not going to live that down, am I?"

"Probably not. It's too tempting to use to tease you."

Just as he was bending down to kiss her smiling lips, they heard a rap on her door.

"Knock, knock."

They sprang apart like two guilty teenagers.

The cop, Officer Benson smirked as he sauntered in. "Sorry for interrupting, but it's time I finished my interview with Miss Klein here."

CHAPTER 30

"We'll tak' a cup o' kindness yet, for auld lang syne."
—ROBERT BURNS

After getting released from the hospital, Kimber had attempted to go back to her hotel room instead of her parents' house. Going home with Gunnar and Traci in tow had felt like too much.

Too many memories. Too many explanations. Too much togetherness, especially since both Traci and her parents had a tendency to speak what was on their minds. The last thing she wanted to do was play referee, or worse, have Gunnar witness it all.

But in her parents' typical bossy way, they'd overruled Kimber's wishes. Mom had been especially persuasive, saying how she wanted to fuss over her but there was no way she was going to be able to do that while sitting in a hotel room the size of a postage stamp, no matter how fancy it was.

She'd ignored Kimber's protests that she didn't need to be fussed over.

Her parents had also said they wanted to spend some time with Gunnar and Traci. Her dad kept joking about he wanted to get acquainted with "Kimber's young man," like she was seventeen or something. Her mother kept talking about how "gorgeous" Gunnar was, but she also kept hinting that she wanted to try to make up for lost time with Traci.

Her parents had good intentions, and everything kind of, sort of sounded reasonable, but it still made Kimber a nervous wreck.

In the end, Kimber had agreed to go home, but had also shared that she really needed some space and couldn't stay up too late, since she, Traci, and Gunnar all had to be at the airport in the morning to catch an early flight back to Cincinnati.

This was after she refused to stay in New York longer.

Her parents weren't exactly wealthy, but they were well off. Well enough to hire a car instead of hailing a taxi to take them all to the Brooklyn brownstone that Kimber had grown up in.

So they'd all arrived on her street in style, which had made more than a couple of their neighbors come out as Gunnar was helping her out of the car.

Noticing that Mrs. Latimer was leading the pack, Kimber inwardly groaned. Mrs. Latimer had always gotten into her business.

"Get ready," Kimber said. "They're going to want to say hello. They can be kind of nosey too."

Gunnar grinned. "Babe. I'm from Spartan, West Virginia. I can handle nosey neighbors. Being nosey is what we do back there."

"Kimber!" Mrs. Latimer called out.

"You go say your hellos and I'll rescue you in a second. I've got this."

And sure enough, he did. While she was asked about her bandage on her head, Gunnar answered questions about dating a super model and assured them that his whole family had the same accent that he did.

Traci was far more awkward, but she was pleasant enough and ignored Kimber's attempts to run interference.

"Kimber, what happened to you?" another lady asked.

Before she could answer, Gunnar swooped in. "She had a little accident, so I think I better get her inside, ma'am."

The ladies smiled at him like he was the cutest thing they'd ever seen while he escorted her toward the door.

After chatting to quite a few people as well, her parents and Traci ushered them all inside.

"Kimber, you go relax," her mother said as she climbed the stairs. "Dad's going to start dinner. I'll be down in a minute to help him."

Knowing her mother was going to want to get the guest bedrooms organized, Kimber nodded. "Okay, come on in. So . . . this is home."

"No, this is you," Traci announced.

Noticing that her sister was staring at the wall next to the fireplace, Kimber tossed her bag on a chair and followed. And then saw . . . her.

Four magazine covers were framed and displayed in the center of a dozen other smaller, framed shots of her.

Kimber was shocked into silence.

"Kimber, baby, look at you," Gunnar said.

"It's like a Kimber shrine," Traci said.

And . . . her whole level of embarrassment had reached a new low. "I swear, I didn't know this was here."

He lightly wrapped an arm around her shoulders. "I'm glad it is. I can't believe I've never seen all this. You look . . ."

"What?"

"Different."

"I know. It's a lot of lighting, makeup, and camera angles."

"I don't think so, Kimber," Traci said, tilting her head slightly to the right. "It looks like you, but Gunnar's right. It's almost like looking at a stranger."

"Let's go into the kitchen. I'm sorry about this." She was not only embarrassed by the whole display but acutely aware that Traci didn't have parents who commemorated her accomplishments.

Gunnar didn't move. "Just a minute. Why are you sorry? I like seeing all of your photos. It's fun to see what you did in your former life."

Her former life. She blinked. He was right. All of this was her former life—not who she was now. "You're right. All this is behind me now. Come on. My parents are waiting."

In the kitchen, her father was digging ingredients out of the refrigerator. "I thought I'd make some pasta. Will that work for everyone?"

"Yep," Traci said. "As long as you let me help."

"Nonsense. You're our guest."

"I'm not real good at sitting around, Charlie."

"Fine. Grab a knife and help me chop." Her dad looked her way. "Kimber?"

"Yes?"

"You just got out of the hospital. Go sit down with Gunnar and rest."

"Come on," Gunnar said. "We can sit in front of your shrine, Kimber."

Going back into the living room, they sat down on the couch. Curling up beside him, she winced.

"I saw that. Are you in a lot of pain?"

"Kind of. But it's not time for a pain reliever. I guess Dad was right. I do need to sit for a while."

Next thing she knew, he was shifting her so her feet were on his lap. He pulled off her boots. Traci had gone to her hotel room, packed her bags, and brought them to the hospital. "Gunnar, what are you doing?"

"Uh, taking off your boots and helping you get comfortable?"

"My mom will be coming downstairs any moment."

"I think she'll survive if she sees her girl getting a foot rub. Settle, 'kay?"

"Okay."

His strong fingers seemed to know exactly where to knead. After a couple of minutes, she stopped complaining, and a couple of minutes after that, she was fighting to keep her eyes open.

"Don't fight it, Kimber. If you want to take a nap, then do that."

"I just want to rest them. It's been a terrible couple of days."

"I know. They'll find out who attacked you. Then it will be better."

"I don't know about that," she said, with her eyes still closed. "It was dark and I didn't really see anyone."

"Try to keep positive."

Finding comfort in her closed-eye world, she said, "Gunnar, the attack wasn't the only hard thing. The shoot was tough. Being around Brett, with his questions and constant chatter was exhausting. Being back and being expected to just pick right up a life that I hadn't been a part of for months was hard too."

"But you did it, right?"

"Yeah." Gunnar was still rubbing her feet. The massage was making her the most relaxed she'd been in a week. "Tomorrow, we'll be on our way back."

"Yep. This isn't going to come out right, but I'm glad I got to come here and see all your pictures."

"They're just pictures. I'm not even sure why my parents put them up."

"Why would you say that, Kim?" her mother asked.

Her eyes popped back open. "Mom, I didn't know you were here."

Looking hurt, she said, "I just walked in. Just in time to hear you say that bit about the pictures. I can't believe you wouldn't think we would display them."

"But you weren't proud of me being a model."

Her mother sat down. "Of course we are."

"But you wanted me to go to college and get a job that used my brain."

Her mother looked over at the pictures. "You're right. You're a smart girl and we thought all this modeling business was just a little hobby. But we were proven wrong, weren't we?" She gestured to Kimber's one-time pride and joy, the cover of *Vogue*. "We learned that things like that aren't just about looks. It's about a woman working really hard and becoming a success in a difficult business." Her voice softened. "I'm sorry you thought we weren't proud. We're very, very proud of you. But of course, from the moment I held you for the first time, I knew you were special. We love you, Kimber."

And just like that, Kimber started crying. "I love you too."

Her mother got up and kissed her brow. "I'm going to get you a cup of tea. Gunnar, do you want anything?"

"No, ma'am. I'll just sit here with Kimber."

"I think that's a good idea."

After her mother joined her dad and Traci in the kitchen, Gunnar pulled Kimber into his arms. "You okay?"

"I think so."

"I think I'll hold you until you're sure, yeah?"

Nodding into his chest, Kimber closed her eyes again and let cleansing tears trickle down her cheeks and stain his shirt.

Even though she realized she was going to be just fine, she decided to lean against Gunnar anyway.

It didn't seem to bother him in the slightest.

CHAPTER 31

"Christmas isn't a season. It's a feeling."
—EDNA FERBER

Four days later

Kimber was pretty sure that Shannon had paid a small fortune for the use of the Bridgeport Community Theater. She'd also put in countless hours designing art for the stage, decorating the auditorium, and cleaning the space.

Dylan had shared that Shannon had also spent more time than he wanted to think about on the phone with all of the children's parents discussing costumes, payment plans, and rehearsal schedules. All this didn't include the many hours she'd spent on tryouts, classes, and run-throughs.

Gwen, who'd joined their little ragtag family a few months ago when their sister Traci had rescued her from an abusive boyfriend, had probably put in as much work as Shannon. Even though Gwen had recently given birth to the baby Traci had adopted, she didn't seem to mind the stress of it all, though. Actually, Kimber thought the nineteen-year-old part-time college student rather relished the opportunity to boss the girls and their parents around.

Kimber had helped as much as she could, but it hadn't been a lot. Shannon and her sisters were still babying her and cautioning her to not risk hurting her head.

Traci, Jennifer, their boyfriends and husbands, and even Shannon's parents had put in time to make the "First Annual Dance With Me *Nutcracker* Gala" a success.

In short, they were all invested now. But at the same time, Kimber reckoned that one of them was going to stuff a sock into Shannon's mouth if she didn't settle down.

They were only halfway through this first dress rehearsal and Shannon was acting as if the little girls were about to appear on Broadway for the first time.

Worried that she'd inadvertently tease her sister about putting stage moms to shame, Kimber elected to stay near the dressing room. She had lots of experience with changing clothes quickly and it was as far from Shannon as she could get.

"Kimber, I need that mouse now!"

It was not far enough. Looking at little Natalie, who was holding the Mouse King head while patiently waiting for Kimber to attach her tail, groaned. "Miss Shannon is sure mean tonight, Miss Kimber."

"She doesn't mean to be. She's just excited," Kimber said as she turned Natalie back around. "You don't have anything to worry about now, though. Your tail is on."

Natalie giggled. "Now all I've got to do is put this big head on."

Kimber stood up and helped her pop it over her head. "Perfect."

"Mouse King! Now!"

"Eek!" Natalie said before scampering to the stage.

When the music started again, Kimber glanced at her notes. "Sugar Plums, you girls ready?"

Shannon's five Sugar Plums, who were the most experienced dancers, stood up and gracefully walked to the door in their toe shoes. Shannon and Gwen had sewn the most beautiful long white tulle tutus for them and the girls looked like willowy angels.

"You girls look perfect. Miss Shannon is going to be pleased. Now, has everyone checked the ribbons on your shoes?" Shannon had warned her that sometimes the girls would forget to secure the ribbons and they could loosen and cause the dancers to fall or injure themselves.

"Yep, we're all set," Bethany replied.

Kimber leaned close. "You look beautiful. I bet almost as pretty as you're going to look tomorrow night at the dance."

Bethany beamed. "Thanks." After making sure that the other girls weren't listening, she whispered. "Does Jeremy seem excited?"

"Gunnar told me they went shopping for new clothes. Since they're guys, I'd say that's a sure sign that Jeremy's looking forward to it."

Bethany giggled. "Good."

"Sugar Plums?" Shannon called out.

"Break a leg," Kimber said as they glided out in perfect unison.

As the music turned to the final round of the "Waltz of the Flowers," Kimber leaned against one of the pillars off to the side and watched them perform their dance. They looked like true ballerinas and were moving in sync. Each of their steps looked flawless—well, as far as she could tell.

"You look a little wistful, sweetheart," Gunnar said as he approached. "Are you wishing you were up there or remembering a dance recital of your own?"

"Neither," she said with a smile. "I can't help but feel proud of those girls though. They look lovely. And, guess what? Jeremy's Bethany is dancing now."

Peeking over at them, his expression softened. "They do look real pretty." Leaning toward her, he pressed a quick kiss to her forehead. "Almost as pretty as you."

She was dressed in black leggings, a light pink Dance With Me T-shirt, and scuffed black flats. Her hair was in a ponytail and she most likely had half her mascara sliding down her cheeks. "Thanks," she said. He was helping to her to see that beauty had nothing to do with looks and everything to do with the happiness that shined out of a person.

"Thank you. When did you get here?"

"About an hour ago."

"Really? I didn't see you come in."

"I wanted to talk to Dylan and Traci for a minute. Then me and Matt were upstairs trying to get some of the lights to work."

Matt was Traci's husband. He was an obstetrician. "Does he know much about electric work?"

"Nope, but it turns out his dad is pretty handy. He came too."

"This really is a family affair."

He grinned. "We've all been saying the same thing. It's great."

"I'm surprised Jeremy isn't here."

"He might want to see Bethany, but he's a fifteen-year-old boy. He's staying as far away as possible from all those girls."

"I don't blame him. Ah, do I want to know why you met with Traci and Dylan? Did something happen that I don't know about?"

His open expression became more guarded. "Not at all. Just better to be on the safe side, right?"

She nodded but still felt compelled to add. "If something is going on I have the right to know about it . . ."

"Of course you do. But it's just a precaution."

It was hard for her not to argue but she'd promised herself to stop questioning everything. She nodded instead.

"Time for bows and curtsies. Where are the Russians?"

"I've got them!" Gwen called out from the other side of the stage. She and Traci had been in charge of the little ones, which was perfect since Officer Traci Lucky excelled at crowd control.

"Do you need to go out there and help?"

Kimber looked at the glob of children all either hopping around or waving to their parents, who were all taking about a million pictures with their smart phones. "No way. I'm on dressing room duty and that's where I'm going to stay."

"Kimber!"

"Yeah, I don't think so," Gunnar said just as she ran out to join the others.

As soon as Shannon flagged her over, Gunnar leaned his head back against the brick wall and pulled out his phone to check messages.

He hadn't lied to Kimber, not exactly. But she had received another note. Traci had intercepted it when it arrived in today's mail and opened it after taking it into the station. It had been just as threatening as the others. But it had also mentioned a Nutcracker Prince, which had given them enough alarm bells that they decided to attend both the dress rehearsals and the recital.

Traci had argued with Gunnar when he'd suggested they simply skirt Kimber away until the play was over. She'd stressed that Kimber needed to live her life, Shannon needed both of them, and furthermore . . . she didn't want Kimber to know about the latest message.

Gunnar had argued, saying that Kimber wasn't going to appreciate being left in the dark, but Traci had been too worried about Kimber's state of mind to consider letting her know.

Gunnar supposed she had a point. Only now, two weeks after

getting home, did Kimber look like herself. She hadn't been sleeping and had been extremely jumpy.

Peeking out, he spied her standing with her two sisters laughing and figured that Traci had a point. Kimber was happy now. Really happy. That counted for a lot.

After checking in with Jeremy, he put his phone away, just as a surge of little girls and their parents moved his way. Shannon and Kimber were in the thick of it, Shannon ordering everyone to be careful with their costumes and Kimber giggling with a girl holding a large mouse head.

He decided to go wait for his girl in the main theater.

Minutes after he sat down, Traci took a seat next to him. "Gunnar, I'm going to need you to get Kimber out of here," she said.

"Now?"

"Yeah. Dylan thinks our guy might be here."

"Where?"

"Calm down. You're not going to go all boyfriend on me. We'll handle this."

"All right, but Jeremy is about to get here. His girl is one of those Sugar Plum fairies."

"That's fine," she said, her voice as calm as ice. "Just go make up something and get her out. Now."

He didn't wait another second. Heading back to the dressing room, he had to stop several times, since all the girls seemed intent on walking in packs and their mothers kept stopping to talk in the middle of the hallway.

Five minutes passed. Then, it was close to seven before he finally made it to the dressing room door. But just as he was about to open it, he saw Bethany, Jeremy's girl.

"You better not open that, Mr. Law. Girls are changing inside."

Of course they were. "Can you do me a favor and go back in and ask Kimber to come on out."

"Okay, but she's kind of busy . . ."

"Just go ask." He attempted to smile and hoped he wasn't failing miserably. "Jeremy texted me. He's on his way."

She brightened. "He texted me too."

When he watched her close the dressing room door behind her, he tried to calm down. On the bright side, if she was in there with dozens of little girls, her attacker was not. That was a plus.

When Bethany popped out again, she grimaced. "I'm sorry, Mr. Law, but I think you're going to have to wait a while. Miss Shannon has Kimber safety pinning everyone's names on the costumes and organizing them."

"It's okay. See you tomorrow night."

Giving him a little wave, she ran out. Another five minutes passed, then another ten as the rest of the girls exited the room.

At last, Shannon opened the door and propped it open. "Gunnar, you're still here?"

"Yeah. You didn't lose Kimber in the mix, did you?"

"No. She's almost done."

"Good. Listen, I'm going to take her out for ice cream, okay?"

"Sure. Y'all have fun. Oh! And I heard you and Matt are the ones who got the lights working. Thanks so much."

"Anytime."

When Gwen motioned her back to the stage, Shannon said, "See you later."

"Yep. See you."

The moment she disappeared from the hallway, everything seemed a whole lot darker and more ominous. The skin on the back of his neck prickled. He had to get her out of there.

"Kimber, how's it going?" he asked as he entered the dressing room. Immediately, he was besieged with the scent of candy, little girl perfume, and the smell of old socks and shoes. "Whew."

She wrinkled her nose. "I know. It's awful, isn't it?"

"Ready?"

"Almost." She hung up another costume then closed the cabinet. "I've been on the clock for hours. Let me run down the hall to the bathroom and then I'll be all set."

"All right, sure." Still unable to ignore the sense that something wasn't quite right, he said, "Hey, how about I walk down there with you."

"To the bathroom? Uh, no. I think I've got this." She handed him her purse. "I'll be back in five minutes. Sit tight," she added as she ran out the door.

Gunnar couldn't help but grin. His Kimber was usually so controlled, he got a kick whenever she did something that was so "normal." After picking up two empty water bottles that had rolled into a corner, he glanced at the time on his phone. It had only been two minutes.

But he couldn't wait around another minute. Picking up her purse again as well as her black puffy coat, he turned off the light and walked into the hall. To his right, a faint stream of light shone out of the auditorium. He could hear faint sounds of conversation floating his way. To his left, he didn't hear a thing.

Another three minutes had passed. He took a step left, then stopped himself. What was he going to do? Stand outside the bathroom door like a creepy stalker? That would freak her out.

Worse, if he mentioned how it was taking her longer than she said, Kimber would probably get annoyed. He wasn't around a lot of women all the time, but he was around enough to know that five minutes in the bathroom usually meant ten. She was probably fixing her lipstick or something—she was often doing that.

Except, he had her purse. And another minute had gone by.

He took another step down the hall. Told himself that he was overreacting. Then walked closer. He couldn't deny it, he was starting to get worried.

"Gunnar? What are you doing down there?" Traci called out. "Is there a reason that you're standing in a dark hallway holding my sister's purse?"

He felt like God had just given him a lifeline. Even if Kimber got mad at him, he was going to risk it. She was too important to him to wait another second longer. "Hey Trace, come here a sec, would you?"

Some of the humor left her expression as she approached. "What's up?"

"Look, I realize I sound ridiculous, but I'm kind of worried about Kimber. She ran down to the bathroom over ten minutes ago. She said she'd be back in five."

As he'd half-expected, she looked skeptical. "Gunnar—"

"I know. Believe me, I know I sound like I'm worrying about nothing. But would you go check on her?"

"You're really worried, aren't you?"

He nodded. "I can't explain it, but something doesn't feel right."

"You know what? Sure. Come on, you can stand outside the door. If she gets annoyed we'll just tell her that's too bad. We care."

"I appreciate it. Thanks," he murmured as they walked the rest of the way. "I'm sorry if I'm acting overprotective. It's just that—"

"I know." Traci reached out and squeezed his arm. "Don't ever apologize for caring so much." She smiled as she opened the door. "Now, I'll be right back."

He braced himself for Kimber to come flying out, chewing on him for worrying. But all that happened was Traci calling Kimber's name.

When the door opened again, everything about Traci was different. "There's blood near the sink and no Kimber. Gunnar, are you sure she went this way?"

"Not positive but about eighty percent sure. Where else would she have run down the hall to use the restroom?"

She picked up her phone. "Dylan, where you at?" After a pause, she said, "Listen. We've got a prob. Kimber's gone."

As she relayed the story, she walked down the hall and turned on the light switch. "Yep. Call in reinforcements. My sister's in danger."

CHAPTER 32

"A merry heart does good, like medicine."
—PROVERBS 17:22

Brett was gripping her wrist so tightly, Kimber was sure he was cutting off all the circulation in her right arm. The pain competed with the burning on her cheek from where he'd slapped her.

She still couldn't believe what was happening. Slight, self-centered, chatty Brett had been the source of all her stalking.

He'd penned notes from Peter, hoping to make her uneasy enough to lean on him more. He'd attacked her after their meal at the restaurant because he'd been so angry that she wasn't going to take any more jobs.

And now she was sure he'd become completely unhinged. All she could do was hold on and keeping hoping and praying that she could either get free of Brett's grip or that Gunnar and Traci would rescue her.

But before she did any of that, she just had to hang on.

"Brett, you're hurting me," Kimber protested for at least the fourth time. "Can't we stop for a few seconds? I need to catch my breath." If he released her, she might be able to fight back and maybe even injure him enough to escape.

But it didn't look like it was going to happen anytime soon. She couldn't find a single ounce of compassion in his expression. Instead, he looked even more determined. He twisted her wrist painfully as he pulled her forward. "Stop fighting me. You're not going to win. Now shut up."

That was easily the nicest thing he'd said since she'd opened the metal door in the women's room and found him leaning up against the sink. She'd freaked out, opening her mouth to scream.

And he had promptly covered her mouth with his hand and called her a long list of profane names.

She'd been so shaken, both by his hand over her mouth and the things he was saying, she'd frozen. That's when he'd slapped her hard enough to make her see stars, then grabbed her wrist and yanked her to the bathroom door.

And what had she done? Instead of anything of worthwhile, all she'd done was say that she needed to wash her hands first. She'd jerked toward the sink, tripping when he grabbed her again, and cut her forearm on the ancient metal faucet. When she'd dared to gasp, he'd hit her hard and again threatened her, telling her to stay silent.

Next thing she knew, he was pulling her down the hall in bare feet and into an alley. All told, the whole abduction had happened in less than five minutes. The only positive was that her cut had bled enough to leave a thin trail on the linoleum floor.

"Brett, please!" When he finally paused, she inhaled, preparing to do whatever it took to escape.

But then she only felt white-hot pain as he hit her again.

* * *

When Kimber woke up, she found herself handcuffed to a latch on her seatbelt. Her other arm was gripped tightly in Brett's right hand, and he was driving through the narrow streets of Bridgeport one handed, barreling toward the highway.

Even though her head was throbbing and she felt hazy, a thousand questions raced in her head. From the most basic, like *why was he doing this* and *how had he known where she was* to the most mundane—*how in the world had he even known where to get a set of handcuffs?*

When he turned and finally released her arm, she whimpered as the blood began to flow again.

He smiled. "Guess you're not so tough anymore, huh?"

"I have never been tough. You know that."

"I know. You've always acted like you were better than me. Better than most of us. Better than all of us." He gritted his teeth as he drove his nondescript gray rental sedan onto the entrance ramp and accelerated.

Realizing he wasn't making a single concession for either the sleet or the oncoming traffic, she screamed. "Brett, you're going to get us killed!"

A semi driver sounded his horn as Brett narrowly managed to swerve into the next lane.

At last, Brett placed both his hands on the steering wheel and started weaving through traffic, Kimber guessed it was safe to talk.

"Brett, I'm not trying to be difficult, but I really don't understand what's going on. Why did you come find me in Ohio?"

"I'm taking you back, Kimber."

"Back to where?" She really had no clue what was going through his head.

"Where do you think? New York." Looking back at the road,

236

he cursed and slammed on the brakes. The car retaliated by fish-tailing. Seconds later, he darted around another semi.

Kimber bit her lip to stop herself from screaming again, but she was really starting to wonder if she was going to make it out of this car alive. Brett seemed determined to kill them on the road.

When he increased his speed and flew through the inter-change she decided to keep an eye out for cops. Surely someone was going to report his driving soon.

"You were my moneymaker, Kimber. I had plans for you. I promised people I'd get you for them. But what did you do? You acted like you didn't owe me a thing."

"This is about my modeling?" She really was floored. Sure, she'd had some success, but she was no Tyra Banks and was never going to be. His expectations didn't even come close to the reality of her career.

"What do you think? Of course it's about modeling. I needed you. I depended on you. I created you. You owe me."

Everything he said was giving her chills. Brett was acting as if she was his property, like she was his Frankenstein or something. Everything inside of her wanted to yell. Wanted to give him a piece of her mind . . . but there was no way she was going to say anything that might make things worse than they already were.

As he continued to weave in and out of traffic, surging forward, braking hard, and then cutting people off, she knew she was going to have to rely on both prayer and the good sense that the Lord gave her . . . and the years of experience she'd had of holding her tongue with her parents.

Kimber also couldn't help but reflect on the recent traumas of some of her new friends. Dylan's sister Jennifer had been viciously attacked and lived in fear for years until her brother's love, her therapist's compassion, and the love of her new boyfriend helped ease the way into beginning to heal her trauma.

Most recently, Gwen had been the target of a drug dealer and her own brother. She'd persevered, though, and was now healthy and looking forward to a much brighter future.

If those two women could survive their harrowing experiences, Kimber knew she could do the same. Besides, she had too much to live for now.

When Brett let out another string of curses, she knew she had to do something until someone on the road called 911 and reported his driving or Traci and Dylan and the rest of the Bridgeport Police Department found them.

When they finally got to a somewhat empty stretch of road, she said, "Where are we going, anyway?"

"Why do you want to know?"

Why did he think? Struggling to keep all signs of sarcasm out of her voice, she shrugged. "Just curious. Are we driving to New York?"

For the first time, he looked unsure. "We're driving as far as we can get today. We need to put as much distance between us and your new family."

"Ah." Pretending she wasn't handcuffed, bleeding, and fighting a killer headache, she crossed her legs. "Well, I hope you have money because I had to leave without my purse. I don't even have my driver's license."

"Like I would ever let you drive."

He was such a jerk. However, since he did look slightly less manic, she figured the conversation was doing them both some good. "I'll have you know that I'm a good driver. I passed my test on the first try. I scored a hundred percent on the written test too."

He nodded. "That doesn't surprise me. You've always been smart."

That almost sounded nice. She was making progress. Pushing back the terrible fear that he was going to take her to some isolated shack where no one was ever going to find her, she sought to keep the conversation going. "You know, you never told me what you've been doing since I left New York. How's Jill?" Jill was his long-time live-in girlfriend who Kimber and all of her friends had regarded as both slightly difficult and also in need of a medal for putting up with Brett 24-7.

He sped up, likely going close to ninety miles an hour now. "Why are you asking about her? What do you know?"

Oh, crap. What had she done? "Nothing," she said in a rush. "I was just asking."

"Jill left me. Did you know that?"

"No. Of course I didn't. I wouldn't have asked if I did. I'm on your side, Brett. You should—"

He pressed on the accelerator, she watched the speedometer edge up to ninety-five, ninety-eight, one hundred. "She said I was too fixated on you, Kimber." His voice turned even more clipped. "She said that I talked about you too much. That I thought about you too much. She couldn't handle it." He looked over at her. "Even though I kept telling her that I wouldn't have been fixated on you if you hadn't left me the way you did."

"I'm sorry. Hey, would you please slow down?"

If he heard a word she'd just said, he didn't let on. "We had a fight. Yelling, screaming. She threw a vase at me. It was Waterford, Kimber. She broke my Waterford vase!"

Cars were honking. She was now afraid to look at the speedometer, she was sure it now read way over a hundred. The little rental was obviously not made to go that fast—at least not very well and in the sleet. This was very bad. She was going to die before she ever told Gunnar that she loved him and that she wanted to help him raise Jeremy. She was going to die before she told her sisters how much she appreciated them. Before she ever looked both her parents in the eye and thanked them for adopting her and loving her.

Then, in the passenger side mirror, she saw some blinking lights. Had help finally arrived?

She had to get him to slow down and focus on her before he did anything even more reckless. Grasping for straws, she pulled up every single hurt emotion she could summon and started crying.

Soon, her tears had turned to real ones.

But it seemed she'd been wrong. It didn't appear to make a single difference to him.

Brett kept ranting about Jill, his pain, Kimber's betrayal, and how much he hated Ohio. Through the side mirror, the lights were brighter. She realized now there were multiple vehicles in pursuit.

Realizing once again that everything about the whole situation was out of her control—with the handcuff locking her to the seat, she wasn't even going to be able to escape if the car crashed and went up in flames—Kimber put her head back against the seat and closed her eyes. She prayed for help and strength. She thought of Gunnar and how even their short relationship had been such a blessing.

She simply let her tears trail down her cheeks. The whole situation was out of her hands.

CHAPTER 33

"'Peace on the earth, goodwill to men,
From heaven's all-gracious King.'
The world in solemn stillness lay,
To hear the angels sing."
—E. H. SEARS

"We're gaining on them," Traci called out as she weaved the flashing police cruiser down the highway. Beside her, Dylan was both talking on the cruiser's radio and typing things into his phone.

From his position in the backseat, Gunnar stayed silent and kept his attention on the gray Hyundai sedan up ahead. There was no way he was going to do a single thing to make either of them regret giving into his pleas to allow him into the car.

Even he knew he shouldn't be in the vehicle. Traci had tried to make him stay behind. But, to his surprise, Dylan had been the one to allow his ride-along.

"As much as I don't want you in our way, there's no way I can ask you to stay behind," he'd said. "If it was Shannon in that car, I'd be doing anything I could to be by her side."

"That's good to know, because there's no way I'm sitting here in this theater while Kimber's in trouble." After seeing her blood on the floor, Gunnar knew he would do whatever it took to help.

"You better keep quiet, though," Traci said with a glare.

"I will. I'll sit in the backseat and won't say a word until you tell me I can pull her into my arms."

Dylan's expression had stayed relatively blank, reminding Gunnar that Kimber's rescue wasn't a sure thing. A lot could happen that was out of their control.

Gunnar knew that. But, he also felt that Kimber's ordeal was going to end on a positive note. After all, from the time Traci had realized that Kimber was gone, things had been on their side. Two people outside had seen Brett pull an obviously struggling Kimber into a gray sedan. After debating whether or not to get involved for fifteen minutes, they'd called the police and had been able to give a pretty good description of Brett's vehicle.

Because of that, the Bridgeport Police had been able to work with other local authorities to be on the lookout for him. After a couple of false starts and some misinformation, Dylan and Traci learned that Brett had been taking Kimber first on the interstate heading north and then on a little-used state highway.

Now their vehicle and several county sheriff cars were getting close. They just had to hope and pray that Brett wouldn't either lose control of his car or hurt Kimber and that he wasn't armed and wouldn't attempt to shoot any of the law enforcement in pursuit.

Every time Gunnar thought about that, he felt weak. That was a lot to ask for. Was it too much?

After a terse discussion, Dylan and Traci agreed to let the local sheriffs take the lead. Their lights were flashing and sirens were blaring.

But it still didn't look like Brett was slowing down or pulling over. If anything, it looked like he was driving more erratically than ever.

Unable to keep his silence any longer, Gunnar blurted, "What's going on?"

"My guess is that this Brett character isn't even aware that he's being followed," Dylan said.

"Seriously?" he bit out. He felt like everyone in twenty miles could hear the sirens on the multiple cars following him.

"I've seen it happen," Traci said, her voice as hard as ice as she continued to follow. "A person gets so set on his or her plans they aren't aware of much around them. Plus, he might be on something. That could do it."

Gunnar swallowed hard. Traci hadn't said anything he hadn't already thought, but it was still hard to hear those words out loud. "He better not be on drugs."

"Sorry I mentioned it," Traci said.

"Oh, hey now. Looks like Brett is aware now," Dylan said.

Gunnar leaned forward, his hands fisted on his knees as he watched the scene unfold in front of them.

The gray sedan swerved, then suddenly braked hard, causing the back end to fishtail. As soon as he righted himself, Brett accelerated and weaved through traffic. One cruiser was on his tail, the other had moved to his left, while the shoulder of the road was on his right. The guy was trapped.

While Dylan talked on the radio again, Traci sped up.

Now they were only about the distance of four cars away. Brett's car weaved again. For a moment, Gunnar thought he was going to veer off onto the shoulder of the road, and maybe even the road just beyond them. But then, whatever the sheriff had called out to them must have finally made an impression because he started to slow down at last.

Gunnar exhaled.

"Come on, Brett," Dylan muttered. "Don't be stupid."

For the next five minutes, Gunnar could hardly breathe. Brett slowed, darted to the shoulder, returned to the road, then finally drew to a complete stop.

The sheriff was on him immediately, yelling something with a pistol raised.

Gunnar could hardly stand to watch from a distance.

Seconds later, the driver door was open and Kimber's agent was exiting the vehicle with his hands up.

Immediately, the sheriff had him against the hood of the car and was cuffing him.

Traci pulled up. Right before she and Dylan exited, she pointed a finger at him. "I know you want to get out and run to Kimber's side, but you're gonna need to hang in there another couple of minutes. Okay?"

"Okay, fine. I don't care where I am, just go get her. Make sure she's all right."

He wasn't even sure if either of them had heard his last words. They were rushing over to the car, Traci leading the way.

Gunnar watched intently as the passenger-side door of the sedan was opened and Traci leaned in.

Gunnar leaned forward too. Waiting for Kimber to get out.

But she didn't. What was going on?

He got out of the cruiser so he could see better.

While Traci was still crouched by the door, Dylan barked an order. Minutes later, one of the sheriffs brought over something that looked like a bolt cutter.

Gunnar sucked in a breath. What had happened to her? He took a step forward, but then forced himself to stay put. He'd promised, but it was killing him.

Traci moved to the side, then Dylan and the other officer leaned in with the bolt cutters. Minutes later, Dylan reached in and carefully helped Kimber out.

She was alive and was standing up.

Tears formed in his eyes as he realized that his prayers had been answered. She was going to be okay.

His world got even better when Traci looked his way and motioned him forward. She met him about halfway there. "Calm down, Romeo. You can see her, but an ambulance is on the way."

"Why? What did he do to her?" A dozen horrible thoughts entered his head. "Is . . . is she okay?"

"She's a little beat up, stressed out, and one of her wrists is raw and chewed up. Brett had her handcuffed to the seatbelt latch. But I think she's going to be okay." She smiled. "She wants to see you."

That was all he needed to hear. Striding past the many law enforcement officers who were milling around, Gunnar reached her side. Pausing impatiently while Kimber's brother-in-law talked quietly to her, he studied her carefully. Like Traci had said, his girl looked beat up and in pain. But she also looked like she was coherent and not too much worse for wear.

He hoped that was the truth.

Then, she turned to him and the best look of wonder filled her eyes. "Gunnar. You're here."

"I had to be," he said as Dylan moved away. Two seconds later, he was gently pulling her into a hug.

She was trembling. "Oh, Gunnar. I . . . I was so scared."

"I know. I was too. But you're okay now."

She pulled away slightly, obviously needing to see his face. "I didn't think I was going to survive. I thought he was going to kill us on that road."

"I know, but he didn't," he repeated as he gently ran a hand along her spine. "You're going to be all right, baby."

Still looking worried, she added, "I never thought I was going to be able to tell you that I loved you. I was so afraid you'd never know that."

Tears filled his eyes as he wrapped his arms around her. "You don't have to worry about that no more," he drawled. "I know now, and I'm so glad I do, because I love you too."

When she relaxed against him, her trembling finally subsiding, Gunnar closed his eyes. He had her back, she was in his arms, and they loved each other.

All he wanted to do was hold her tight and never let her go.

CHAPTER 34

"When they saw the star, they rejoiced."
—MATTHEW 2:10

Twenty-four hours later, Kimber felt as if everything that had been so broken in her life was at last coming together. Her rocky relationship with her parents had been smoothed over at last. Her stalker was gone, her career was now tucked firmly in her past, and Brett, her loser agent, was now safely behind bars.

She wasn't beating herself up about her future anymore, either. A lot of soul searching had taken place during Brett's wild ride. Most importantly, she'd realized that she didn't need to have a smooth, set-in-stone plan for her future. No one cared what she wanted to do or what her name meant in modeling circles—especially not the people who loved her. They just wanted her to be happy.

She thought that was a pretty good thing to concentrate on as well. Being happy was a wonderful goal.

So, while her life was currently a little messy, it was slowly mending together nicely. Kimber had a feeling her future wasn't always going to be perfect and well put together. Instead, she thought that it was going to be more like her wrist now. A little scarred but just fine. Instead of perfection, she was going to settle with living in the real world.

She was actually starting to think that maybe her scars gave her a little bit of character anyway.

"Do you want more tea?"

Kimber looked up at Jeremy. Since Shannon was going crazy at the theater near Dance With Me, getting ready for the last rehearsal before tomorrow night's Nutcracker performance, Gunnar had brought Kimber to his house for the day.

She'd taken a long nap and then had been hanging out and watching TV on the couch in Gunnar's living room for most of the afternoon. Well, now she was hanging out with Jeremy. Gunnar had had needed to do some work in his office, so Jeremy was "Kimber sitting."

Gunnar's phrase, not hers.

Looking up at the teenager, who had really come out of his shell of late, she handed him her mug. "Thanks. That would be great."

"No prob."

When he returned, a mug in one hand and a plate of sugar cookies in the other, Kimber sat up straighter. "You have cookies too?"

He gave her another grin that spoke volumes about how silly he thought she was. "Your friend Jennifer brought them over while you were sleeping."

"That's so sweet." As usual, Jennifer had made something so simple into small works of art. "Oh! They're nutcrackers!"

Still holding that plate, he nodded. "I guess they're for the ballet."

She gave him a break and took the plate so he could sit down at last.

Looking at the simple white outlines on each, Kimber said, "These cookies are perfect. I like my cookies light on the icing."

"Not me. I like them chock-full of frosting."

"That makes sense," she said as she plucked a cookie off the pile and set down the plate on the coffee table. "I used to like lots of frosting too. Hey, where's yours? Aren't you going to have some?"

He shook his head. "Nah. They're supposed to be for you."

"Of course I'm going to share with you." She held out the plate. "Take one."

After a second's hesitation, he took two. "Thanks." He bit down and smiled. "They're good."

"So are you ready for tonight's dance?"

A shadow filled his eyes. "I guess. Gunnar picked up Bethany's corsage while I was at school."

"Did you choose the wrist corsage?" She'd recommended that style when they'd talked about the dance a couple of days before.

"Yep. And I picked pink roses."

"Good job. What about your clothes? Are you all set?"

"Yeah. I'm wearing khakis, a button down, loafers, and a navy blazer."

Jeremy looked like he didn't know whether to be excited or worried about the outfit. Smiling softly, she said, "Sounds like Gunnar took you shopping, as well."

"Yeah. My friend Phillip told me what everyone was wearing." After peeking down the hallway, he added, "Gunnar was really nice about it. He didn't even complain about how much all the clothes cost."

"That's because I'm not going to complain about clothes, Jeremy," Gunnar said as he walked into the room and joined Kimber on the couch. "Besides, we can't have you looking like you don't know any better. I mean, you are taking the head Sugar Queen or whatever she is to the dance."

Kimber shared a look with Jeremy, who rolled his eyes. "Bethany is the lead Sugar Plum Fairy, Gunnar. You need to remember that."

"I'm trying." He ran a hand over his eyes. "There's just been a little bit going on lately."

Kimber winked at Jeremy. "I guess we could give you a break then. What do you think, Jeremy?"

Jeremy grinned. "Yeah, maybe."

"Thanks, guys," Gunnar said sarcastically.

After talking a couple more minutes, Jeremy took off to his room, saying that he needed to go get ready.

When they were alone, Gunnar kissed Kimber lightly on the lips. "How are you feeling?"

"Pretty good." She actually felt like she'd gone for a wild ride with a royal jerk across southern Ohio, but she didn't see any sense in dwelling on that.

He reached for her bandaged wrist. "What about this? Do you want some pain reliever?"

"I'll take you up on it later. Right now, all I want to do is sit in front of your fireplace and just appreciate that I'm here." She loved how he encouraged her to simply relax.

"That's all I want to do too." Lowering his voice, he said, "Yesterday scared the heck out of me. I can't tell you how many prayers I said when I was in the back of that police cruiser."

"I said quite a few prayers too. I was pretty sure Brett was going to get us in a wreck. All I kept thinking about was how stupid I've been, overthinking about everything in my life. I was so afraid I wasn't going to get the chance to make changes." Knowing Gunnar was listening intently, she shifted so she could be nestled more securely in his arms. "But most of all, I just wanted to see you and my sisters again. I didn't realize how alone I was until I met Shannon and Traci. And now I have you too."

"Yes, you do. I'm going to do everything I can to keep you near, Kimber. I don't intend to ever let you go again."

When he said things like that, she felt like swooning. "That's one thing you're not going to have to worry about. As far as I'm concerned, you saved me from my former life. I'm not going anywhere."

When he kissed her again, she wrapped her arms around his neck and held on tight.

CHAPTER 35

"A merry heart does good like medicine."
—PROVERBS 17:22

The gym was covered with a ton of white tulle, streamers, glitter, and about a thousand stars hanging from the ceiling. Obviously a bunch of kids and probably just as many moms had spent all day decorating the place.

Jeremy supposed it was real pretty. The lights were dim, the music was good, and everyone looked like they were having a great time.

Unfortunately he was starting to wish he hadn't come. It was now a quarter to nine. Bethany said she would be there by now but she wasn't. He didn't blame her for being stuck at rehearsal, but he still wished she would have at least texted him or something.

At first, after going to Finn's dinner and arriving with the popular senior's huge group of friends, Jeremy had been feeling pretty good. No one had questioned why Bethany had to arrive late. Instead, everyone had acted impressed—both with the fact that she had a starring role in the ballet and that he was her date.

But after a while, everyone had started dancing and he was now standing by himself near the door.

He felt like a loser.

He was pretty sure that out of everyone in the room, he was the only person who was standing alone. He hated that.

"Jeremy, are you okay?" Mrs. Keeperman asked as she approached.

His favorite teacher, who usually only wore baggy khaki pants, old-school Converse tennis shoes, and sweaters was dressed up in a dark-purple dress. She was even wearing high heels and red lipstick. It was enough to spin him out of the cycle he'd been living in for the last two hours. "Wow, Mrs. K. You look great."

She rolled her eyes. "Everyone's been teasing me from the moment I got here. That's what I get for not wearing my usual clothes."

He shrugged. "Maybe so, but you still look nice." Feeling like a dork, he said, "Are you having a good time?"

"Even though I've almost tripped twice, I'm pretty sure that I'm having a better time than you are. You look like you'd rather be anywhere else."

"I'm okay."

"I could have sworn that you had a date for this shindig. Did I get that wrong . . . ? Or did something happen?"

"No. I do have a date. I mean, I thought I did . . ." His voice drifted off. What was there to say, anyway? He had a plastic container holding a flower corsage in one hand and a silent cell phone in the other. If Bethany had been trying to get a hold of him, she would've by now. "I'm probably not going to stay very long."

Her expression sobered even more. "For what it's worth, I'm sure sorry about whatever happened. But I'm glad you came here anyway."

"Why's that?" The words escaped before he could stop them.

Mrs. Keeperman shrugged. "I've always thought we get too much credit for doing the easy stuff. Who cares if you do things that everyone expects you to do or always say the right thing because no one will get mad? But doing that hard stuff? The things that hurt and cause pain and maybe even make someone think twice about you? Well, that's what counts in the end. At least that's what I've always thought."

Had he done that? Thinking about learning to survive those other foster placements, it had been hard. Learning to trust Gunnar enough to be himself? That had been harder, but it had been worth it.

Was he doing that now, believing in Bethany and waiting around for her even though she might never show up? Maybe, but he wasn't sure about that. "Uh, thanks?"

She chuckled. "No problem." She looked like she was about to say something more but groaned instead. "Oh, great. I just got flagged over by Mr. Pauly. He better not be about to ask me to hunt down some wandering kids. My feet are going to kill me."

She left without another word, but her grumpy statement had sparked a smile out of him. It looked like she'd been taking her own advice and her "hard stuff" was walking around the gym in high heels.

"Jeremy, what's going on?" Phillip called out as he and three other guys approached. "Did you not see us waving for you to come over?"

"Sorry, no. I was um just talking to Mrs. Keeperman."

"We saw," Mark, another one of his buddies, said. "We decided we better come get you."

"Why?" He realized then that their dates weren't standing nearby. Like not at all. "Wait, where are your dates?"

"Ellie, Carson, and Alyssia ran to the bathroom together," Mark said. "I don't know where everyone else is."

"Bethany's over near the back," Phillip said.

"What? I didn't see her come in."

"That's what I told her. She walked in the back door and was looking for you. When I saw you were up here, I told her I'd come get you."

"Wow. Thanks."

Phillip grinned as they started walking through the crowd. "By the way, you owe me."

"Because?"

"Because Erik Mason has been circling her like a shark. It's obvious that she's sick of him already."

Craning his head, Jeremy switched from trying to locate Bethany to searching for Erik—who was one of the few guys in the school who made sure to tell Jeremy that he didn't hang out with foster kids. "What's Erik been doing? Has he been touching her or something?"

"Not anymore," Connor said. "When he tried to put his arm around her waist, she glared at him."

"Good. I can't believe all this has been happening while I was on the other side of the gym."

"It doesn't matter. She came here to be your date."

"Yeah."

Phillip pulled him over to the side. "Look, I've got to go. Carson's coming back. But listen, Carson has told me what Bethany's told her. She really likes you, man. You need to stop worrying so much, it's all good now."

He nodded as the guys left. Some of their dates looked his way, but to his surprise, none of them were looking at him like they wished he was dead. Instead, a couple of them even almost smiled.

Then, at last, he found Bethany. She was in a dark-red dress that was fitted at the top and had a full skirt that brushed the tops of her knees. Her hair was in a complicated-looking bun. She looked like a ballerina and the prettiest girl in the whole gym.

She was also staring directly at him.

Everything inside of him kind of shut down and then opened again. He liked her. He liked her a lot. And what did it matter if half the school was going to be gossiping about them? They already were.

And hadn't he been through a whole lot worse? Thinking of Kimber and Gunnar, he felt his cheeks redden. What did a little bit of embarrassment have to do with what they'd just gone through?

All the sudden, he stopped worrying about what everybody thought and started through the crowd.

Jeremy knew the instant Bethany realized he was walking directly toward her. Her eyes widened and then she smiled.

He felt his confidence rise and he picked up his pace. "Sorry," he murmured as he almost ran over a pair of freshman.

Still obviously watching him, Bethany's smile grew.

And that had been all he'd needed to see. It was going to be okay. Whatever happened next, it was all going to be okay.

Hopefully.

"Hey," he said. "I'm really sorry I didn't see you walk in. I was standing at the other door."

"It's okay. I meant to look for you right away, but everyone started talking to me. And my phone died. I'm sorry I didn't text you."

"It's fine." And that was true, because it was fine now.

She smiled up at him. She had on more makeup than usual and her brown eyes looked bright.

"You look really pretty."

"Thanks." She looked away.

"I brought you a corsage."

Her eyes widened. "Have you been holding it this whole time?"

He nodded. "Yeah, but it's okay. Here." He handed her the

box, silently thanking Kimber for suggesting a wrist corsage instead of one that had to be pinned on. He could only imagine how awkward that would be, with half the school watching him attempt to pin the flowers on the tiny strap of her dress.

She carefully opened the plastic container and pulled out the flowers. He set the box on a nearby table and helped her put it on her wrist. When it was in place, she looked up at him and smiled. "I love it. Thank you."

Even though he felt all their friends watching them, he reached for her hand. "It looks better on you than in the box."

She laughed. "So . . ."

"So do you want to dance?" he asked. When she nodded, he carefully led her through all the other couples who were slow dancing.

Holding her hand in his, seeing his buddies' looks of approval, Jeremy felt like everything in his world had changed again.

This time for the better.

CHAPTER 36

"It is never too late to live happily ever after."
—UNKNOWN

It had been the craziest night. Rehearsal had been so long and chaotic, which was saying a lot since everyone knew that Miss Kimber had been abducted the night before. Everything that had gone wrong had, and one of the girls in her main ballet had come down with strep throat and had to quit, which had meant that they'd had to rechoreograph the whole thing.

By the time they'd finished the run-through, Bethany had grabbed her dress and followed Gwen into a private bathroom in the back of the building. Gwen had let Bethany store her things there. She'd even offered to take Bethany's dance things back to the dance studio at the end of the night so she could head right over to the dance.

She'd been so ready to get out of there and go to the dance,

Bethany had hardly cared if Miss Shannon was going to be mad at her or not.

When she'd finally walked into the gym, she'd thought Jeremy was going to be at the door. When she didn't see him at first, she'd really thought Jeremy had decided to skip the dance. Or worse—that he'd take some other girl and was going to ignore her the whole time.

Of course, that had been stupid. He was there, he'd just been waiting at the other side.

And now, here she was, with her hands linked around his neck, his hands loosely holding her waist, and they were swaying to Bruno Mars. It was awesome.

Even better than all of that, he hadn't looked away from her once, like he didn't want to be anywhere else in the world than with her. And that was perfect, but she didn't want to be anywhere else either.

"Hey, are you okay?" he whispered.

"Yes."

"Sure?"

"Very sure." She smiled up at him. "I'm really glad you still wanted to go to the dance with me even though I had to come so late."

He looked away, like he was trying to come up with the right words but he couldn't think of what they were. "I wasn't sure what to do about twenty minutes ago, if you want to know the truth. A couple of hours ago, sitting at home, I started thinking that maybe I shouldn't have made Gunnar buy me clothes for it and everything."

"You look really nice."

He rolled his eyes. "Whatever. What I'm trying to say is that I didn't know if you were going to show up. I thought maybe you would ditch me."

"I wouldn't do that."

"I was being an idiot."

"I'll tell you about rehearsal later, but for now, I'll just share that it was terrible. I'm glad we're dancing now."

"Yeah. Me too." He pulled her a little bit closer. And his hand kind of felt heavier on her back, like he suddenly didn't want to let her go. Looking troubled, he said, "I kind of lied about worrying about my clothes. The fact is, Gunnar said that there was no way I couldn't not come." He lowered his voice. "He told me that I needed to see this through."

"This?"

"You and me."

She liked the sound of that. She liked that they were a "you and me." It sounded permanent. Good.

As more couples joined them, the space got even more confined and he pulled her closer so the couple to her right didn't knock her over. Now her chest was practically touching his and her lips were almost against his neck. She could feel the heat from his body and smell the soap on his skin. It felt good to be right next to him. Good and a little intense. She wondered if everyone around them was watching.

"Sorry," Jeremy said when he stepped back. "I thought he was going to step on your foot."

"I didn't mind." When he smiled at her, she gathered her courage. "Hey, uh, Jeremy?"

"Yeah?"

"Why did you worry so much?"

"I guess I got scared. I let all the crap that I was worried about in my head get the best of me. I started thinking that maybe you'd get smart and would want someone better."

Now he was starting to confuse her. "What do you mean by better?"

"You know. A guy who isn't a foster kid with no parents and not a lot of money."

"Stop. You're not that."

"That sums me up, Bethany."

"You're more than that. And you can't help either of those things."

"Maybe not."

"I know you can't." Before she could stop herself, she added, "And one more thing. I don't care that you're 'just a foster kid.' You think about things more than most other boys. You are more mature. You don't do stupid stuff either. I like how you are, Jeremy. I don't want you to change."

"I'm going to get adopted soon."

"When you do, I'm going to go to the ceremony with you. It's going to be great."

He chuckled then smiled at her. "If we weren't dancing in the middle of the whole school, I'd kiss you for saying that."

"Maybe you should kiss me anyway."

"You won't get mad?"

"Why don't you kiss me and find out?"

And so he did. Right there during the last dance of the night.

CHAPTER 38

*"Without love and laughter there is no joy;
live among love and laughter."*
—HORACE

Months later

After much discussion, they'd decided to keep the meeting to the three of them. It felt right—like how they'd started. Sitting in the living room of Kimber's house, the beautiful, modern house that Gunnar had built for someone else but later married Kimber in, Shannon giggled.

Kimber shared a smile with her. It was a fact. Traci Rossi was hopeless at opening champagne bottles.

At last, on her third attempt, the cork went flying through the air.

Shannon clapped and cheered, which had earned her a put-upon glare from her sister.

"You know, for a know-it-all cop, you sure can't open a bottle of champagne too well," Kimber said.

"Ha ha. I didn't grow up drinking fancy stuff like this. A beer has always been good enough for me."

"We could have split a six pack, Traci," Shannon said. It wasn't like any of them were big drinkers anyway.

"No, I agree with you. This is a special occasion," Traci said as she carefully poured the sparkling wine into the three flutes. Picking up her glass, she raised it high. "It's not all that often three sisters get to celebrate two years of knowing each other."

"Amen to that," Kimber said as she reached for her own flute.

Shannon picked up her own, thinking Traci had, indeed, made a very good point. Tonight marked the second anniversary of the first day that they'd met.

She'd had every intention of making a big deal about their first anniversary the year before, but life had gotten in the way. She'd still been all moony over her newlywed status. Then there had been Gwen, her baby Bridge, Traci's adoption of him—and then her engagement and quick marriage to Matt.

In the midst of it, Kimber had been working nonstop, taking just "one more modeling job" again and again. Now, here they all were, married, and Kimber was a perfectly happy stay-at-home mom to Jeremy. It turned out that she loved carpooling, helping with homework, volunteering at the dance studio, and Jennifer's cooking lessons.

They were all doing really well.

Kimber cleared her throat. "Ah, Shannon? I don't know if you noticed, but we're all sitting here, waiting to say cheers."

"Sorry. I was just thinking . . . well, never mind."

"Take your time," Traci said. "I've been doing a lot of reminiscing myself lately.

Taking a deep breath, she began. "I wish I could think of the right words, but as far as I'm concerned, there are no words to sum up how I feel about these last two years. All I can say is that I love you both dearly and you've made my life better. Cheers."

"I love you both too," Traci said. "Cheers."

"Cheers," Kimber said. As usual, she was the least demonstrative but also the one who was fighting back tears.

After taking a sip, Shannon smiled. "Oh, my goodness, this is the *expensive* stuff. Where did it come from?"

"Where do you think? Bev," Traci said.

The house mother who took in Traci at the group home in Cleveland had visited them two weeks ago, saying she needed to see just how they'd all turned out.

It had been a great visit, and now Shannon felt like Bev was yet another relative into their already large and varied family. She, Traci, and Kimber had laughed that between Kimber's parents, Shannon's parents, Traci's Bev, and all of their in-laws, they now had more family than they knew what to do with.

Reflecting on that, she said, "Sometimes I feel like I went from being an only child with two doting parents to having two sets of parents, a fairy godmother, a husband, two new brothers—among other people."

"I feel the same thing," Kimber said. "So much in my life has changed. I went from living with a bunch of models and focusing on my career to being a wife and mom and . . . well, everything."

"I've learned a lot from both of you," Traci said quietly. "You taught me to trust myself and other people. And now I have Matt and Bridge and Gwen."

Shannon smiled. "I love how much you love Gwen."

"She would be hard not to love."

Looking at both of her sisters, Shannon wondered if she'd ever felt more at peace. Yes, she loved her parents, and her husband Dylan was everything she'd ever dreamed a husband could be. He loved her for everything about her, flaws included. She never felt that he loved her in spite of them.

But as she gazed at her two sisters, she decided that there was something special about sharing blood. There was something in their genes that was irreversible, that was meant to be. And somehow, they'd manage to find each other.

Putting her champagne flute down, Kimber said, "What's going on, Shannon? You got quiet all the sudden."

"I was just sitting here thinking how amazing it is that we're sitting here, so happy with our lives. We've each found men who we really love and are planning futures all in the same city. And if it wasn't for one little DNA test, we wouldn't have found each other at all."

"I think about that all the time too," Traci said. "But, you got something wrong, Shannon."

"What was that?"

This time it was Kimber who spoke up. "It wasn't just a little DNA test. It was you reaching out to us. It was you taking that first step. You're the reason we're all together."

"It was also you two being willing to give up so much to move here. To give us a try."

Kimber chuckled. "And now look at us. Three peas in a pod."

Three peas in a pod. It was a silly expression but one that felt fitting—because that's what they had become. In spite of everything, they were three unique women who fit together imperfectly.

But she'd long ago decided that perfection was overrated.

Tucking her legs under her, Shannon said, "Well, we've got the whole night to ourselves. What should we do?"

"That's easy," Kimber said. She picked up the remote control and tossed it to Traci. "Pick a movie. I'm going to go put on sweats. And yes, I brought y'all some sweatpants and old T-shirts too."

As Traci started flipping the channels, Shannon said, "That's what you want to do? Put on old sweats and watch a movie?"

"And eat ice cream," Traci said. "Don't forget that. Oh! How about *You've Got Mail*?"

Kimber rolled her eyes. "I've only seen that four or five times."

Looking delighted, Traci smiled. "Me too. So it's perfect, right?"

Shannon was about to disagree when she realized that when she was little, moments like these were just what she'd always wanted.

Time to do nothing. Just sit with two people she cared about. Because she could.

And right then, right at that moment, she realized something for the first time.

These were the moments you couldn't put a finger on, couldn't really explain, but that meant everything.

These were the moments that counted.

They counted for everything.

"Don't eat all the cookies and cream!" she shouted.

When Traci and Kimber just laughed, she followed them upstairs. Because what they did didn't really matter.

All that mattered was that her sisters understood just what she meant—and she had a feeling that they always would.

That was all that mattered. Maybe it was all that ever had.

The End

Excerpt from

EDGEWATER ROAD

RUMORS IN ROSS COUNTY, BOOK 1

CHAPTER 1

It had been a really bad idea. Staring at the five vehicles parked haphazardly in the long driveway leading to her neighbor's farmhouse, Jennifer pressed hard on her Camry's brakes and seriously contemplated turning around.

But the two guys drinking beer on the front porch had already seen her. One of them waved.

If she turned around, Jennifer knew that John Bennett would find out. And when he did, he wouldn't let it slide, because that was the way he was. Shoot, he'd probably show up at her front door tomorrow morning and ask her a dozen questions about why she hadn't parked and gone in.

He might even decide to stop by later that night.

Though she'd only spoken to John, who also went by Lincoln—his better known and preferred nickname—a couple of times, Jennifer had already gotten the feeling he didn't suffer fools. Or liars, which was what she would be if he asked why she'd decided to show up at his house without calling first.

Jennifer wasn't typically a liar, but she knew herself well enough to realize that she'd feel so foolish, she'd start making up all kinds of excuses that were as flimsy as a sheet of tissue paper.

So she had to go inside and do what she came to do.

Feeling a weight on her chest, Jennifer carefully pulled off to the side of the driveway, leaving plenty of room to turn around. That wouldn't be hard to do. Lincoln's house was on a full two acres, just like her own. There was plenty of space for parking.

And, it seemed, parties.

Turning off the ignition, Jennifer came up with a plan. She was going to walk up to John's front door, say hello to his friends, deliver this really bad idea, and then hurry home.

Feeling the men's eyes on her, she walked around to the passenger side, opened the door, and pulled out her whole reason for being there. One triple layer chocolate cake with a chocolate mousse filling and a creamy white seven-minute-frosting. It was a beautiful dessert, if she did say so herself.

She'd baked it for Lincoln. As a thank you present. She'd thought it was the kind of gift her grandmother, Ginny Smiley, would have delivered back in the day.

But now that Jennifer thought about it? She was starting to get the feeling that MeMe would have done no such thing.

It was just another example of how her grandmother had been far cooler than she could ever hope to be.

The longer she lived in MeMe's old Victorian farmhouse, the more aware Jennifer became that she really hadn't known her grandmother all that well.

Then again, there was a lot to know about MeMe. She'd had a really interesting life. Even at eighty years old she'd been far more confident and vivacious than Jennifer, Ginny Smiley's namesake.

Yep, Jennifer was plain, store-brand vanilla, while her grandmother had been a lot more like one of those crazy Ben and Jerry's flavors that were filled with ten different mix-ins and cost double the price. Side by side, there was no comparison.

"Hey."

Startled, she turned to face one of the men who'd come over

to help her unload the U-Haul when she'd moved in next door a week ago. He'd shown up barely ten minutes after Lincoln had stopped by. Lincoln had pulled in her driveway to introduced himself but then had quickly realized she was moving in all by herself. That she was completely alone.

He'd frowned when she'd told him that she was fine and didn't need a single thing.

Seconds after that, he'd sent a text, and then his friends had arrived.

Now, looking at the man dressed in a long-sleeved T-shirt and worn jeans, Jennifer couldn't remember what his name was. All she could recall was that he'd been a lot easier to talk to than John Bennett.

"Hi . . . I'm sorry but I forgot your name. Was it Ben?"

He scowled. "Bo."

"Oh. That's right." She smiled weakly. "I won't forget it again." That was, if she had a reason to talk to Bo anytime in the near future, which she doubted. "My name is Jennifer."

"I didn't forget." She watched him study her face, drift down to her shoulders, her chest, then zero in on her cake server. "What you got there?"

"This? Oh, it's a cake."

"You brought over a cake?"

"It's a thank-you cake. For John."

His brow wrinkled. "Who?"

"Oh! I mean Lincoln. I baked a thank-you cake for Lincoln." Yes, she had now shared that she had a cake in her hands three times.

When Bo tilted his head, like he was trying to comprehend such a thing, she rushed on. "I know. I bet he would have rather had a six pack of beer or something. And I should've called before I drove over here. I didn't know he was having a party."

Bo looked over his shoulder like this was news to him too. "Huh. I guess you could call this a party."

When he looked back at her, she realized that the heels of her cute mules were slowly sinking into the ground. "Hey, you know what? Maybe I should deliver this later."

"No way. Lincoln's probably wondering what's taking you so long."

So long? "To do what?"

"To come up to the house. Come on." He turned and started walking.

Her heart sinking like her heels with every step, Jennifer followed.

The closer she got to the door, the more she regretted her decision, which was saying a lot.

There now had to be at least a dozen people standing on the front porch and they were all looking at her like she was a strange creature that had just appeared from the woods. Even the other men who'd helped her unload the van looked surprised to see her.

And no wonder. She was wearing a pair of navy wool slacks, an ivory sweater, and beautiful, impractical, turquoise suede mules. In her hands was a plastic cake carrier. She looked like she was going to a church social. Not this . . . this, whatever *this* was.

Right as reached the front steps, one of the men tagged Bo. "What you got there?"

"Jennifer here has a gift for Lincoln." He looked down at her hands. "It's a cake," he added, sounding as if it was a foreign word.

"She going in?"

Bo nodded. "Yeah. Where's he at?"

The guy shrugged. "Ain't no telling. But I wouldn't bring her inside."

"Don't see as I've got a choice. I'm not going to just leave her out here."

Yep, they were talking about her like she wasn't standing there right in front of them all. Jennifer was starting to feel like a stray dog no one wanted around.

It was time to finish this visit and get back home where it was safe and quiet.

She cleared her throat. "Bo, since you don't think I should leave this with you, I'm going to head on in. I'm sure my delivery won't take but a minute."

Bo looked appalled. "Hey, now—"

Ignoring him, she walked through the door.

And entered a whole new world.

Though the house wasn't much to speak of on the outside— kind of an old red sprawling ranch—inside it was decorated in vintage fraternity style. Mismatched couches, scarred coffee tables, beer cans littering all manner of surfaces . . . and she was pretty sure there was more than one couple making out in the back corners.

There was also a group of men playing cards at a massive table near the kitchen. Lincoln was one of them.

As she stood there, pretty much gaping at everything in wonder, the door opened and shut behind her.

"Come on, then," Bo said, sounding irritated. "He's over there. Let's get this over with."

When he started walking, she kept by his side, though it was a bit of a challenge, given that Bo was a good six inches taller than her and she was in mules with kitten heels and holding a three-layer cake.

Those heels made little clapping noises on the wood floor.

Lincoln looked their way. And then did a double take.

After saying something under his breath, he threw his hand of cards on the table and stood up.

"Here he comes," Bo said.

"I noticed," Jennifer muttered.

As he came closer, Lincoln pulled out his cell phone and studied the screen with a frown. Then he shoved it into his jeans pocket.

"Jennifer, what's wrong?" he asked.

Oh, any number of things. Starting with the fact that she was holding a chocolate cake while a couple on a nearby couch next to her seemed to be minutes from pulling off the rest of their clothes. Lord, she hoped they'd wait at least ten more minutes.

"Nothing," she said in an almost-cheerful voice. "I brought you something."

Lincoln glanced at his phone's screen again before he studied her closely. "Did you call?"

She met his gaze. Noticed for about the fifteenth time that his eyes were really blue. Dark blue, like lapis.

Then the woman on the couch moaned.

Oh! She needed to get out of this room. Clearing her throat again, she attempted to find her voice. "John. I mean, Lincoln, sorry but I didn't text or call. I guess I should have, though. Anyway, here." She thrust her container toward him.

He took it easily enough, but he held the red Rubbermaid cake server like it had a bomb about to go off inside of it. "What is this?"

"It's a cake, Lincoln," Bo announced. "She made you a freaki—" He looked over at her again. "A chocolate cake."

Lincoln was still holding the container gingerly, like it might explode. He frowned. "I don't understand."

"It's a thank you present." When he still only stared at her, she added, "You know, as a thank you for calling all the guys to help me carry all my boxes and furniture into the house last week. It was really nice of you."

"It was no big deal."

"Well, it was to me. You and all the guys really made my life easier." She smiled at Bo, so he'd see that she hadn't forgotten that he'd carried her desk inside.

Lincoln ran a hand through his coal-black hair. "No need to thank me for helping you out. I promised Ginny we'd look out for you."

Ah. He hadn't done the favor for her, he'd done it out of obligation to her dead grandmother. And . . . that made the awkwardness of this whole errand complete.

Swallowing the lump of embarrassment, she nodded. "Well, I think I'll be going now. Have a good night." Turning around, she closed her eyes. Have a good night? She wasn't at one of her mother's friend's houses.

Was she ever going to learn to be less self-conscious? A little bit more composed? A little bit more like her grandmother?

She increased her pace. Kept her head down as she walked by the couple on the couch. Ignored the stares as she strode to the front door, her heels once again clicking against the hardwoods, each step echoing in the suddenly quiet room.

"Jennifer."

She paused, mentally debating whether she wanted to turn around and face Lincoln in front of all his friends or keep walking.

She decided to get the heck out of there.

She opened the door. Felt the cool breeze bite her cheeks.

A large hand gripped the edge of the door as it swung open. "Jennifer, wait," Lincoln said.

She could feel his breath on her neck. Goosebumps rose, not from the cold air but from his proximity.

"Yes?"

"Jennifer, turn around, babe."

Babe? She wasn't a fan of that word. Wasn't a fan of being called that either.

So why did a part of her insides melt a little when she heard it from his lips?

How come she pivoted on her heels right then and there, just like she had no option?

They were barely standing eight inches apart. Close enough that she had to raise her chin to meet those blue eyes. "Um, yes, Lincoln?"

Humor lit his gaze before he visibly put his game face back on. "I'm gonna walk you out."

It was dark. There were all sorts of men lurking around his house. She might have social issues, but she wasn't a fool. She nodded. "Thank you."

Taking her arm, he guided her out and pulled the door shut behind him. Almost immediately, she could hear the noise level rise inside.

The five men on the porch abruptly stopped talking and watched them.

Lincoln acted as if they weren't even there. "Where's your car, honey?"

She pointed to the driveway, where her reliable gray Camry still sat at the end of a long line of vehicles.

"How come you parked so far away?"

She shrugged, not wanting to admit how close she'd come to turning around.

He sighed and started down the stairs, still holding her arm in his heavy hand, like he was afraid she'd dart off without him.

They stayed silent as they walked. She was doing her best not to thank him a second time for walking her out in the dark. And John? Well, who knew what was on his mind?

When they reached her vehicle, he held out his hand. "Key?"

"Oh, there's no need." She patted her pocket. "It's keyless entry."

"You going to be okay getting home?"

She was a grown woman. It was a three-minute drive back to her grandmother's farm. The farm that was barely a mile away. So, all in all, it was pretty silly question.

But it still made her feel cared for. "I'll be fine." Looking up into his eyes, she smiled softly. "Now, you have a good night, John."

"It's Lincoln."

"I didn't forget." Unable to stop herself, she chuckled at his irritated expression before opening her door and slipping inside.

Lincoln stepped away, but she knew he watched as she turned around and slowly drove back onto the main road.

She'd been the one who'd delivered a thank-you cake, but she had the strangest feeling that Lincoln Bennett had given her something too.

She just wasn't sure what it was.

Acknowledgments

When you write a series based on a town you no longer live in, feature a ballroom dance teacher when you don't know how to ballroom dance, and have a number of police officer and social worker characters even though you have no background in law enforcement or social work . . . well, you can imagine the amount of help an author has to have! I've been blessed beyond measure to have so many people give me their time to answer innumerable pesky questions.

First, thank you to Alex Napier for answering many, many questions about his work as a cop in a number of Cincinnati-area police departments. I'm also grateful to a longtime reader and friend, Marilyn Ridgway, for long ago telling me about her work as a child advocate in the court system. I'm also grateful to dance instructor Yvette de la Torre for her continued dance lessons—this time, helping me fumble through the cha cha. Yvette, you're a gem!

A big thanks also goes out to Lynne Stroup, my first reader extraordinaire, who always helps get manuscripts in shape for the editorial team at Blackstone.

Once again, I'm beyond thankful to the team at Blackstone Publishing for taking my stories and turning them into beautiful books to be proud of. Thanks especially to my editor, Ember

Hood, who always seems to find the right things to say; to acquisition editor Vikki Warner, who is always beyond kind and encouraging; and to the marketing and publicity teams, especially Hannah Ohlmann. I also must mention Alenka Linaschke who designed the book's cover and helped bring the Dance with Me studio to life.

No acknowledgment letter would be complete without mentioning my agent Nicole Resciniti—who is everything an author could ask for—and my wonderful readers, both new and longstanding. Finally, I'm so grateful to have a relationship with the Lord. He's blessed me with the ability to write and the security of knowing that I'll never have to write a book alone. I'm always so grateful for that gift.